A Sheltering

M. S. Power

EDINBURGH AND LONDON

*For Peter and Natalie Curran,
the most loyal of friends, 23 July 1994*

Copyright © M.S. Power, 1994
All rights reserved
The moral right of the author has been asserted

First published in Great Britain in 1994 by
MAINSTREAM PUBLISHING COMPANY (EDINBURGH) LTD
7 Albany Street
Edinburgh EH1 3UG

No part of this book may be reproduced or transmitted in any form or by any means without permission in writing from the publisher, except by a reviewer who wishes to quote brief passages in connection with a review written for insertion in a magazine, newspaper or broadcast

A catalogue record for this book is available from the British Library

ISBN 1 85158 616 4

Typeset in Bembo by Litho Link Ltd, Welshpool, Powys

Printed and bound in Great Britain by
Biddles Ltd, Guildford and King's Lynn

Contents

Winter	7
Spring	51
Summer	83
Autumn	129

. . . and yet, as is the way with fools and cruel men, all they are left with is silence, an awful silence in which they can but shelter their guilt.

Visits and Visitations
of Arthur Apple

Winter

One

Winter lumbered into the valley, cautiously at first, presaged by flurries of driving sleet from the Atlantic, and by great glowering clouds laden with snow. Old people clad themselves in layers of thick woollen clothes which, curiously, gave them all the same round, plump shape no matter how gaunt their actual bodies might be. Many of them spent the short daylight hours staring out of their windows with dim, watery eyes wondering how severe the season would be; wondering, too, if they would survive it since death came frequently to the valley at that time of year: it was, people said, a matter of nature taking its course just as most of the children seemed to be born in the spring, and there was nothing much they could do about it. And as they stared the old women prayed, prayed rapidly with thin, cracked lips, trying to get everything said, while the old men left the praying to their womenfolk, and watched the coldness seep into the ground, watched with a steady defiance as though daring God to make His final move against them.

In the fields surrounding the village cattle stamped their feet and lowed and steamed, their breath as thick as the blue-brown smoke that rose from the chimneys and blanketed the whole valley, all but obscuring it from view, and the dogs the men would use to drive the cattle into barns were silent and fidgety, given only to gentle whimpering as they tiptoed across frozen yards, their coats already shaggy and dull.

The valley itself was fertile enough to support what

livestock the villagers kept but just about useless for cultivation, the soil shallow and flint-ridden, and the fierce gales that hurtled down its length from the sea bringing with them the smell of fish and the taste of salt saw to it that little but the coarsest grazing survived. Sometimes, usually in early spring for some unknown reason, there would be so much salt on those winds that it would settle when there was a lull, and those who did not understand the quirks of the place often surmised it was a freak covering of frost. What trees there were stood scattered, aloof from each other, bent crazily by the storms, their leaves fragile things that clung to the branches for a while but soon gave up the unfair struggle and blew away, and the birds that sometimes roosted in them took on the aspect of exotic fruits, their talons grasping the bark, balancing themselves with genius.

The houses, mostly one-storey, were built close together and in a straight line, yet they didn't seem to be huddled, and, although identical for the most part, they managed to convey an air of individuality just like their occupants. Because of its location at the foot of the mountains, in good weather it was a pretty place and it had once been mooted that it was to be put on some tourist list, but the villagers were having none of that, and gave the men from the tourist board short shrift, even threatening to stone the foreigners if they came, so the idea was dropped and the proposed road into the village abandoned, leaving the people content enough in their isolation.

In the highest mountain the river had its source. It didn't pass through the village, though. Just before it reached the cemetery it veered off to the right, flowing through the outlying farms before swinging back again and resuming its original course to the sea. It had no name, this river. Not as far as the villagers were concerned at any rate. They called it simply 'the river', but that was said with respect, the same respect that imbued their tones when they said 'the doctor' or 'the priest'. And with that respect came a certain awe, for the villagers endowed the river with inexplicable mystical powers, useful for explaining away strange happenings, even better for taming recalcitrant children with dire threats of what the river might or might not do to them if they failed to behave. In the colder months the river was referred to as 'he', but during those rare spells when the weather was balmy and kind and everyone was feeling content, it miraculously became 'she'. So, it was 'should have known that would happen with him being grumpy at the time', but as the cattle swelled and prepared to give birth, lazing on the banks of the river and sucking its sweet water, it was 'ah, she's the purest of pure and filled with them things that give heart and bone', whatever that meant.

At the point where the river curved back onto its original route and set sail for the sea, Mr and Mrs Biddlecomb had their store, one end devoted to the sale of all things imaginable, the other utilised as a pub, and it was here the men would gather of an evening to gossip although they didn't think of it as such: they 'discussed' matters, which was something quite different, wasn't it?

It was the coldest day anyone could remember, with a coating of white snow like an old man's beard covering the branches, and the edges of the river frozen, when the police came to take him away with them. They made a great show of it, coming in two cars no less: a pair of burly Gardai in one, another couple and an Inspector in the other. They even put a blanket over his head as they bundled him into the first car although there didn't seem much point in doing that. Perhaps they knew that a man's dignity had something to do with the cast of his eyes and they didn't want him to have any vestige of dignity left if they could help it. Billy Maken swore he saw them putting handcuffs on him, but Billy Maken was always one to embellish the truth and no one else saw any handcuffs so he was probably exaggerating about that episode too. And although it was a Sunday, it was still a working day but none of the men went to the fields. They stayed in the village and lined the street, watching the sorrowful drama with their women, finding it hard to believe but telling themselves that seeing was believing.

And when the cars had gone, bumping along the road that led from the village and doing little zigzags to avoid the potholes, and the women had gone to their homes, the men gathered in Biddlecomb's store, leaning on the bar, nodding sagely, each waiting for someone else to speak, to make the first comment that would loosen everyone's tongue. Mr Biddlecomb himself obliged as he waited for the heads to settle on the beer before passing the tall glasses down the counter. 'So, there you are,' was what he said, but that was enough to set the ball rolling as he probably knew it would be.

'Aye, there you are,' said Jim Haughy, which didn't add much to the conversation, but Jim Haughy seldom did.

'Who'd have thought it, though?' Tom Feeney put in.

'Just goes to show, doesn't it?' Cahal Brennan added.

'Show what?' Billy Maken wanted to know.

But none of the men seemed to know what it showed, and it was Mrs Biddlecomb, perched on her high stool at the shop end of the room that suggested, 'That you never know with folk. Never know what's going on inside them,' she said.

And the men nodded some more, and one of them agreed, saying, 'That's the truth, Mrs Biddlecomb. That's the truth and no mistake.'

Mrs Biddlecomb shifted her huge buttocks on the stool. Both her hips had been replaced in the last year and continued to give her trouble. Not that they caused pain. They didn't. It was just that Mrs Biddlecomb was suspicious of what she called 'unnatural bits' within her and worried herself by constantly wondering when they might snap and leave her sprawling. 'And now that we know the truth,' she went on, wincing a bit, 'now that we know the *truth*, what about little Christy Codd?'

The men looked away from her, some of them taking to supping their drink, others taking inordinate care about lighting their pipes.

'I didn't think you'd like that,' Mrs Biddlecomb said, looking grimly satisfied.

'No need to bring that up now,' her husband admonished.

'Every need,' Mrs Biddlecomb insisted.

'Later,' Mr Biddlecomb said. 'When things have settled down.'

'Oh, that's you all over, Mr Biddlecomb,' Mrs Biddlecomb snapped. 'Always the one for putting things off, especially when you know you're in the wrong.'

'Nobody's in the wrong,' Mr Biddlecomb defended himself.

'All of you are in the wrong,' Mrs Biddlecomb told him, told all the men. 'Every last one of you is in the wrong and you'll all end up paying for it one day. You mark my words. One day you'll all have to pay for it.'

And the men knew Mrs Biddlecomb was right, and were ashamed, and one by one they finished their drinks and left the pub, muttering goodnight but not meeting Mrs Biddlecomb's bright accusatory eyes.

'Satisfied?' Mr Biddlecomb said when everyone had gone.

'Huh,' grunted Mrs Biddlecomb, but, yes, clearly satisfied.

Two

Willie Little was born in the village of Ifreann, but when his parents uprooted themselves and set sail for England in search of their fortune they took him with them. It was a decision they mulled over for some time since Willie was not the brightest of souls and having to lug him around with them could prove both a trial and a hindrance to their plans for greatness. Indeed, it was almost settled that he would go to stay with his Auntie Maude in Dublin when that benevolent lady was unkind enough to have a mild stroke, and take to her bed, and decide that was where she wanted to stay indefinitely, cosseted and tended by her one unmarried daughter, a girl so plain there was little chance she would ever make her way to the altar other than in a box. So, Willie Little was taken to Manchester and did quite well for himself, getting a job when jobs were hard to come by, while his father did less well, and soon tired of the city and his family, and one day just vanished never to be heard of again. A year after Mr Little took off, Mrs Little caught something that was called the bug, and succumbed to it, taking only a couple of weeks to die.

When he was forty-five Willie Little returned to Ifreann, moved back into the now derelict little cottage, and in a short space of time appeared never to have left the place. But he had certainly changed. The shy, stupid boy who had been dragged across the Irish Sea was now a taciturn creature, and his silence now gave the impression more of cunning than stupidity. He had also, somewhere along the way, lost his left arm. Of course, everyone was dying to know how that had come about: it wasn't exactly a blemish that could be overlooked, especially since Willie liked to carry the preserved limb around with him from time to time, neatly packed in an old fiddle case. But no one had the nerve to come straight out and ask him directly, so for months they just speculated, often arriving at outlandish conclusions, until, one evening when the bar was full, Mrs Biddlecomb, unable to bear the weight of her curiosity any longer, asked him bluntly, 'Tell us, Willie, how come you lost that arm of yours?'

It was as though they were all about to eavesdrop at the confessional. The store went deadly quiet, and all the men craned their necks to have a good look at Willie's face as they anticipated his explanation.

Willie shrugged. 'Dunno,' he said to Mrs Biddlecomb.

'What d'you mean – you don't know?' Mrs Biddlecomb demanded, sensing a rebuttal and not about to stand for that.

'Just dropped off of a night, didn't it?' Willie said quietly, his face serious. 'Went to sleep with it sticking to me and woke up to find it lying in the bed with me, down around my knees.'

Tommy Stack sniggered, thinking this must be a joke. 'You're joking,' he said. 'You're having us on, aren't you, Willie?'

But Willie wasn't having them on, it seemed. He gave Tommy Stack a baleful look. 'Not joking,' he said. 'That's how it was exactly,' he emphasised. 'You needn't believe it if you don't want.' And from then on he stopped carrying the fiddle case about with him.

It was just after the start of the year, a bitter but windless Sunday with everything snapping and crackling in the cold, and great sea-birds swooping stiff-winged across the brittle sky, eyes unblinking, seeking scraps from the frozen landscape, when Willie Little, thinking mildly about Father Cunningham's sermon comparing the coldness of the season to the frigidity of men's hearts, but nonetheless walking briskly along the riverbank, his one arm swinging, came across the body of

May O'Mahony lying under the old willow that wept into the river. Under the circumstances Willie was very cool about his discovery. He paused in his stride and frowned. He pursed his thin lips and stared at the body for a while. Then he crouched on his hunkers and studied death, stroking his chin. And when he was satisfied he strode off as if he'd seen nothing out of the ordinary. For the whole of that day he said nothing to anyone about May O'Mahony stretched out on the riverbank – although this wasn't too surprising since it was his wont to be secretive, having learned the hard way that it is better not to be the one to announce bad news, and get oneself inextricably implicated in all the trouble that was bound to follow.

So, it wasn't until dusk, when May's mother, Hannah, took herself out onto the village street and started asking anyone she could find if they'd seen her daughter that the rest of the villagers knew that something was amiss, and only when Hannah came to Biddlecomb's store and asked there did Willie own up to his find. 'Yeah,' he admitted. 'I seen her.'

'Where, Willie?' Hannah O'Mahony wanted to know urgently.

'It was down by the river, under the willow.'

'What time was that?'

'This morning. Just after Mass.'

'This morning!' Hannah O'Mahony said. 'What in God's name was the girl doing down there in the morning?' she asked, mostly of herself.

'Nothing,' Willie volunteered. 'She weren't doing nothing. She were, well, sort of sleeping, I think.'

'Sort of sleeping, you *think*!' Hannah O'Mahony half screamed at him. 'Dear Lord, are you God's first fool or what, Willie Little?'

'Didn't you think to take a closer look at her?' Mrs Biddlecomb demanded.

'You mean to say you just left her lying there?' Davey Shortt said.

'Didn't it dawn on you that there might be something amiss with the girl and she not being all there in the head?' Leonard Midden asked.

'Did you just step over her like she was meat?' Patrick

Farrel wanted to know.

Bombarded with all these questions Willie Little retreated into one of his surly moods, slitting his eyes and tightening his lips, and they stopped questioning him since they knew that once Willie took the hump like that there was no way they'd get anything useful out of him.

'Hadn't some of ye better go and take a look and see if she's still there and what ails her?' Mrs Biddlecomb suggested finally.

So off they traipsed the lot of them, all except Mrs Biddlecomb whose hips would never have stood up to the track, Patrick Farrel leading the way and the rest of them jogging along behind him; and as they passed down the street some of the women and most of the children joined the party, making quite a procession out of it, the torches many of them carried giving the whole scene a macabre religious flavour.

'All we need now is Father Cunningham with the monstrance and it'd be like Corpus Christi, wouldn't it?' Stevie Carroll said, but no one answered him – thinking, maybe, it was too close to sacrilege to dare reply.

May O'Mahony was still lying there under the willow, stiff as a board now with a sprinkling of frost on her eyelids. Of course Hannah O'Mahony started to wail, and as she wailed Mrs Finch, the midwife, came into her own, pushing her way through the gathering and kneeling by the little curled-up corpse, and putting her fingers in all the right places to tell if there was any breath left in it. She made tiny clucking noises for a while, and shook her head a lot, and then announced that May O'Mahony was well and truly dead, as if they hadn't all guessed that already.

'So, what do we do now with her?' Davey Shortt asked nervously, he, like almost everyone else, a bit shaky and bewildered to find himself in the presence of unexplained death.

'Get her back to the house, of course,' Mrs Finch said, heaving herself to her feet by planting both hands on her knees and pushing hard, and then backing away to let the men pick up the body. 'Go on,' she ordered no one in particular. 'Pick the poor wee child up and get her back to the house and out of this cold,' she said, giving a shudder herself maybe from the cold or maybe because it just dawned on her that May couldn't have cared less about the cold at this stage.

Harvey Motion, the woodsman, who was built like an oak and always liked to be in the thick of things, picked May O'Mahony up as if she was a feather, and off they all trooped, back to the village, but more silently now, even the children stopping their larking about. Not that any of them felt what could be called deep sorrow since none of them had really known the dead girl, or her mother for that matter, since Hannah was a woman who didn't forgive easily, and held a grudge against the rest of the villagers, and seldom spoke to any of them if she could avoid doing so. Years ago, when she was just sixteen, she'd got herself into trouble, as they put it, and given birth to a boy child, and brought a terrible shame to her father, and wasn't it just as well and a great kindness that her mother was dead and didn't have to witness this disgrace. And even though that child was taken from her and adopted, she carried with her the reputation of a slut, and was ostracised, and made a mockery of by the young lads who had nothing better to do than taunt her in their cruel, ribald way, the more so since Hannah for some unknown reason would never reveal who the father of her child had been.

Hannah must have been thirty when her father died, leaving her alone, which was probably a relief for her since her father had been a bitter man and treated her like something of a slave, a skivvy, people put it. She shed no tears when he died and that made matters worse since she was now called brassy and unfeeling into the bargain. 'As hard and brassy a woman as ever I saw,' Mrs Biddlecomb used to say, and that was the opinion of nearly everyone.

And then, incredibly, Hannah got pregnant again, and again refused to say who was responsible. And she flaunted herself, proud of her bulging tummy, defiantly staring in the eye anyone who dared even hint they were about to belittle her.

And so, little May was born, and God took his revenge on Hannah by making the child deaf and dumb and blind from the day she was born. And maybe Hannah believed in this wicked retribution for she kept May indoors most of the time with something akin to a dog collar round her neck and a length of string attached to that, and the string affixed to something solid so that she wouldn't go bumping into things. Sometimes in summer she was let out into the garden with the string tied to the fruitless apple tree, but that was as far as she ever got from the house. Even Mass was dispensed with in her case since she would be sure to disrupt things, with no one willing to hang onto her when Hannah went up to communion, and God alone knows what she'd have done if she was allowed up near the altar rail. Bitten the priest's hand off probably. Sometimes the villagers would see her ashen little face gaping sightlessly out of the windows, but not often, and that was all they knew of her so, now, it was difficult to mourn her. Yet, any death in the village was an unnerving occurrence since it brought home to everyone that it could visit at any time, and who would be next?

With May O'Mahony laid out on a bed, and Hannah wringing her hands and mutely beseeching God for forgiveness of something only she seemed privy to, and Mrs Finch doing what she called 'examining' the child like she was a curious specimen the likes of which only cropped up occasionally, the men went back to Biddlecomb's.

'Well?' Mrs Biddlecomb demanded instantly, peeved that her hips had prevented her from going along to the viewing.

'Oh, she was there all right. Just like Willie said.'

'And?'

'And dead.'

Mrs Biddlecomb clapped her chubby hands to her cheeks. 'Oh, my Holy God,' she exclaimed. 'Dead?'

'Dead.'

'And frozen solid,' Leonard Midden elaborated.

Mrs Biddlecomb made little tutting noises. 'Dead and frozen solid. Poor wee mite,' she said at last, quietly and to herself.

But some of the men heard her and nodded their agreement with that sentiment, and took their time for a while about supping their porter as though guzzling it like they usually did would be showing disrespect, and they wouldn't do that, not even towards Hannah O'Mahony's child, just in case the same thing happened to them when they passed on. And they didn't seem to have much to say to each other, which was unusual, and it took Tommy Stack, Mick Stack's younger brother and about as pessimistic, to break the ice and voice what most of them were thinking. 'Means, I s'pose, we'll have to tell someone.'

No one answered that.

'*Have* to get the doctor over,' Tommy Stack added, pleased he was having all the say to himself for a change.

'He'll want the Gardai brought in,' Davey Shortt pointed out.

The men sucked in their breath at that one, each of them seeing their lives disrupted, and questions asked which they wouldn't want to be answering.

'And I suppose that Hannah will be wanting Father Cunningham to bury her,' Mr Biddlecomb said gloomily.

'Won't do that, will he?' Mrs Biddlecomb pointed out.

'Why not?'

'Child was a bastard, wasn't it? Can't go burying a bastard just willy-nilly in the graveyard.'

'Oh, no. S'pose you're right.'

'But it'll have to *be* buried,' Tommy Stack said, getting back into it. 'Can't just leave it lying around to rot, can you?'

'And Father won't bury anyone unless it's all legal and above board,' Leonard Midden added as though he hadn't been listening to what they'd been saying.

For a while, then, they all stayed silent, turning the problem over in their minds, their dread of outside intrusion far greater than their sympathy for the dead child.

'I don't suppose – ' Mr Biddlecomb began, but then decided he couldn't suppose whatever it was had illuminated his thoughts, and added, 'No. Forget it,' and turned his back on the bar and pretended the bottles needed to be straightened, and busied himself with that.

After another while Patrick Farrel said, 'Maybe –' and then he, too, stopped and shook his head.

But, oddly, all the men seemed to guess what he was leading up to, and some of them nodded hopefully, encouraging him to give tongue to his thoughts, and he did seem on the point of speaking again, licking his lips fast, when Mr

Biddlecomb gave a jerk of his head in the direction of his wife, and said, 'We'll sort all that out,' quite quickly and in a loud enough voice.

'You'll have to,' Mrs Biddlecomb said.

'We will,' Mr Biddlecomb told her.

Only after Mrs Biddlecomb had heaved herself off her stool and plodded from the shop did the men start to discuss the matter again, huddling together, heads bent, conspiring.

'The way I see it,' Patrick Farrel began, 'the way I see it is this: the child's dead and nothing's going to bring her back. Right?'

The men nodded willingly, and chorused, 'Right.'

'So,' Patrick Farrel went on, more confident now that he had backing, 'what's the point in dragging all them outsiders into it, getting the doctor and the Gardai involved? You know what they're like. Having us all running round in circles, they will, asking us things we don't want to be telling them.'

Again the men nodded, and some said, 'Right,' again too.

'Be different if she'd been – well, you know – been sort of normal,' Mr Biddlecomb pointed out.

'Or if someone had killed her,' Leonard Midden suggested.

'Exactly.'

As he so often did when trying to wangle his way out of something, Mr Biddlecomb now blamed God. 'God wanted her and took her. Simple as that,' he said.

'You're right, Mr Biddlecomb.'

'Dunno,' Enda Murphy said.

A few of the men rounded on him, one of them demanding, 'What d'you mean, you don't know?'

'Hannah's still going to want Father Cunningham to give her a burial, and if *he's* told . . .' he let his words trail off significantly.

That set them thinking again, and to help them think Mr Biddlecomb refilled a couple of glasses and never asked for payment, which was a great rarity. Then, 'Hannah'll understand,' Patrick Farrel said eventually, although there wasn't that much conviction in his voice.

But Mr Biddlecomb brightened. ''Course she will,' he agreed.

Davey Shortt grunted. 'She'll just have to.'

''Course she will,' Mr Biddlecomb repeated.

But just as the men were congratulating themselves and beginning to relax, and see their way out of the dilemma, Mrs Finch appeared in the doorway, looking stony-faced and more gloom-laden than any of them had ever seen her. She stood in the doorway, and put her hands on her hips, and stared at them.

'Well?' Mr Biddlecomb demanded.

'Youse had better know now,' Mrs Finch said. 'Little May was strangled,' and then she added, 'and whoever strangled her, done her too.'

'What d'you mean – done her?' Davey Shortt asked.

'Shut up, Davey,' Patrick Farrel ordered, and Davey wilted. 'You mean she was – ?' Patrick Farrel began.

Mrs Finch nodded fiercely. 'That's just what I mean,' she said. 'One of you lot raped her and then you strangled her, and her not yet fifteen years old,' she added, and then left abruptly, slamming the door, and leaving the men agog.

It took a very long time under the circumstances before anyone spoke. Then, frowning into his beer, Matty Burke muttered, 'Sweet Jesus!'

Someone said, 'You can say that again.'

Matty Burke obliged. 'Sweet Jesus!' he repeated even more fervently this time.

'That changes things,' Mr Biddlecomb observed fatuously, taking a drink himself, a very large whiskey, and downing it in a single gulp. He grimaced as the alcohol burned his gullet. 'Changes things a whole damn lot.'

But as most of the men were nodding morosely in agreement, Patrick Farrel shook his head, and told them, 'No it don't.'

''Course it does,' Mr Biddlecomb snapped, not liking to be contradicted, especially now that he had a drink in him.

Patrick Farrel, however, continued to disagree with his big head. 'Means only that more than ever we've got to keep this to ourselves and not have outsiders poking around.'

Mr Biddlecomb sucked in his breath so quickly he almost choked himself. 'Ooooh,' he managed to squeeze out at last.

'Can't see us keeping *this* to ourselves. Not if May was strangled and done.'

'Why not?' Patrick Farrel asked reasonably. 'We were going to keep it to ourselves before we knew all that, weren't we? So the only thing that's changed is that *we* know she was – '

'Can't see Mrs Finch standing for that,' Davey Shortt observed.

'She'll do what she's told, won't she, Tim?' Patrick Farrel asked Tim Finch, giving him an ominous look. 'Women do what their menfolk tell them,' he added.

Tim Finch squirmed, and sucked on his pipe as though he was getting energy and courage from it. 'I'll try – ' he began.

'Trying isn't enough, Tim. You've got to show her who's boss,' Davey Shortt told him, which brought a wry look from most of the men since Davey Shortt was well known as the most henpecked man in the village.

'Easy for you to say,' Tim Finch said into his beer.

'Don't tell us you're afraid of her?' Tommy Stack asked.

'I'm afraid of no one,' Tim Finch said, getting riled and working himself up for a fight like he usually did when slighted.

'I'll have a word with her,' Patrick Farrel announced, and that seemed to satisfy everyone.

'What about Hannah, though?' Mr Biddlecomb wanted to know. 'She's going to want a proper funeral for May, and that means telling Father Cunningham, and he's not going to keep his mouth shut. Couldn't, could he? Him being a priest and all.'

'You going to talk to Hannah too, Patrick?' Leonard Midden asked.

'I'll talk to Hannah,' Farrel affirmed. 'She'll understand.'

'I still say she'll want a proper funeral for May,' Mr Biddlecomb insisted.

'We'll give the girl a proper funeral.'

'And how do we do that, might I ask?'

'It'll be a proper funeral. All right, without the priest, but it'll be a proper funeral all the same. Hannah won't want no fuss,' Patrick Farrel said, as if he was sure what he was talking about.

'Can't see it,' Mr Biddlecomb said.

'Just take my word for it,' Farrel said, and finished his beer and strode out of the shop.

No one ever found out what exactly Patrick Farrel said to Hannah O'Mahony and Mrs Finch, but whatever it was it did the trick, and the two women agreed to stay silent.

And so it was that the villagers buried little May O'Mahony, and true to their word they gave her a very nice funeral. Even the weather seemed to collude for it was remarkably still on the day. Uncannily so. Some of the very old villagers nodded solemnly to each other as if they understood the reason for the weather's clemency and agreed that it was, when all was said and done, a sign that what they were doing was for the best under the circumstances. But there were those who wrung their hands and insisted it was a dreadful way to be going on, wicked and unforgivable, something that would surely haunt them for the rest of their unnatural lives.

Nevertheless the whole village turned out for the funeral, salving their consciences by bringing gifts to place in the grave beside the child. And Patrick Farrel himself said the prayers, and did a good job of it too, sounding properly solemn, and not making any mistakes when he came to the tricky words, and leading the hymn without once getting out of tune.

When the ceremony was over, and the graveyard quiet and deserted, the rain came down with a vengeance, making the new mound of reddish clay spatter over the flowers Hannah O'Mahony had placed on the grave, flattening them, giving the pale yellow petals the appearance of having being wounded, giving them, too, an appropriate appearance of death.

Within a week the earth had levelled itself off. Bert Slattery and Dick McCormack were detailed to grass it over, and they did this expertly, taking sods from under the hedge that surrounded the cemetery and positioning them with great precision, and stamping on them, even clipping the longer blades of grass, so that when they had finished there was no clue that anyone had been buried there, no clue either that May O'Mahony had ever existed.

Three

Surprisingly, it took some weeks for the men to realise there was something they had overlooked, and it took Mrs Biddlecomb to bring it home to them, and she did it with glee, taking her time before coming to the point. She chose a Saturday evening when the store was full and then, settling herself on her stool like a broody hen and waiting for a lull, she said loudly enough to be sure everyone could hear, 'And I suppose you're all thinking how clever you've been and that it's all over now,' and immediately lowered her head and pretended to be concentrating on her knitting.

Flustered, Mr Biddlecomb was the first to recover. 'What you talking about, woman?' he demanded.

Mrs Biddlecomb pretended not to hear.

'You hear me?' Mr Biddlecomb demanded, not liking to be put down in such a way in front of everyone.

Mrs Biddlecomb folded her knitting carefully and stuck her needles into the ball of wool before looking up. 'What I'm talking about is what Mrs Finch said to you all when she told you about poor May being strangled and done.'

'And what was that, pray?'

'Oh, forgotten have you?'

'Would I be asking if I knew what you were on about?'

Mrs Biddlecomb sighed and spoke as though to an idiot, slowly. 'What she said was that one of *you* lot strangled and done little May.'

Well, it was as if Biddlecomb had gone round the store and slapped each and every one of them in the face. Jaws dropped and eyes gaped and the only sound for quite a while was Connor Neill's asthmatic breathing.

'She was off her head when she said that,' Mr Biddlecomb managed to splutter eventually. 'Just like you are now, woman.'

'Fine. Fine,' Mrs Biddlecomb said, getting down from her stool and trundling towards the door that led to her kitchen in the back. But at the door she stopped and turned. 'Fine,' she said again. 'I'm off my head if you want. But if one of *you* lot *didn't* do it – who did?' she asked, and with something suspiciously like a cackle she left them.

'Jesus, you know, she's right,' Davey Shortt said, but waiting until Mrs Biddlecomb had closed the door and was out of earshot.

And all of a sudden the men found themselves taking sidelong glances at each other, but not holding any gaze lest it be interpreted as an accusation. Nonetheless, Willie Little got edgy, and insisted, 'Well, I couldn't strangle a cat with me one arm, so none of you need be gawping at *me*,' he said, feeling quite grateful for his infirmity and becoming brave enough to stare out anyone who dared look him in the eye.

'No one said it was you, Willie,' Mr Biddlecomb said to pacify Willie who was a good customer when he had the money.

'Doesn't stop them thinking, though, does it?'

'No one's thinking it either.'

'Better bloody not.'

And so they fell to wondering who might have killed May O'Mahony and raped her, not discussing it, mind, just thinking about it, and keeping their thoughts to themselves, sheltering their innocence in silence.

But as the days passed it was noticeable how edgy everyone was getting, snapping at each other when they did speak, and spending longer hours in their fields away from each other, and drinking quickly when they did go to Biddlecomb's, and then leaving with only a nod.

And fathers questioned their sons and were relieved when

they were convinced of their innocence, but it made bad feeling between father and son and the young bucks got together and moaned at how they were always getting blamed for everything these days and how it would have to have been someone really sick to do what was done to May and none of *them* were that sick in the head, were they?

'Can't go on like this,' Mr Biddlecomb was forced to remark to his wife as business dropped off.

'Don't you talk to me about it,' Mrs Biddlecomb huffed. 'I'm the one that's off her head, remember.'

'Oh, for God's sake, woman!'

'And don't you dare bring God into it neither. It's your own sake you're thinking of as ever. The day you start thinking about God, Larry Biddlecomb, the Almighty'll get such a shock He'll probably strike you dead from nerves.'

Mr Biddlecomb glared at his wife but made no answer to that. He knew her well enough to know there was no point in talking to her when she was in one of *those* moods: all he'd get was more abuse, and he had enough troubles as it was, he told himself. So he waited until the night when Mrs Biddlecomb was tucked up nice and warm and cosy, and the aches easing out of her fat body. Then he sat on the side of her bed and put his head on his hands, giving deep sighs like a silent lament. He'd tried this tactic before and it had worked, so maybe it would again. And it did although Mrs Biddlecomb let him suffer for a while just to teach him a lesson.

'So, what are you going to do?' she asked at last.

Mr Biddlecomb shook his head forlornly. 'I just don't know,' he said in a quiet, woebegone voice.

Mrs Biddlecomb relented. 'Well,' she said. 'Well, now if I was you I'd get all the men in here together and talk it out. Got to clear the air one way or another.'

'You think?' Mr Biddlecomb asked dubiously, not really fancying having to discuss the matter at all.

'What else can you do? Just go on wondering all the time who did it and never knowing for sure?'

'S'pose you're right.'

''Course I'm right.'

'I'll do that then.'

'Good.'

'It wasn't me, you know,' Mr Biddlecomb added, as if he'd just thought of it.

Mrs Biddlecomb gave him an odd look. 'You think I don't know that? Strangle her you might, but the other – never find the energy for it, would you now?' she asked with a vicious grin, leaving her husband to redden and somehow finding his innocence an embarrassment.

But Mr Biddlecomb took his wife's advice nonetheless and called all the men together in the shop one Tuesday night when a gale was blowing and rain the size of pebbles clattering from the sky. And he dressed up for the occasion, putting on a tie and his best braces that his cousin had sent him from California, gaudy things in red with posey starlets ranged down their length.

'All right, all right,' he said in a loud voice when everyone was assembled, and looked a little taken aback when all the men fell silent. He floundered for a while, looking for words he was unaccustomed to using, but which he felt the occasion called for. 'Now then,' Mr Biddlecomb continued, lowering his voice to an appropriately conspiratorial level, 'we all know that it was a terrible tragedy, that business with little May O'Mahony, and I'm not saying we didn't do the right thing by keeping it all to ourselves, but the thing is – ' and here Mr Biddlecomb felt the need of a quick drink from the whisky he had had the foresight to prepare for himself. Fortified, he went on, warming to his task, ' – but the thing is, as Mrs Biddlecomb said to me only the other day, the thing is that until we know for sure who done it we're always going to have that wondering hanging over us, aren't we?' He stopped for a breather and was gratified to see some of the men nodding in agreement. But only some of them: the others clearly weren't so sure about delving into the matter again which they thought had been neatly swept from memory as soon as May O'Mahony's body had been buried. And seeing this, Mr Biddlecomb asked, 'Would any of you disagree with that?' and, of course, those that had not nodded said nothing, keeping their heads well down, for fear they might be asked to explain why they disagreed. 'Good,' Mr Biddlecomb said, pleased he seemed to be getting somewhere.

'So what you suggesting, Mr Biddlecomb?' Davey Shortt wanted to know.

That set Mr Biddlecomb back on his heels for a bit. He hadn't planned to suggest anything. He had meant for someone else to come up with suggestions. But he got out of it neatly enough. 'Oh,' he said expansively. 'It's not for *me* to suggest anything. It has to be a unanimous agreement, and all ideas will have to be listened to and weighed and discussed.'

'Difficult that,' Willie Little put in.

'What's difficult about it?' Mr Biddlecomb demanded.

'Just think about it,' Willie said.

There was silence for a while, and some of the men even put on faces as if to give the impression they were thinking about it. Then Leonard Midden, never one for concentrating on anything for too long, asked, 'What's your drift, Willie?'

'I know what his drift is,' Jim Haughy put in, since he was a great one for letting on that he understood everything when in truth he was as slow as anyone to grasp any idea.

Willie Little knew this so, with a smile, he said, 'Well, you explain it to them then, Jim, will you, they not being that bright?'

Jim Haughy reddened. 'Better coming from you,' he said.

And since Willie was in a good enough humour he let it go at that. He took time to light his pipe though, fumbling more than was necessary. And he puffed for a while before explaining. 'Very simple. Like – well, let's take it that you, Mr Biddlecomb, that you did it. Well, you're not going to say you did, are you? So, you'll be the first one to be pointing the finger at someone else. Just like the rest of us if one of us did it.' Willie tapped his pipe in the brass ashtray set into the counter.

'He has a point,' Patrick Farrel pointed out.

Mr Biddlecomb, perhaps at the moment overly sensitive, and stung by his being used as an example as the possible perpetrator, wasn't about to have that. 'Not really,' he insisted. 'I mean – you just look at us. None of us would do something like that. We'd *know* if one of us did it.'

'You reckon?'

"Course. *I'd* know if any of you did it. I'd surely be able to tell. I mean you – none of you – could do that sort of thing and stay the same as you always are. Bound to change you, that sort of thing is. Got to. Stands to reason.'

'You're saying it's got to be someone who doesn't come in here then, are you?'

'I'm saying that's the most likely way of things.'

'So who does that leave?'

It didn't leave many, and keen as they were to find a suspect none of the men were all that anxious to suggest a name lest they might also be called upon to inflict whatever punishment was decided upon. So, more as a joke than anything else, David Batty said, 'What about Olly Carver then?'

That made them smile and broke the tension for a while, since Olly Carver, despite his fiercesome appearance and prowess with a gun, was as gentle a creature as one could wish to find. Besides, Olly had the ear of God, people said, and he could tell when winter was about to start long before there was any hint of it in the air. In the autumn, regardless of what the weather was like, when the first smoke curled up from Olly Carver's chimney you could stake your life that the next morning there would be the first fine white covering of frost on the ground. It never failed. But how Olly knew was anyone's guess, but know he did, and once smoke was spotted all the other fires and ranges in the village would be rekindled, and old people would curse poor Olly gently, blaming him for the onset of winter, but they did so quietly, to themselves, keeping their curses intimate.

Olly lived some way from the village, away from the sea and high up in the hills. Rumour had it that he had killed his wife trying for a son since she died in childbirth having borne him thirteen daughters, although nobody dared say as much to his face. And when she died Olly became more or less a recluse, if you can be a recluse surrounded by thirteen of the best-looking young women God ever created, and the only time people really saw him was when he led his tribe down into the valley each Sunday morning for Mass, the lot of them practically filling the chapel by themselves.

When something was needed from the shop Olly sent his daughters, four of them anyway, usually Heather and Myrtle and Hazel and Holly since they were the eldest and could keep an eye on each other. It was always a bit of an occasion when the Carver girls came shopping, all neatly turned out and each of them carrying a little wicker basket, and the young men seemed to be able to sniff their coming, like animals do when in heat, and when they appeared the boys would stroll in twos and threes behind them, their hands in their trouser pockets, maybe hoping to make their manhood seem bigger and more potent, making adolescent mating noises with their tongues, or what they thought such noises should be. But the Carver girls always ignored them, keeping their pretty heads bowed, which made everything more exciting, and when the girls had finished shopping and returned home the young men would watch them till they were out of sight and then gather outside Biddlecomb's and arouse each other with lurid and impractical tales of what they would do if ever they got one of those Carver girls to themselves.

'Ha, you can forget Olly,' Patrick Farrel said. 'Might as well suggest old Davey Allen.' That really made them laugh since Davey Allen was ninety if he was a day and had to be lifted from his bed every morning by his spinster sister and dumped in a chair by the window, where he stayed until he was humped back to bed again of an evening.

Other names were mentioned but dismissed after little debate, and it was as though everyone knew from the beginning who they were going to end up blaming, but were leaving his name until last, hoping someone else would come up with it. And to make things easy Patrick Farrel asked Willie Little, 'That morning you saw May lying there, Willie – you didn't notice anyone else around, I suppose?'

Willie Little got the message all right, but he wasn't going to jump into anything head first. He screwed up his face as though thinking hard. Then he slowly shook his head. 'Can't say I did.'

'You're sure now?'

Willie shook his head some more. 'Can't say I did.'

'Think, Willie,' Mr Biddlecomb urged.

'I *am* thinking.'

'Shut your eyes and see the whole thing again in your mind,' Mr Biddlecomb suggested, since he'd heard somewhere that was the best way to remember things.

Willie shut his eyes.

The men waited.

'You know something,' Willie said eventually, opening his eyes. The men leaned forward.

'What, Willie?' Mr Biddlecomb asked quietly, like he was unwilling to wake someone from a trance.

'I think there *was* someone there. Can't be sure, mind. But something seems to tell me there was someone – hiding, sort of.'

'Think, Willie. For God's sake, will you think. Who could it have been, would you say?'

Willie Little closed his eyes again, playing their game. And now, keeping his eyes closed, he said, 'I think it was Christy Codd.'

You could hear the hiss of breath being released from all their lungs.

'Christy Codd. I'd forgotten about him,' Leonard Midden lied.

'Funny I never thought of him,' Davey Shortt lied.

'You're sure it was Christy?' Patrick Farrel wanted to be sure.

'Sure as I can be,' Willie Little lied.

And the rest of the men just nodded, preferring to do their lying in silence.

Four

Christy Codd was one of those unfortunate creatures on whom God had played a mischievous trick, giving him beautiful looks and a brain not worth a whit.

Christy lived with his mother in the cottage closest to the cemetery. When he was two and diagnosed as being terminally stupid, his father, Dermot, had taken Christy's two elder brothers with him to Canada to look for work. He had promised, of course, as all those who emigrated from the village did, to send money back for his wife and idiot son to join him, but he never did. True, he did write occasionally at first but filled his letters with excuses rather than cash. Once he sent presents at Christmas, perhaps to soften the blow when even the letters stopped, and for years now nothing had been heard of any of them. So, it was left to Mrs Codd to raise her crazy son, and she did so as well as she could, doing sewing and darning at which she was very good, and helping with the lambing, while he, Christy, did heavy chores for he was a fine strong young man now, and obliging to a fault, and did exactly as he was bid without demanding too much for his labours. But you had to keep an eye on him just the same. You couldn't just say, 'Christy, chop me some wood, will you, like a good boy,' and leave him to it because you'd end up without a tree standing within a mile of you; or say 'Christy, be a pet and pick a few of them apples for a pie,' and expect him just to gather you a handful. The tree would be stripped and you'd be left with baskets of apples just for the rotting.

Just as the young bucks lusted after the Carver girls, so the young girls of the village hungered for Christy Codd. It was a time when big hands meant a big cock, and Christy had hands like shovels, which led the girls to dream of the size of what might be hanging between his legs. The twins Daphne and Delphinium Leary were the worst for teasing him. You'd never have taken them for twins, though, Daphne being a thin, weedy girl, pinched in her spotty face, and with one eye that kept looking at the other to see what it was up to, while Delphinium was huge, and impossible to clothe since every available garment was far too small for her bulk, and when she stretched (which she did quite often since that was the way the pretty girls in the magazines posed, wasn't it?) her blouse or woolly top would ride up and reveal a great belly criss-crossed with tiny blue and red veins, making her stomach look for all the world like some monstrous bloodshot eye.

They weren't the most popular pair either, being spiteful and vindictive, aware that they were ugsome to behold, aware, too, that they were likely to remain spinsters all their lives, unless they found some blind eejit to marry them, which was unlikely, and so be left to suffer the jibes and loneliness that spinsterhood brings. So maybe that was why they were unkind to Christy, always taunting him, egging him on, trying to make him make a bigger fool of himself than he normally did, ever ready to make a grab for his cock and get him going. Oddly enough though, Christy never fell for their wiles. Probably he didn't realise what they were up to. He would just stand there and grin idiotically at them, and agree with everything they said in his silly way. On one occasion Delphinium did manage to get his thing out and play with it for a while, her ugly eyes popping out of her head as it swelled and grew in her fingers, but Christy just thought it was all a great joke, and ran off down the street, guffawing like a lunatic, his penis flopping about his knees like a stallion's. Leonard Midden witnessed the incident and reported it at length in Biddlecomb's, exaggerating the details, of course, and making everybody laugh their heads off.

'Just goes to show you, doesn't it, that our Christy might

be stupid but he's not completely mad,' Patrick Farrel said.

'Not mad enough to give that ugly fat cow the length of him anyway,' Davey Shortt said, giving Willy Little a sly look since it was rumoured Willie had had it off with Delphinium once or twice.

Mind you, it wasn't just the young girls who had an eye for Christy. There were some of the older women who would not have said no to a dally with him. Christy, you see, for all his dimness, was a gentle soul, and considerate, and those were attributes their menfolk lacked, things they yearned for and dreamed about, if only briefly. And their menfolk saw this, saw the occasional look of longing in their eyes as Christy passed, and they couldn't understand what any healthy woman could see in a moron. And what they couldn't understand worried them, and what worried them they disliked, so it was easy for them to dislike Christy. True, they never admitted this and seldom showed it. They tended more to use poor Christy as a goad to anger each other, saying things like, 'Saw young Christy Codd over at your place this afternoon, and him looking very pleased with himself.'

'Cleaning out the barn, I had him.'

'Oh, sure. Sure. Of course, of course, of course.'

'You getting at something?'

'Me? No. What's there for me to get at?'

'So what are you on about then?'

'Nothing. Nothing really. Just that smile on your woman's face – that because the barn was being cleaned out, you think?'

That sort of thing. So, in an odd way, they could dislike each other whenever they wanted by disliking Christy first, which made everything that much easier to manage. Stopped them hanging on to any anger they felt towards each other. Father Reynolds, who came back from the missions in Fiji once to visit his mother one last time before she died, called it a sort of Celtic voodoo, and maybe he had a point.

There is something extraordinary in the make-up of man that makes him shudder when confronted by abnormality in others, that makes a childlike absence of malice accusatory. As though to negate this feeling he derides innocence, equating it with weakness. In his arrogance he detects a fearful threat in anything that smacks of timidity or gentleness, and he denounces it with mockery, using a buffoon's abuse to conceal his brutishness, and conjures up within himself an awful righteousness that permits him to destroy simplicity.

And so it was with Christy Codd. Once he had been nominated the men found it easy to call up reasons for their wicked decision, each reason a warped vindication of what they planned to do. Yet, as men accustomed to witnessing the process of death, they were appropriately solemn about evil intent since death, they suspected, could be contagious, and they knew whoever was chosen to revenge themselves on the unfortunate Christy would be marked with the finger of doom. So it was agreed that things would be let lie until after Christmas, left until the emigrants who returned home each year had gone back to wherever they had come from. 'Give us time to think about it and be sure,' was how Mr Biddlecomb put it, although he knew full well there'd be precious little thinking done about it, not about the justice of it at any rate.

'And not a word to any of the women,' Patrick Farrel warned.

'God, no,' everyone agreed.

'Should decide now, though – I mean, shouldn't we decide now who – ' Leonard Midden began before stumbling over his thoughts.

'We'll think about that too,' Mr Biddlecomb put in quickly.

'And about how,' Davey Shortt said.

'And about how,' Mr Biddlecomb agreed.

And that decided, it was amazing how quickly they seemed able to strike it all from their minds, and return to drinking, and talking about other things, and joking.

Yet from that night on until he was killed, the men were especially kind to Christy. They stopped mocking him and poking fun at him, and they paid him more than he asked for when he jobbed for them, and they saw to it that their wives sent little gifts to Mrs Codd, pies and bread and some nice brown eggs. And Patrick Farrel warned Mrs Leary to keep her randy twins away from Christy, saying it was sinful the way those girls were going on like bitches in heat, they were, and if one of them did end up with a child in her belly not to be looking for sympathy, because there wouldn't be a drop of that coming.

If Christy Codd noticed the change he didn't show it. He was his simple self as ever, ever smiling in his silly way, ever obliging. When the fragile membranes of his mind that ensured sanity had snapped they had also mercifully removed any knowledge of pain, and Christy lived happily for now in his painless world, probably not even aware that people were being especially nice to him. 'Thank you, Christy,' they said politely when he did some work for them, and Christy smiled back the way he had always done regardless. And even when he made a botch of something he wasn't sworn at or hit across his shoulders with whatever came to hand. 'Don't you worry your head about that, Christy. You did the best you could, didn't you?' was how that was dealt with.

And as his mother, Mrs Codd, too, was smiled upon, and, in the way mothers like to do, she credited her son with the pleasant change. 'You're a good boy, Christy Codd, aren't you?' Mrs Codd asked, speaking to Christy in the same sing-song, baby way she had spoken to him since the day he had been dragged from her with forceps. 'Of course you are,' she went on, as ever not expecting or waiting for an answer. 'The best little man in the world,' she told him, and Christy, standing six foot and a bit more and towering over her, gurgled like a delighted infant. 'And would you just look at what Mrs Keogh sent up for us! Look at that, Christy! The grandest pie you ever did see, isn't it? Of course it is.' Mrs Codd sliced the pie and sniffed. 'Gorgeous,' she said. 'Just gorgeous. And the biggest bit for my Christy, isn't that right?' She cut a wedge of the pie and put it carefully on Christy's plate, licking her finger. 'Mmmm,' she said. 'You're going to just love that, Christy,' she told him. 'You'll think your Mammy can't cook at all after you've tasted that, won't you?' she said playfully, knowing Christy would never be capable of any such thought. 'People are good to us, aren't they?' she went on, taking a small piece of pie for herself, and savouring a mouthful. 'Of course they are. People are really kind to you and me, and it's all your doing, Christy,' she said.

And on and on she went, right through the meal, playing her harmless little game, deluding herself that Christy could understand every word she said and was, in some way, contributing to the conversation, giving responses to her questions that she herself gave, and even asking questions of his own that she herself asked.

And Christy, whether he understood or not, ate his pie with relish, and smiled brightly, his lovely blue eyes shining with the happiness of it all.

Five

Christmas was a grand time in the village of Ifreann. Not that it had much to do with Christ although everyone did go to Mass on Christmas morning and Father Cunningham was at his very best when his church was filled, forgetting about hell and retribution for the time being, and concentrating more on the fact that Christmas was a time for giving – a point he made just before the collection-plate started circulating. No, Christmas was grand because the wanderers, as they were called, came home, home by the bus-load, all in their fine new suits and polished shoes that were clearly too tight and pinched their feet mercilessly, and with great wads of money bulging in their pockets. Small matter that they worked all hours of the day and night, and slept in hostels, eight to a room, in London or Coventry or Sheffield or New York even, and half of them were up to their eyeballs in debt to the money-lenders. And the presents they brought? Outrageous things. Clothes that didn't fit since they were bought for someone remembered from a year earlier and no thought given to the fact that they might have grown up or grown wider, but they could be let out, couldn't they, or taken in? And perfume for sisters, rare scents with exotic names like Eau de Cologne and Nuit Bleue, whatever that was. Oh, and lavender water, buckets of it, for grandmothers, since grandmothers always got lavender water whether they wanted it or not. And there were toys galore for the younger children, marvellous toys that they couldn't understand and couldn't make work and didn't know what to do with, but wondrous nonetheless.

And the drinking that went on was something to behold, each wanderer trying to outdo the other with generosity, buying round after round, and none of your porter either, the hard stuff. They only drank whisky and brandy and rum as if this gave them status, and Mr Biddlecomb, red-faced and sweaty and beaming, happily supplied them, and slept the sleep of the mighty after he had counted the takings.

Of course, with so much drink inside them of an evening many of the men fell to getting maudlin, and tears were shed, but this was part of the enjoyment. And sometimes they laughed at the strangest things like when Matt Gillsenon reported that Mickey Murray had been killed by breaking his neck when jumping from his neighbour's bedroom window. That brought great guffaws for Mickey Murray had always been a one for sewing his oats and there were one or two youngsters up and down the coast that bore an uncanny resemblance to him, and when all was said and done it was a fitting way for him to go, wasn't it? Better than being crushed by one of those bloody great machines they used for laying the tarmac like had befallen Tim Hyde. That must have been terrible. Crushed like that and the eyes of him popping out of his head to see what was going on about him, and him already well dead.

But then, like everything else, it came to an end. The money ran out, and the wanderers had to leave and make more for next year. And the buses lumbered back to the outskirts of the village and collected them and took them away, and they weren't so jolly now, their sore heads being only a part of it.

And by January it was almost as though they had never been home. Except for the old women. They remembered all right. And you'd see them standing by their windows, hugging themselves, hugging the memory of their sons and grandsons, and knowing that was probably all they would now be left with, that memory.

The weather didn't do much to help raise the spirits either, for it was always at its worst during the first three months of the year, raining like it would never stop, and the river churning itself into a frenzied tantrum, flooding the fields, and the wind cutting into every nook and cranny, and so bitter it would freeze you where you stood given half a chance.

And there were deaths too that season, three in all. Old Davey Allen went, just going off as he dozed in his chair, which was a relief for his sister since it meant she didn't have to heave him back into bed any more of an evening. And Betty Clarke too. She keeled over while collecting her eggs. It was a couple of days before she was found and one of her chickens had laid an egg in the hood of her cape, which everyone thought was quite a nice touch since Betty had been very fond of her chickens, giving each of them a name and thinking of them as her children. And Sissy Williams went but that was expected. She'd been getting ready to go for ages, burning stuff that she didn't want anyone to see, nothing for them to poke into, as she put it. She must have known exactly when her time was up because they found her in her bed with her hair all nicely arranged and her very best nightdress on, and her rosary beads prettily arranged between her bony old fingers. But there were births to look forward to, which was a good thing, so not everything was bleak.

But things looked bleak enough for Christy Codd, although a few of the men were having second thoughts about it all, particularly Willie Little, who kept saying things like, 'Oh, I dunno about that,' and shaking his head like someone with superior knowledge of such things. But whether he was doing this because he was genuinely worried or just because he wanted to seem important was anyone's guess. Liam Gillsenon, Matt's younger brother, didn't seem all that keen now either, but he was still floating on the promises his brother had made over Christmas to get something organised by way of a job in Leeds, so it could have been that which made him reluctant to participate. And Harry Copter, who was going through one of his religious spells, visibly quaked when Christy Codd's name was mentioned, and started muttering platitudes to God whom, during these infrequent spells, he regarded as something of a chum.

But for the rest of the men the terrible decision had taken on curious proportions. It had become something of a primeval sacrifice, a pacification of whatever god dealt with the salving of consciences. And, in the way stupid men do, they convinced themselves that the suffering of a lesser being would expiate the death of an innocent. It also meant, of course, that once Christy Codd had been taken care of none of them could ever accuse each other of killing May O'Mahony, which was what they wanted in the first place. And to make things easier for them they started contriving stories about Christy, telling each other he'd been acting strange since May was found dead, saying he looked very jittery, which was untrue, and saying hadn't he been hanging about the church a lot like a man with something awful to confess, which was true. Christy did seem to spend quite a bit of time lurking near the church but even he must have known that Father Cunningham only came from the town on Sundays and big feast days, so what he was doing there was a mystery, and the mysterious was just what the men needed to validate their decision.

In March they decided they couldn't put it off any longer, and Mr Biddlecomb became very business-like about it. 'Right, now,' he said when all the men concerned were there. 'What we've got to do is decide who's going to do it.'

Willie Little cackled. 'And how are you going to do that?' he asked. 'You're not going to be daft enough to ask for volunteers, are you?'

Clearly Mr Biddlecomb had been hoping for just that. He reddened and blew loudly into his handkerchief before saying, 'Of course not.'

'Good,' said Willie. "Cause I couldn't see you getting any.'

'We've got to do this properly,' Mr Biddlecomb went on, and in place of volunteers he asked for suggestions.

'What I think,' Davey Shortt said, 'what I think is that whoever gets to do it should be – ' he paused, trying to think of the word he wanted, but starting all over again when he couldn't call it up. 'What I think is that we shouldn't know who does it,' he concluded.

'You mean he should be anonymous?' Mr Biddlecomb asked.

Davey smiled widely. 'That's the word. What was it again, Mr Biddlecomb – anon – '

'Anonymous,' Mr Biddlecomb repeated.

'Anonymous,' Davey Shortt said slowly, chewing on the word like it was a jelly.

'That's a good idea, Davey,' Mr Biddlecomb said. 'Very sensible. What do you think?' he asked, looking round the store.

'How are you going to manage that one?' Willie Little wanted to know.

'Easy,' Mr Biddlecomb snapped.

'Tell us then,' Willie insisted.

'I know,' Leonard Midden said, seeing Mr Biddlecomb starting to redden again, and pleased with the chance to make his presence felt. 'What we do is this. I heard about this somewhere. Don't know where. Somewhere – '

'Get on with it, Leonard, will you?' Mr Biddlecomb said.

'You draw straws and before putting the straws into a jug or something you mark one, or make one shorter or something, and whoever gets that one does it.'

There was silence for a while before Patrick Farrel said, 'It could work.'

'Don't have no straws,' Mr Biddlecomb said, sulking a bit.

'Doesn't have to be straws.'

'What then?'

'Anything. Bits of stick. Anything.'

'I've got matches,' Mr Biddlecomb said.

'There you go,' Leonard Midden said, delighted that his idea was being considered.

'I've got red ones and black ones. What about if I put just one black one in and all the rest red, and whoever gets the black one –' He stopped at that.

And now that it had come down to it the men shifted their feet uneasily, and stopped looking at each other again. One of the gas lamps made a sudden pop, and went out, making them all jump, 'Damn stupid thing,' Mr Biddlecomb said mostly to himself, and went to fix it. And when he'd done that, he asked, 'Well?'

'Oh, I dunno about that,' Willie Little said.

'I wasn't asking you, Willie Little,' Mr Biddlecomb snapped.

'Who was you asking then?'

'Everyone.'

'Well, I'm part of everyone, amn't I?'

'Shut up, Willie,' Patrick Farrel said, but kindly enough, and Willie shut up obligingly.

'What do you think, Thomas?' Mr Biddlecomb asked Thomas Meehan.

Thomas Meehan was a man everyone trusted, a big man with a lush black beard and black eyes that made him look fierce enough, but which belied his gentle and often wise nature. He was the only fisherman who owned land, twenty acres he got when he married Kathie Docherty. But he showed little interest in the land. 'The sea owns me,' he'd say, and the other fishermen would nod as if they understood what he meant by that. And when someone remarked, 'Can't beat owning a bit of land,' Thomas Meehan would look at them in his peculiar sad way but say nothing. Indeed, Thomas Meehan seldom said much, keeping himself to himself and doting on his family, which was probably why his opinion was prized. Now, Thomas Meehan just fixed his gaze on Mr Biddlecomb's face and tugged at his beard a bit, and made a grimace that indicated that he hadn't heard enough yet to be sure.

'Suppose we do what you say,' Patrick Farrel went on. 'Supposing we do each of us take a match and the one who gets the black one takes care of things. It's got to be that none of us knows *who* gets the black one so that none of us knows either who – you know what I mean.'

'That's fair enough,' Davey Shortt said.

'Very fair,' Mr Biddlecomb conceded, perhaps peeved that he hadn't said it himself.

'Dunno about that either,' Willie Little said.

'For Christ's sake, Willie!' Mr Biddlecomb exploded.

'Just saying,' Willie said.

'Well, don't.'

'Okay. Have it your own way. Just means we'll all be wondering who got the black match, that's all. Won't be any further forward.'

'You don't have to wonder if you don't want to,' Mr Biddlecomb insisted.

'No,' Willie agreed. 'Don't *have* to, but will.'

'Well, you can wonder as much as you please, Willie Little. I'm getting the matches ready and that's it.'

'Please yourselves,' Willie said.

Mr Biddlecomb got the matches and counted the heads of the men, dropping one match for each of them into a tin and shaking the tin well. 'Now, remember,' he said sternly. 'If you get the black one keep your gob shut. Don't let any of us know you have it,' he warned, and put the tin on the counter.

As each man came to choose, Mr Biddlecomb made him look away and only then raised the lid a little. And after he had chosen each man left the store without a word, many of them not even looking at their match until they were outside and alone. And when they were all gone Mr Biddlecomb opened the tin fully and stared at the single match remaining. He let out a long, low moan. He poured himself a drink and swallowed it. 'Thanks be to God,' he sighed, wiping beads of sweat from his brow with the cloth he used to wipe down the bar. He took another drink. Then he gazed for a while at the red top on the match, breathing deeply. He used it to light his pipe. Striking it on the stone floor and watching the bright white light. Then he sat down for a while, amazed at how shaky his legs were.

It was a terribly windy night that night as though all the elements had decided to become involved in the decision and condemned it. The east wind whipped down the valley, rattling windows and lifting great wodges of thatch from the roofs and sending them scudding down the potholed street like devilish whiffmagigs. There were claps of thunder, too, not loud ones, but low rolling rumbles that promised far worse to come. And the rain from the sea, thick and saline, soaked itself in everywhere, making the cattle in the barns panic and bellow as it stung their great brown trusting eyes, making the collie dogs whimper, making those who could not sleep cough quietly to themselves in tune to the gale and wonder when this bitter season would be over and done with.

And the women whose men were out at sea clad themselves in black oilskins and clasped heavy shawls about their heads and went to the cliff-top and stood there, gazing out to sea, hoping for a glimpse of the small prow lights that signalled the safe return of their men. But soon the salty spindrift seared their worried eyes, and they were forced to turn their backs to the sea, which was an awful thing to have to do for it was like they were turning their backs on their men.

Six

It lasted five days and nights, that storm, battering the valley, the thunder making the very ground shake, and the lightning striking the elm in the cemetery and cleaving it in half, leaving one bit standing and the other crashing down onto Sam Gogarty's headstone. And perhaps it was this, and her dreaming of it, that made Mrs Codd think she heard a strange noise and sit up in her bed with a start. She cocked her head and listened, hoping for a repeat of the sound that had awoken her. 'That you, Christy?' she called, for sometimes Christy went down to the kitchen at night for a drink of water and quite often he dropped a jug and broke it. When she got no answer she clambered out of her bed and wrapped one of the blankets about her, and downstairs she went, calling, 'Christy? Christy? Christy?' as she went.

When she got to the foot of the stairs she was surprised to find the front door open, swaying in the wind, but not banging against the wall since Christy's wellingtons prevented that, acting as a buffer. The kitchen door was also open and she now saw Christy flat on his back on the floor by the range, a terrible wound in his chest and blood gushing from it. 'Christy!' she screamed, and made a run for him. Down on her knees, bending over him, cradling his lovely head in her arms, she rocked him, trying desperately to think what to do. She pulled the blanket off of herself, made a pillow of it, and put it under his head, smoothing his brow as though wiping the young man's worries away with her gentle touch. 'Talk to me, Christy,' she pleaded in a tiny voice, some wicked hope tricking her into thinking he might just be sleeping, but Christy was well past talking to anyone any more. Then, as though the realisation of death in her hands suddenly came to her, she let out a dreadful scream, and took tufts of her hair in her hands, tugging mercilessly at them. She stood up, twirling about the place, screaming and calling Christy's name all the while. And then she stopped. She stopped and stared in disbelief at the man standing in the shadow of the dresser, still with the gun in his hands. 'What – ' she began, and that was all that came from her, for the man raised the gun and fired, and took most of her head away. She collapsed beside her son, and as life shivered out of her she grabbed Christy's hand, maybe thinking she could lead him to heaven in the way she had led him through every step he'd taken on earth.

Hannah O'Mahony was at her window watching the storm with the fascination that only the demented seem to have for such things, and saw the man coming down the street from the Codds'. She didn't seem to recognise him, or gave no sign of that anyway, but she thought to herself what a brave man he was to be out on a night like this, walking through all that storm with his lovely rolling gait like all his life he had passed through such weather. She let the man pass through her vision and stopped her eyes from following him: he might not have been real, after all, and Hannah didn't want to be following the sight of phantoms disappearing into the dark.

The next morning the storm abated, simmering down to an eerie keening as though lamenting.

And there was lamenting, too, when the news of the tragedy became known, and all the villagers made their way to the cottage where the Codds had lived, and stood outside, the women on one side, huddled, praying with tight, chapped lips, some weeping at the awfulness of it all, the men clustered in groups on the other side, shaking their heads as though surprised, but neither praying to God nor talking to each other, since prayer would be a mockery and words were difficult to find. But they kept their vigil for many hours, until someone pointed out that the Gardai would have to be sent for.

And so the Gardai were called, and they came, two of them at first, a sergeant and a constable, just to see what all the fuss was about. They were shocked by what they saw, and spent a lot of time scratching their thick red necks, and officiously telling the villagers to keep back. 'Keep back now, the lot of you. Can't have you destroying the evidence before the Inspector gets here,' they said, sounding very important.

'How's he goin' to know he's got to come if you don't send for him?' Willie Little asked.

'He'll be along, never you fear,' the Constable said, eyeing Willie and maybe wondering if he should be arrested for his cheek.

'Only asking,' Willie Little said in his defence.

'Just you leave things to us,' the Constable told him. 'We know what we're doing.'

And the Inspector did come eventually, and he brought with him two more Gardai, men not in uniform, young men, slim young men with bright faces who seemed to know what they were doing too, and who spent a lot of time down on their knees peering at the bodies and at everything close by them. They did strange things like taking measurements and contriving angles and photographing the position of the gun in Christy Codd's hands, a shotgun that Christy's father had used to shoot rabbits and crows before he had taken off with his two other sons and vanished from the face of the earth.

And when they had finished doing whatever they had to do, they set themselves up in Mr Biddlecomb's store and started interviewing everyone, being gruff and quite unfriendly about it as though everyone they spoke to was a definite suspect. But they didn't learn much since the women knew nothing and the men weren't saying anything except Leonard Midden who couldn't resist the temptation to philosophise. 'I'll tell you what, Inspector. That's something that's been just waiting to happen for a long time. Wasn't Christy a mad one. Never right in the head.'

And that was as much as the Gardai learned, but they

seemed content enough with that. And as evening drew in, and the starlings screamed into the old yew tree near the church, they left, taking the bodies with them.

But while the death of Christy and his mother was much discussed by the women over mugs of strong black tea, the men, gathering as was their wont in Biddlecomb's, never mentioned it although each of them longed to know how come Mrs Codd was killed too. But they couldn't ask that, could they? Who could they ask? Only one of them knew the answer to that and he wasn't likely to tell anyone, was he?

After about a week word came from the town that the matter had been closed. Christy was blamed for shooting his mother, blamed for shooting himself, too, but that was his concern. But he'd done it all when of unsound mind, they said, which made it sound better, less gruesome anyway, and took a lot of the guilt off poor Christy's chest.

And that resolved the Codds could be buried, and everyone turned out for that, listening quietly as Father Cunningham, standing tall and sombre and solemn as befitted the occasion, read prayers from a thin black book which he held at arm's length in his blue fingers, cocking his head and moving the text this way and that having abandoned his spectacles which constantly clouded over in the drizzle, his white surplice flapping about him like some exotic gander trying to take flight.

'. . . *cineres ad cineres*,' he intoned, looking rather ashen himself in the cold, but sounding confident enough as well he might on such familiar ground.

The melancholy ceremony concluded, the dead well and truly committed to the merciful hands of God, the holes filled and the flowers, such as they were, neatly laid out, the villagers drifted away, the women immersed in muttered sympathy, the men silent, making for Biddlecomb's and the comfort of familiar, less foreboding surroundings. They even tried to normalise the event by drinking the health of Christy, which was an odd thing to do but none of them saw anything extraordinary in it. But if they thought that would set them all back on an even keel they were wrong. If anything things were worse now, but maybe time would lend a helping hand. Anyway, that was all they could hope for.

Spring

Seven

It was as though a benevolent god had waved his arm and obliterated winter, and erased all memory of it also. Overnight the wind dropped and the weather warmed. Primroses appeared in the hedgerows, making the laneways and the riverbank pretty. Birds scavenged for twigs and moss and fluff, and at night the vixens yodelled their piercing call, setting the dogs to barking, their yapping sounding hoarse from lack of practice. And the old people who had survived took to smiling again, albeit thinly, and blankets were strung out on lines to air and they flapped away like the sails of a beached schooner. Lambs were born and gambolled in the fields, bleating their hearts out. And Maisie Midden had her baby a bit early but both of them were fine, and she told everyone she was calling the child Elizabeth which some folk thought was a bit grand for such a wizened ugly little creature. But you couldn't tell: she might grow up to be pretty enough and merit such an extravagant name. Unlikely given the looks of its parents, but possible.

In early May Willie Little brought the news. 'Heard the news?' he asked in Biddlecomb's, knowing full well that none of them had.

'What news is that then, Willie?' Mr Biddlecomb asked.

'You haven't heard then?'

'Don't know if we have till you tell us, do we?' Mr Biddlecomb answered with a glare.

'Someone's been and bought the Codds' cottage.'

That made all the men listen, made them suddenly look uneasy, too.

'Thought that was going to some aunt or something up in the city,' Patrick Farrel said.

'Did too. But she couldn't be bothered with it.'

'So who bought it?' Davey Shortt asked.

Willie Little shrugged. 'Dunno. Someone. Foreign, I think.'

'You mean foreign foreign or just someone from the city?'

Willie shrugged again. 'Dunno,' he said.

'Don't know much do you?' Mr Biddlecomb said.

'Know someone's bought the place, don't I?' Willie retorted.

'Doesn't tell us much.'

'Tells you someone's bought it.'

'Wonder who it is?' Leonard Midden wondered aloud.

'Soon find out. Soon enough anyway.'

'Suppose you're right, Willie.'

But they didn't find out for a while, and certainly not soon enough as far as they were concerned. But they did have something to talk about since within a few days a van arrived with strange men in it, and they started doing wonderful things to the cottage, replacing windows, re-thatching, painting inside and out, and putting in a blue bath which was something unheard of.

'A *blue* bath,' Davey Shortt reported with something approaching awe in his voice. 'And a basin and shit bowl in the same colour.'

'You're kidding!'

'I'm not.'

'A *blue* bath?'

'Swear to God, and a basin and shit bowl to match,' Davey insisted.

'Wouldn't like that,' Tommy Stack said. 'Not blue. Wouldn't fancy having a shit in a blue bowl. Wouldn't seem right, would it?'

'Have to ask your arse that,' Willie Little told him, and everyone had a great laugh at that.

But the men didn't laugh quite as much, didn't laugh at all in fact when the man who had bought Codds' cottage arrived. Although friendly enough he didn't have much to say for himself, and made it clear from the beginning that he didn't want much truck with anyone and intended to keep himself pretty much to himself. He came to Biddlecomb's from time to time, but didn't join the rest of them. He stood apart, making one pint last him all evening. And he was unnerving since, although he said little, he appeared to listen a lot, and gave the impression everything he heard was being stored away most carefully.

Even Father Cunningham seemed thrown by the man. During his Sunday sermon his eyes kept flicking back to the stranger's face, and he got all tied up with his words on many occasions, and there wasn't the customary fire in his voice either when he went on about hell and all that stuff.

'Something funny about him,' was how Connor Neill put it.

'Funny about who?' Mr Biddlecomb asked, pretending not to know.

'Him.'

'Oh.'

And that was another thing: they still hadn't found out his name, which was irksome. None of them came right out and asked him since they didn't do that sort of thing, and the stranger never volunteered it. And he got no post so Jim Ridgen didn't prove himself a fount of information.

'What you mean by funny, Connor?' Davey Shortt asked.

Connor Neill sucked air through his teeth and grimaced. 'Don't rightly know.'

'Makes you laugh – is that what you mean?'

''Course not. I mean – well, creepy. Like he knows things and isn't letting on.'

'Puts the frighteners on you, does he?'

'Damn right he does. Anyway, got to be something odd about any man that buys a house where two folks have been killed,' Connor said before realising what he was saying, and he wilted under Mr Biddlecomb's accusatory glare.

'And has a blue bath,' Patrick Farrel put in to save the

situation and make them laugh again.

'Well, all I can say is that we'll find out all about him before he finds out anything about us, and that's for sure,' Mr Biddlecomb announced.

'That's for sure,' someone agreed.

'Hope you're right,' Willie Little said, putting a damper on things again.

'For Christ's sake, Willie!'

'Just saying I hope you're right. What's wrong with saying that?'

Kevin Keogh, who never had much to say for himself, which was probably why the men tended to heed him when he did speak, coughed suddenly and said, 'Can't help feeling I know him from somewhere.'

'What you mean from somewhere, Kevin? You ain't ever set foot out of the village since the day you were born.'

'I know. I know. Still have the feeling I know him from somewhere though.'

And that gave them pause for thought, and you could see them all thinking, rattling their brains but getting nowhere.

'Well, you know what Father Cunningham always says,' Mr Biddlecomb said.

'What's that, Mr Biddlecomb?'

'All will be revealed. That's what he always says. All will be revealed.'

'Yep,' Willie Little agreed. 'That's what he says all right. Heard him say that many a time myself.'

'There you go,' Mr Biddlecomb said, beaming.

'Only he means everything will be revealed after we're dead, and a fat lot of good that's going to be to any of us.'

He wasn't an old man, the stranger. Maybe thirty-five or forty at most. But he did look older than that. His hair was white, although he did have a fine bushy head of it and eyebrows to match, brows that met over the bridge of his long thin nose and gave him a curiously permanent sorrowful look. And his face had an unhealthy grey tinge to it and was gravely lined like that of someone who had suffered a great deal, or been swamped by worries, or spent a time, a long time, in prison or somewhere like that shielded from the sun. And when he walked he walked slowly, measuring his paces almost, very deliberate about it, the way the fishermen tended to walk on their first day home after a long spell at sea as if half expecting the ground to lurch and sway and heave under them and they without a decent rope to hang on to. He was very deliberate when he spoke too, on the rare occasions he did say anything, placing his words carefully in the air, just as he did his feet on the ground, a bit like a man unused to speaking at all, a look of mild surprise playing on his face when he finished a sentence. The clothes he wore caused a bit of comment also for although they were sober enough the cut of them was strange, definitely city clothes but sort of old-fashioned, like clothes from an old magazine, and not something you'd ever expect to see in the country certainly.

But for all that the man seemed comfortable with himself and with his surroundings, and fitted easily into the rhythm of the place. Oddly, he seemed to spend many hours in about the graveyard, staring at the headstones, and writing things down in a little notebook he always carried. It wasn't just the old headstones he looked at, the new ones too came under his scrutiny which just about put paid to Kevin Keogh's theory that he might have had ancestors buried there, or thought he had.

'Maybe that's it,' Kevin Keogh said one evening. 'Maybe that's why I think I've seen him before.'

The men looked puzzled, and eyed Kevin, waiting patiently for him to explain since Kevin wasn't a man to be hurried.

'Maybe he *has* a relative buried up there, and maybe it was the relative I knew. Maybe he just looks like him.'

'Lot of maybes there, Kevin.'

Kevin Keogh nodded, and blew a stream of smoke ceilingwards from his briar pipe. 'Life is, isn't it? Full of maybes.'

'Maybes and ifs,' Willie Little said, and Kevin agreed with him, nodding.

'As you say, Willie. Maybes and ifs.'

'If only he – ' Mr Biddlecomb began but stopped abruptly as Kevin Keogh wagged his pipe at him, and Willie Little let out a fiercesome cackle.

'There you are, Mr Biddlecomb. See? Just like Kevin and me was saying. Another if.'

'I was only going to say – '

'You were going to say if something,' Willie pointed out maliciously.

Mr Biddlecomb got testy. 'I *know* what I was going to say, Willie Little. I don't need you to tell me.'

'What was it you were going to say, Mr Biddlecomb?' Patrick Farrel wanted to know.

'Can't remember now,' Mr Biddlecomb said in a huff, turning on the tap and engrossing himself in the interesting process of washing glasses. But this was an old trick of his, and the men knew it, knew too that if they left him alone for a while he'd get round to telling them what he had been about to say anyway. And sure enough, as soon as he'd washed a few glasses and put them up on the shelf behind the bar Mr Biddlecomb stuck his thumbs in the cord of the striped apron he fancied himself in and said, 'If only he'd speak to us more we'd get an inkling of what he's up to.'

'Aye. And who he is,' Kevin Keogh said.

'All will be revealed,' Willie Little said with a wicked grin, and that set Mr Biddlecomb back into a bit of a huff again.

But before any revelation could take place the stranger had to take back-stage in the men's thoughts for a while because Thomas Meehan was drowned at sea, and death at sea was a terrible thing since often the body was never found, and no burial was possible, and the widow and children were left in an awful limbo, often giving to wondering if the man wasn't just floating on his back somewhere, still alive, waiting to be found and rescued. And it was the practice in such tragedies for the missing man's wife to go up to the cliff-top anyway, and stare out at the grey unfriendly ocean, and wave an arm, just in case her man was out there and might see her and find a little comfort in that.

They did find Thomas Meehan, though, but only after four days, and by then he'd been battered on the rocks and was in a terrible mess. Dead, of course, but in a terrible mess too which made everything worse, much worse because there was something wickedly sinful about inflicting pain on a body already dead even if it was the sea and the rocks that did it. Or so the villagers thought anyway.

After Mrs Finch, the midwife who knew a thing or two about bodies, and Kitty Mercer, who looked after the church and was a dab hand with a needle, had finished with him, Thomas Meehan didn't look too bad at all. Sure, there were scars and rock etchings on his handsome dark face, but all the blood had been wiped away and the wounds stitched in the same criss-cross pattern Kitty Mercer used to stitch up the chicken's arse at Christmas. And they'd combed his lovely wavy black hair, and dressed him in his good white shirt and good navy blue suit, and put shoes and socks on his feet, and even a white hankie sticking out of his top pocket.

The funeral was special too, even more special than the funerals of other fishermen who had been lost at sea, for Thomas Meehan had been well liked by everyone, and had always been the one to help out in a crisis without expecting any favours in return. So Peadar Taigh Donnelly, who made the coffins, did an artist's job, carving little fishing-boats with sails hoisted high on the rim of the lid, and polished the wood to a wonderful sheen, and burnished the brass handles till you could have shaved yourself in the reflection they gave. And he carved Thomas Meehan's name on the lid too, and burned out the letters with a hot poker so that they stood out, dark and glowing against the pale softwood of the coffin.

And Father Cunningham's voice was quite choked with emotion as he gave a little talk when the prayers were finished, saying that God must not be blamed since He worked in mysterious ways and what He did was always for the best. And wasn't it something to be thankful for anyway that Thomas Meehan was at peace now, warm and dry in the caress of Jesus and with all his earthly suffering behind him? And wouldn't he be there waiting to welcome his loved ones and be getting everything ready for them? Of course he would.

And when Father Cunningham finished his eulogy and sprinkled the coffin with holy water, they filled in the grave, being solemn about that too, and making sure not to just heave the clay in so that it would echo hollowly on the coffin and give offence with that awful sound but putting the shovels close to the box and letting the earth slip off it gradually. And when that was done everyone came up and shook Mrs Meehan's hand and told her if there was anything they could do to relieve her pain all she had to do was ask. And they came up to me too, and shook my hand, since I was Thomas Meehan's only son, his only child in fact.

Eight

I was fourteen then, and a grand big lad for my age. That's what my Mam thought anyway, although she never actually said it to me. But when my Dad was a week in the ground she wrote to my Auntie Maeve in Gooseneck, Arizona, and left the letter lying around so I took a quick peek at it. 'Young Aiden's just fourteen now, and a grand big lad for his age,' she wrote. 'He's such a comfort to me, and he looks the image of my poor Thomas, and I've such hopes he'll turn out to be as good a man as his father was, God willing.' So, there I was, fourteen and a grand big lad for my age, and a comfort to my Mam which was a nice thing to know.

I'd finished with school, of course. Most of us lads finished with school at fourteen since there were other more important things to be done. Only the very bright lads stayed on, going to the town, and even maybe on to university, but there wasn't many brainy enough for that although quite a few thought they were. The rest of us had to work, and for me that meant tending the cattle and the sheep my Dad kept on the three fields his father had left him. Insurance, my Dad always called those fields and animals like he'd known all along he wasn't going to live to a natural end, like something told him the sea was going to take him. And with him gone now responsibility for them fell onto me since Mam was delicate with a sickness on her chest and couldn't do heavy work like some of the other women. Anyway, I was a man now, man of the house, and the other men started treating me different, and stopped thinking of me as a boy, although they still called me Young Aiden, and probably still would be calling me that when I was ninety if I lived that long.

There's an awful lot of work with sheep. They have to be wormed and dipped and shorn, and they need their feet done, and their tails have to be cut to stop the blowflies laying their eggs in the dirt that might gather there. And when they lamb you have to be with them every minute of the day and night in case they have a difficult birth. If you're not there to help you could lose both the sheep and the lambs and that's a terrible loss to any farmer. You can time the lambing though, not letting the ram hump them too early, so that the lambs arrive when the worst of the winter weather is over, or is supposed to be over. That way you don't have to keep the stock cooped up, shielded from the cold, but can let them off into the fields as soon as they're born, and watch them leap and spin all over the place.

I was doing that the first time the stranger spoke to me, watching the lambs leap and spin all over the place. It was early in May, and the sun was warm enough, and I was sitting on the stone wall that I'd helped my Dad to build three years earlier, swinging my feet and thinking to myself that I wouldn't give up this sort of life for anything.

'The shepherd looks upon his sheep with the eyes of Christ.'

I spun my head round and saw the stranger staring at me. 'Huh?' I said.

'Something I read.'

'Oh.'

'You're Thomas Meehan's son.'

'That's right.'

'I was sorry –'

'That's all right,' I told him, not wanting to be reminded of my Dad on a nice day like it was, making me gloomy all over again.

'Can I?' the stranger asked, pointing to the wall.

I shrugged to say I didn't mind, and he climbed onto the

wall beside me, and joined me in looking at the lambs playing. And that's all we did. Looked, and listened to the sounds that echoed across the valley, the birds singing as they gathered food for their fledglings, the yap, now and again, of fox cubs mock-fighting close to their dens on the edge of the woods, and once the terrified scream of a young rabbit caught off guard by a marauding stoat.

Finally, 'I gotta go,' I said and jumped down off the wall.

The man nodded, but stayed where he was.

'See you,' I said.

'No doubt.'

I started to walk away, but turned and looked at him hard when he called after me, 'I enjoyed our time together.'

'Yeah,' I said. 'Yeah.' And to tell the truth I had enjoyed our time together also. Don't ask me why. I just did, but for some reason I didn't want to let him know that.

I was feeding the dogs round the side of the house when Patrick Farrel and Davey Shortt came to the house that evening. Mam met them at the door, and nodded to them without saying anything as they took off their caps.

'Eh, Young Aiden about?' Patrick Farrel asked.

Mam frowned. 'Why?'

Patrick Farrel gave a quick laugh. 'Just want a word with him, Kathie. That's all.'

Mam chewed on that before telling them, 'Round the back,' and watching them as they backed away from the door and came round the house, keeping their caps in their hands.

'Ah, Young Aiden,' Patrick Farrel said. 'How's everything?'

'Fine, thanks.'

'Grand pair of dogs those,' Davey Shortt observed.

'They do their job,' I told him.

'Got names, have they?'

'Bess and Sam,' I said.

'Bess and Sam,' Davey Shortt repeated. 'Good names those.'

'Eh, Young Aiden, tell me – ' Patrick Farrel began, and

then took a sigh and started all over again. 'Hear you were up there with that stranger this afternoon.'

I took the empty bowls from the dogs and ran them under the tap before answering. 'That's right.'

'Asking questions, was he?'

'No.'

'Oh. I see. Just sort of talking?'

'No.'

'Must have said something,' Davey Shortt put in.

'No.'

'Nothing?'

'Just sat there together, looking and listening.'

'Just sat there looking and listening?' Patrick Farrel asked.

'Like I said.'

'Must have told you his name, I'd bet.'

'No.'

'Asked you yours, though.'

'He knew it already.'

'Ah.'

I put the bowls up on the window ledge out of reach of the dogs and faced the two of them. 'That all?'

Patrick Farrel nodded vigorously. 'Oh, yes. That's all.'

'Right,' I said. 'Got to get inside now and help Mam some.'

'Of course. You're a good lad, Young Aiden.'

'Try to be,' I told them, and left them standing there. Best advice I can give you, lad, my Dad used to always say, is keep yourself to yourself, and keep what you know to yourself too. And that's what I was doing.

It wasn't until I finished my tea and was thinking about bed that Mam asked, 'What'd they want, those two?'

'Patrick and Davey?'

'Of course.'

'Don't know rightly, Mam. Asking me about that stranger who's taken the Codd house over, that's about it.'

'And why should they be asking *you* about him?'

'Seen me with him today, that's why.'

'You were with him?'

'Yeah. He came up to the field and sat on the wall with me.'

Mam suddenly looked worried. She pulled a chair up close to mine by the table and took hold of my hand. 'You must be careful, Aiden,' she said, like she knew something I didn't.

'Careful of what, Mam?'

'Of, well –' Mam stopped there.

'Of the stranger?'

'Well, yes,' Mam said, but making it clear there were other things she wanted me to be careful about too.

'He seems all right, Mam,' I told her.

'But you don't *know* him,' Mam insisted.

'All we did was sit on the wall and listen to things the way Dad and me used to listen to things sometimes.'

'It was different when it was your Dad,' Mam said quite sharply, and then got up and started tidying things up, tidying up things that didn't need to be tidied up like she always did when she was agitated about something.

I watched her for a while like I'd seen my Dad watch her on occasions like this, and then I stood up. I put my arm around her and kissed her on the cheek. 'Goodnight, Mam,' I said, and I waited until I'd reached the door before turning and adding, 'Mam? Don't you worry about me. I'll be careful. Real careful.'

Mam smiled at me then, a saddish smile, and came to me carrying that saddish smile all the way with her across the room, and put her arms about me. 'I pray you will, Aiden. You're all I have now, you know.'

'You worry too much, Mam.'

'Of course I worry,' Mam said, standing back a bit and staring at me like she was seeing me for the first time, or maybe for the last time and wanting to take every detail about me in. Then, abruptly, she went back to her tidying up again.

'Women!' I mocked, like I'd heard my Dad mock my Mam sometimes, and Mam looked up in surprise, and with fright in her eyes. Then she spotted me grinning, and threw a drying-up towel at me, and I could hear her giving little laughs to herself, and little sobs too, as I walked along the passage to my room.

Night's a funny time for me. I think a lot at night. Do *all* my thinking at night really. All snugged up in my bed with the quilt that had been in our family so long no one could remember where it came from, and it smelling faintly of lavender all the time since that was what was wrapped in it when it was put away during the summer months, pulled right up to my chin, and over my head when a storm was raging when I was younger. And lying there with my eyes tight shut I could go back over everything I wanted to think about, and back over some things I didn't want to think about as well, and hearing things different too, getting other meanings from words, meanings that I hadn't noticed when I'd heard them spoken. That happened the night my Dad was buried. I was in bed but I might as well still have been at the graveside since I could hear very clearly things that were being said, like when Eamonn Doherty who had been skipper of the boat my Dad fell from said to Noel Keegan who had been on the boat that night too, but whispering it, 'Can't understand it, Noel. Still can't understand it. No reason for it, see? Fine, calm night, like you know. Saw him standing one minute with his back against the winch just gaping out at the sea and the next minute he was gone.'

'What you saying, Eamonn?'

'Dunno what I'm saying.'

'You saying he went 'cause he wanted to go?'

'Dunno what I'm saying.'

'You saying he killed himself? That's what you're saying, isn't it?'

'If it wasn't Thoman Meehan we was talking about I'd say yes.'

And when the two of them saw me looking at them they stopped their talking, and hung their heads like they were praying the same as everyone else. But I thought about that when I was in bed. I thought about it a lot, and wondered about it too since I remembered that my Dad had been a bit funny for a few weeks before the accident, moody which wasn't like him at all, and snappy, even with my Mam.

But I'd think too about how Mam and Dad told me they'd met, and that would cheer me up. They told me about it lots of times, maybe forgetting that they'd ever told me at all since it was a precious moment for them and every time they spoke about it made them happy. It would start by Dad asking me, joking of course, when I was going to marry and settle down. And Mam would interrupt and say something like, 'What, and have him all tied down like you keep telling me you are?' And Dad would hoot with laughter at that, knowing it to be untrue, and say, 'Biggest mistake I ever made, that was, letting your Mam talk me into marrying her.' And Mam would put her hands on her hips and say, '*Me* talk *you* into marrying me? Well, I like that. Kept after me for best part of three years he did. Begging me. Took me up yonder to those hills and said to me, Glory, glory, glory but you're the most beautiful creature God ever did create, that's what your Dad said to me Aiden.' And Dad would give in then and look at Mam with his big soft eyes, and say, 'And wasn't that the truth of it though. And you still are.' And they'd hug each other, and just stand there swaying in their love.

Or maybe I wouldn't let my mind start thinking at all. Maybe I'd just lie there with one eye on the window and watch the nightly shapes that went whiffling past: owls that flew across the moon, seeking eatable stars, and swooping and diving, their great shapes swooping and diving on my walls. And bats, loads of them, soundless but for the whirr their wings made, their shadows fearsome things, like monsters, and threatening, and sometimes making me duck under the quilt as though those grey reflections could harm me.

But always, every night, like it was part of her getting ready to go to bed, Mam would tiptoe in and make sure I was all right. Sometimes we'd talk a bit, but mostly I'd pretend to be asleep and feel her tucking me in safely, and kiss me on the brow, and tiptoe out again. I don't know why I did that – pretend to be asleep, I mean. Something seemed to tell me it was the right thing to do, so I did it.

Nine

Mr Biddlecomb was the first to break, and give in to the urges of his curiosity. One Friday evening when he could stand it no longer he sauntered the length of the bar, trying to look nonchalant, and stopped dead in front of the stranger. 'Everything all right?' he asked for openers.

The stranger nodded. 'Fine.'

'Like it here then?'

'Fine.'

Mr Biddlecomb gave a little cough. 'Eh, we don't know your name, do we now?' he asked.

The stranger smiled a thin smile just to show Mr Biddlecomb he knew he had broken his resolve not to be nosey. 'Does it matter?' he asked finally.

'Doesn't *matter*,' Mr Biddlecomb said gruffly. 'Be civilised if we knew, though.'

'Civilised,' the stranger said mostly to himself, and seemed to think about that word for a while, because, 'Civilised,' he repeated, louder this time as if wanting everyone to hear. Then, 'Well, to be *civil*,' he said, stressing the word, 'I can tell you that for years,' he paused, 'for a lot of years, people have called me Johnsey.'

Mr Biddlecomb gave a small glance of triumph at the men eavesdropping from the other end of the bar. 'Johnsey,' he repeated in case they hadn't caught it. 'And would that be Johnsey like in a surname or would it be Johnsey like we'd be saying Jimmy or Mickey – you know, friendly-like, that way?'

'Just Johnsey,' the man said.

'Just Johnsey,' Mr Biddlecomb repeated, clearly disappointed. Then he bluffed away his frustration. 'Well, if Johnsey it is, then Johnsey it is.'

'That's right.'

Emboldened perhaps by Mr Biddlecomb's modest success Willie Little asked, 'And what would bring a man like you, Johnsey, to a place like this, if it's not asking too much?'

The stranger turned his head and gazed at Willie, and for a moment it looked as though he might say it *was* too much to ask. But then his eyes relaxed, and something like a twinkle played about them but whether this was a good or a bad sign was difficult to tell. 'A man needs to find himself,' he said enigmatically.

'Lost then, are you?' Willie Little said, thinking himself funny.

'Something like that,' the man said seriously, and then added, 'or a part of me at any rate,' and with that he finished his drink, and nodded, and strode from the bar.

'Well, what d'you make of that?' Mr Biddlecomb asked, clearly confounded.

But none of the men seemed to know what to make of it, or if they had any ideas they weren't proclaiming them. Only Kevin Keogh had something to say. 'Still say I've met him somewhere before,' he said.

'You keep saying that, Kevin,' Patrick Farrel pointed out.

'I know,' Kevin Keogh conceded, but that was as much as he would say.

'You don't suppose – ' Connor Neill began, but then shook his head and went back to picking his nose.

'Don't suppose what?' Mr Biddlecomb asked. 'And would you stop picking your nose and me with my tea not fully digested yet.'

'My nose,' Connor said with a surly look.

'My stomach,' Mr Biddlecomb retorted. 'You don't suppose what, anyway?'

'You don't suppose he was *sent*, do you?' Connor asked, rolling a glob of snot between his fingers and staring at it.

Kevin Keogh nodded. 'Could be,' he said.

'Sent for what?' Mr Biddlecomb demanded, knowing full well what they were getting at but not daring to admit it.

'Say what's on your mind, Connor,' Patrick Farrel said.

Connor Neill stared at his ball of snot and looked as though he might take a nibble on it. Then he flicked it away, ignoring Mr Biddlecomb's fiercesome gaze. 'Sent to find out things. Been different if it'd just been Christy, but his Mam too. That's awful. That's wicked. Maybe that's why he's here.'

You'd have thought the Devil himself had come into the bar and struck them all dumb. There wasn't a sound. Not a movement either. Not for several minutes anyway, and the leaky tap dripping into the metal basin that Mr Biddlecomb slopped out the glasses in sounded like the clang of a cracked bell.

'Pshaw!' Mr Biddlecomb scoffed finally. 'Who'd have sent him?' he asked as if the question was unanswerable, and with no answer it became irrelevant.

'Never know, do you?' Connor Neill said.

'God, maybe,' Willie Little suggested, trying to be funny again.

'Shut your gob, Willie,' Patrick Farrel snapped, and Willie shut his gob instantly as though it just dawned on him that maybe his suggestion wasn't quite so funny after all. 'Got to find out more about him,' Patrick Farrel went on. 'Got to.'

'But how? How do we do that? He's not giving much away, is he?' Mr Biddlecomb pointed out. 'You heard yourselves – had to practically squeeze a name out of him even, and that wasn't much of a name either now, was it? Johnsey. Could mean anything.'

'We'll have to find a way. That's all,' Patrick Farrel insisted.

'Easier said than done.'

'Could get that Young Aiden to help us,' Davey Shortt said. Patrick Farrel nodded.

'Why him?' Mr Biddlecomb wanted to know.

'Been talking to each other, haven't they?'

'Have they?'

'They have. Seen them myself. Me and Patrick. Sitting up

there in the valley field talking away.'

'Didn't know that.'

'You do now.'

'Dunno about that,' Willie Little put in. 'Just like his Dad he is, that boy. Close. Very close.'

'Thomas Meehan was a fine man,' Mr Biddlecomb said stoutly, not being one who liked talking ill of the dead.

'Not saying he wasn't. But he was close. Never got anything out of him that he didn't want you to know. And the boy's the same.'

'Maybe. Maybe not,' Patrick Farrel said. 'He's one of us, isn't he?'

'Born and bred,' Mr Biddlecomb said.

'Who's going to put it to him then?' Peadar Taigh Donnelly asked, he being the coffin-maker and having something of an affinity with death, and liking to get things done quickly before time ran out.

'I will,' Patrick Farrel volunteered. 'I will.'

A number of men sighed with relief.

'How you going to put it?'

'I'll think about that.'

'Still can't help thinking I know that man from somewhere,' Kevin Keogh insisted, but he'd had quite a bit to drink now, and was mostly muttering to himself.

Mr Biddlecomb leaned over the bar. 'Gives me the creeps, he does, the way he keeps on saying that,' he whispered to Patrick Farrel.

'He's an old man,' Patrick Farrel replied as though that explained everything.

'Old or not he still gives me the creeps. You think he really *does* know him from somewhere?'

Patrick Farrel shrugged. 'Who knows.'

'Gives me the creeps,' Mr Biddlecomb said for a third time, and gave a little shiver to emphasise his feelings. 'Makes it sound like Johnsey or whatever his name is could be someone back from the dead.'

'God, Mr Biddlecomb, you're really letting him get to you,' put in Willie Little who'd been eavesdropping, and Mr Biddlecomb glared at him and turned away.

But as in everything they did, the men dallied a while before going any further with the matter. And it was between the time of their deciding to try and find out more about the stranger and their doing something about it that odd things started to happen in the village.

To begin with, two of Patrick Farrel's best breeding cows were found drowned in the river. They'd been drinking there all their lives and no such woe had befallen them. Besides, there was only a few inches of water at that spot so how they came to drown was a mystery. It was as though, Billy Maken said, as though the two cows had simply decided they'd had enough and laid themselves down in the water to die.

'And had to be my two best ones, of course,' Patrick Farrel lamented, seeming to have shrunk a few inches since the tragedy and looking more pithecoid than ever. 'Always the way though, isn't it? Always the best ones that have the jinx on them.'

'Oh, that's always the way sure enough,' Mr Biddlecomb agreed although he didn't feel that much sympathy for Patrick Farrel since Patrick Farrel was a wealthy man by any standards, wealthy and mean which was probably why he was wealthy in the first place.

'Never spend a penny when half a one would do,' they said about Patrick. 'And he'd be grudging you even the half,' they usually added.

But that wasn't the case with Cahal Brennan or Tom Feeney or Jim Haughy. They were poor men, struggling to make ends meet and keep enough food on the table. So when they all found that some of their lambs were missing it was serious. And it wasn't as if they were killed by foxes or stray dogs that sometimes came in packs from the town. There would certainly have been carcasses lying about if that was the case. But the lambs just vanished into thin air with not a trace of them to be found. 'Could be the owls,' Willie Little said. 'That happens,' he added quickly and defiantly as he saw some of the men getting ready to belittle his view. 'I know it happens. They come down on them great wings of theirs and stick their claws into the lambs and lift them off their feet, lift them clear into the sky, and away with them.'

'Take a hell of a big owl to do that,' Cahal Brennan said, half wanting to believe it possible since owls were something he could protect the rest against even if it meant sitting up all night with his shotgun.

'You seen some of the ones we've got around here?' Willie Little asked, spreading his hands wide apart like an optimistic angler. 'That's the size of them with their wings spread, and I'm not joking. Size of bloody great eagles they are. Swear to God. Size of bloody great eagles.'

But it wasn't owls or bloody great eagles that made Seamus Goff's dog turn on him without reason or provocation, and take a chunk the weight of two pounds of mince out of his thigh, that was for sure. 'Best damn dog I ever had too,' Seamus lamented, having to stand all the time now and wincing if anyone so much as brushed against him. 'Had him this last seven years, must be. Grand sort of dog. Clever. Think for itself, it did. Then it just turned on me. No warning. Nothing. Just lunged himself at me and took a chunk of me thigh away with him.'

'Not foaming or anything, was he?' Willie Little wanted to know, happy enough to keep things stirred.

'Naw. Nothing. Looking up at me and wagging his tail one minute, and having a meal off of me the next,' Seamus Goff explained, shaking his head at the mystery of it all. 'Fair broke my heart having to shoot him like that.'

'Must have done,' Mr Biddlecomb sympathised.

'Did.'

And there were other things, too. Like the Shortts' new baby coming down with a terrible rash that covered it from head to toe and which no one could explain, not even Mrs Finch who knew every sickness known to man and beast, not even the doctor who came all the way from the town in his brown-coloured Standard just to say he hadn't a clue what it was or how the child could have come by it, and making them take the child back to the town with him, to the hospital, and on them getting there the rash just disappearing, and them looking like fools, and coming home in a hire car which cost them a fortune, and the rash back again as soon as they set foot in the village, and the poor child screaming its head off like it had been scalded or something.

And there were some things that could have been explained reasonably enough, things that would not have needed to be explained at all were it not for them coming on top of everything else. Like all the chickens and ducks in the village not laying for weeks on end like they were frightened of something, sticking together in huddles, silent and watching every movement about them with beady lidless eyes. And the gaping holes that appeared in the fishermen's nets as they tried to haul in their catch, and them not being able to do a thing about it as the silver fish slithered through the holes and swam off, flicking their tails and laughing like.

'All we need now is for the cows to dry up and we can all settle back to starve,' Connor Neill said, and wished he hadn't for the very next day the cows started drying up.

'You and your big mouth,' Mr Biddlecomb said to Connor Neill.

'Can't blame me,' Connor insisted.

'You said it.'

'Might have *said* it, but – '

'Well, you shouldn't have said it, you fool.'

And then the worst thing happened. Just as dusk was settling down Hannah O'Mahony came racing down the village street, her hair streaming behind her, and her white as white like she'd seen a ghost, and then tripping up and falling, and lying in the street until Mrs Finch saw her and came running to her aid, yelling for others to help. It took them ages to get any sense out of Hannah. It was like she'd forgotten every word she'd ever learned and was reduced to moaning and sort of spitting and rolling her eyes, and waving her arms in the direction of the graveyard. Not, indeed, until night had well and truly set in, and the big white moon had risen and was rolling across the sky, and Hannah was propped up in her own bed with a couple of pillows behind her and a hot drink inside of her, that the truth of the matter came out, and it was a truth the men of the village could have done without since it put the fear of God into them.

Hannah, it seemed, was coming back from the bog astride her donkey and it all laden nicely with baskets of turf on either side of it. And as it was still bright enough, and a nice evening to boot, Hannah had decided to go into the cemetery to say a prayer over the unmarked spot where poor little May was buried. She did this regularly enough and wasn't expecting the shock she got. On the very spot where May was buried someone had put up a little wooden cross, just where the little girl's head would be. And as it was still bright enough, small white stones, like the ones that littered the coast, had been laid out on the grave and they read, A Child of God.

Well, when Patrick Farrel reported this to the assembly in Biddlecomb's store there was near enough panic. Not mad panic or anything. A silent panic, all of them panicking inside themselves, and some of them starting to quake and shiver, and some of them so shocked they froze and couldn't even get their glasses up to their lips.

To his credit Mr Biddlecomb recovered quite quickly. 'Anyone else see all this?' he asked.

'Don't think so,' Patrick Farrel said. 'Why?'

Mr Biddlecomb gave a shrug with his mouth. 'Could be she was just seeing things.'

'Hannah O'Mahony doesn't see things that aren't there,' Willie Little pointed out.

'Maybe she did this time,' Mr Biddlecomb snapped back.

It was Willie's turn to shrug. 'Well, if she said she saw it, I'd bet she saw it.'

'She certainly saw *something*,' Patrick Farrel confirmed. 'Only got to look at the state she's in to know that.'

'Maybe the light playing tricks on her?' Davey Shortt suggested hopefully, but as soon as he said it he knew it was a stupid thing to say, and was glad when everyone chose to ignore him.

It was Mrs Biddlecomb who asked Patrick Farrel, 'Not been up yourself to take a look then, Patrick?'

Patrick Farrel shook his head.

'Why not?' Mrs Biddlecomb now asked, knowing full well why not.

'Too dark now,' Patrick Farrel said.

'Too dark?' Mrs Biddlecomb asked, raising her voice. 'A fine bright night like it is tonight? Clear as day it is, if you ask me. Clearer than a lot of days we have.'

'Night's no time to be going into graveyards,' Mr Biddlecomb told his wife, and gave a little nod of his head as Patrick Farrel's eyes thanked him.

'Why not?' Mrs Biddlecomb persisted.

'Because it's not,' Mr Biddlecomb told her.

'Don't tell me you're all afraid?' Mrs Biddlecomb started to laugh, a low cackling laugh that she used when she wanted to deride someone.

'Don't be stupid, woman,' Mr Biddlecomb said.

'Well, go on then. Off with the lot of you. Up to the graveyard and find out once and for all what all this is about.' She paused and enjoyed the discomfort her words were causing, then added, 'Unless, of course, you *are* all afraid of –'

Mr Biddlecomb threw his towel onto the bar and undid his apron, pulling it off over his head. He glared at his wife, and kept glaring at her when he said, 'Come on then. Let's go up and see what's to be seen.'

'Oh, no, I'm going nowhere near that graveyard at this time of night,' Willie Little said. 'Not on your life, I'm not.'

'Well, stay here then,' Mr Biddlecomb said, furious at Willie since he was having a hard enough time of it as it was to summon up the courage to go there himself.

But most of the men went with Mr Biddlecomb, and it was a bit like a funeral procession they made of it, sticking close together, and keeping in step so as not to trip each other up, and for all the size of their big boots being silent about it too, perhaps scared they might disturb whatever whiffmagigs might be lurking in the hedgerows. They didn't speak either, and when Connor Neill coughed they all jumped, and gave him fearsome looks and cursed him under their breath.

Like thieves they crept into the cemetery, and moved between the headstones, most of them crouched down for some obscure reason. And when they got to the plot where May was buried they stopped and stared, and let the breath ease out of their lungs. There was nothing untoward there. No cross. No pebbles. Nothing. Just the unidentifiable plot like it always was.

'Shit,' Patrick Farrel said with relief.

'Told you,' Mr Biddlecomb said.

'Let's get out of here,' Davey Shortt said.

They were almost jolly when they got back to the store, giddy certainly, cracking jokes and slapping each other on the back.

'Nothing,' Mr Biddlecomb announced mostly to his wife. 'Like I said, Hannah was just seeing things,' he added.

He was greatly pleased with himself until Willie Little gave a low, mooing sound, and said, 'You mean like an apparition?'

'I – ' Mr Biddlecomb began.

'Terrible things apparitions,' Willie interrupted. 'Terrible entirely,' and that put most of the men back into a gloomy mood since Willie was right: apparitions were indeed terrible things, things of the spirit that came from God or the Devil, and mostly from the Devil as far as the men of Ifreann were concerned. And to make matters worse Mrs Biddlecomb started by blessing herself extravagantly and muttering incantations to herself, getting on Mr Biddlecomb's nerves.

'Will you stop that, woman,' he ordered.

'Maybe it's what we all should be doing,' Willie Little said.

'Shut up, Willie,' Patrick Farrel said.

'Just saying – '

'Well, don't.'

And later, when Mrs Biddlecomb had gone to her kitchen taking her mutterings with her, and the men had calmed down a bit with the help of a few drinks, and a bit of courage had seeped into them, they put their heads together and talked about it all calmly, putting a bit of logic into it, as Kevin Keogh said. They didn't get very far though, since logic seemed to have little role to play, and the more they talked the more they drank, and it was probably the drink that made the difference and got them all to thinking that since such things had never befallen them before it must be the work of some newcomer, and that meant the man they knew only as Johnsey.

'Got to be him,' Mr Biddlecomb decided. 'Always felt there was something about him. Something not right.'

'He can't have stopped the hens laying and the milk from flowing,' Connor Neill said. 'Can he?'

'No knowing what a person like that can do.'

'Stretching it a bit, though,' Willie Little said.

As though aware that he was stretching things a bit, and none too keen to be reminded of it, Mr Biddlecomb rounded on Willie. 'Would you ever get off your backside and go away home before I stretch your bloody stupid neck for you, Willie Little,' he said.

Willie's temper was about to flare. His jowls reddened like a turkey-cock's and little specks of saliva formed in the corners of his mouth. But before it all got the better of him, Bert Slattery intervened, taking Willie's side.

'Willie's right, you know, Mr Biddlecomb. No way that Johnsey fella could make the chickens stop laying or the cows giving up milk,' he pointed out again. And had he left it there things might have sorted themselves out. But he didn't. After a sigh and a bit of a think he added, 'Unless he's some sort of devil himself, of course.'

It was just the ammunition Mr Biddlecomb needed. 'That's it!' he exclaimed, beaming so wide his smile looked like a wide white hammock strung across his fat round face. 'You've hit the nail in one, Bert!'

'Arra, come off it, Mr Biddlecomb,' Dick McCormack said, spitting first to clear his mouth. 'Into devils and all that sort of shit now, are we indeed?'

'And why not?' Mr Biddlecomb wanted to know. 'There's always been folk that got powers from the Devil himself, right since – oh, since way back.'

'You're meaning like witches and magicians and things, eh, Mr Biddlecomb,' Willie Little put in, enjoying himself as he always did when he suspected Mr Biddlecomb was soon to make a fool of himself.

'Merlins, Willie. Not magicians. Merlins and witches, like you say.'

Kevin Keogh was nodding. 'That would explain him knowing things he shouldn't know right enough,' he said sagely.

'Exactly,' Mr Biddlecomb said with a touch of triumph in his voice.

But he wilted, and defeat loomed, when Willie Little said, 'You mean about May and Christy Codd and his Mam?'

All eyes turned to Willie Little and then, when all they got from him was a smug sort of stare, to Mr Biddlecomb, searching his face for an answer. But Mr Biddlecomb was looking baffled and a bit scared into the bargain. 'He *can't* know about all that,' he said finally, but not sounding too convinced.

'Come on, Mr Biddlecomb,' Willie Little persisted. 'Thought we were putting some *logic* into this.'

'We are, but –'

'Well, if it's the Devil who's behind him then he *has* to know all about what's been happening. Stands to reason, doesn't it? The Devil's not going to keep that sort of news to himself, is he now?' Willie Little paused to let that sink in before adding, 'And if he *does* know – about May and all – if he *does* know then we're all in deep shit trouble.'

'He has been spending lots of time up in that graveyard, rooting about, hasn't he?' Cahal Brennan asked.

'That doesn't prove –'

'Proves he's *interested* in what's up there.'

'Tell you what, Mr Biddlecomb – why don't you come right out and ask him. Like you did when you found out his name,' Willie Little suggested.

'Couldn't do that, could I?' Mr Biddlecomb protested.

''Course you could. Just say – hey, Johnsey, you in league with the Devil, are you? Bound to find out that way,' Willie concluded, enjoying himself enormously. 'That's what I'd do if I was you. First chance you get, just ask him straight out.'

And the first chance Mr Biddlecomb got came sooner than he would have wished. No sooner had Willie Little finished speaking than the door opened and Johnsey came in. Mr Biddlecomb must have taken this as some sort of demonic omen. His face went white as a sheet, and he very nearly dropped the glass he was holding, did drop it in fact but managed to catch it again before it smashed on the floor. Even Willie Little who'd been having the time of his life stirring things up for Mr Biddlecomb looked taken aback, and tried to make himself inconspicuous, crouching low over the bar, his nose almost in his drink. The rest of the men, too, hunched themselves over the bar, not daring to look at Johnsey but longing to, their necks aching as they kept their eyes off him.

To make matters worse Johnsey didn't go to his usual isolated place at the end of the bar. He made straight for Mr Biddlecomb, making Cahal and Kevin move quickly out of the way to let him through, slopping their drinks in their hurry.

Mr Biddlecomb opened his mouth as if to speak but only a strange guttural bark emerged. He shut his mouth quickly again, swallowed and coughed, and tried again. 'Johnsey?' he managed.

Johnsey stared at him with grey unsmiling eyes, and held the stare for several minutes. Then, abruptly, he blinked, and said, 'Changed my mind,' and spun on his heel and left the store.

'Oh, Jesus,' Mr Biddlecomb sighed, blessing himself with the words.

'You must have frightened him,' Willie Little said, quickly getting back into the swing of his mockery.

But Mr Biddlecomb wasn't in any condition to notice mockery. 'He bloody frightened me, I can tell you,' he confessed. 'Did you see those eyes?'

But no one had seen those eyes which gave Mr Biddlecomb the chance to exaggerate. 'Bore right into me, they did. Right into my bloody soul.'

'No wonder he was frightened then,' Willie Little had to say, but Mr Biddlecomb ignored him, maybe didn't even hear him.

'And all red and fiery round the edges.'

'Oh, that'd be the fires of hell burning in them,' Willie Little opined.

'Oh, you can joke if you want, Willie Little,' Mr Biddlecomb said. 'But I'm the one who saw them, and I'm telling you –'

'You know what, Mr Biddlecomb? You're cracked,' Willie Little said, and got off of his stool and went home, shaking his head and chuckling a bit to himself.

And most of the other men went off home at that point too. Perhaps they were wondering if what Mr Biddlecomb had been saying was true and were frightened by it. Only Patrick Farrel and Davey Shortt stayed behind, and when Mr Biddlecomb had refuelled the stove the three of them pulled up wooden chairs and sat round it, gazing at the glow, seeming to be mesmerised by it. And suddenly there in the low warm light the three of them looked older in the way men do when fright takes hold of them, and they seemed to shrink a bit, become smaller and vulnerable and weak things as if whatever secrets had kept them going had been exposed and rendered them defenceless.

'You really do think he does know, don't you?' Patrick Farrel asked Mr Biddlecomb at last.

Mr Biddlecomb nodded but said nothing as though he didn't trust what words he might utter.

Patrick Farrel sighed.

And Mr Biddlecomb sighed.

And Davey Shortt twisted his buttocks in his chair and scratched his armpit and then sighed too.

'You know what that means?' Patrick Farrel asked.

Mr Biddlecomb nodded.

'Means we'll have to do something about it,' Patrick Farrel explained anyway.

'About him,' Davey Shortt corrected. 'About Johnsey.'

Mr Biddlecomb nodded and sighed again.

And then they took to sitting in silence again, bemused men and dangerous because of their confusion. Mr Biddlecomb closed his eyes, perhaps wondering how things had come to such a pass and how he had become mixed up in them. And Patrick Farrel closed his eyes too, maybe trying to see on his eyelids a way out of the predicament. But Davey Shortt kept his eyes open, watching the other two with sidelong glances, not thinking of anything since he was a one for doing what others told him to do since that was the way to a quiet life, he'd found.

Summer

Ten

Summer was a lazy, droning, hazy time, a time when bees, weighed down with cargoes of nectar, flew greedily from flower to flower, their buzzing guttural like crazy little juggernauts; a time when birds, free at last of their tormenting, ravenous chicks, their craws and bellies filled, spent hours preening themselves in the sunlight, their feathers gleaming; a time when the river, clean now of the winter silt, took its time about flowing to the sea, ambling through meadows as though it had all the time in the world; a time when the women of the village had time to chat more and doing it in a friendlier way, forgetting minor hostilities and wearing cotton dresses that sometimes fitted, and when the young girls gazed at themselves in mirrors and wondered if they were about to become beautiful; a time when the men took to strolling through the fields and casting proud eyes over their stock, content that they had money in their pockets now that the lambs and calves had been sold. It was a time when days were endless and warm, and nights short and calm, and people slept with just a sheet thrown over them. 'God, but it's good to be alive,' was what people often said, and sounded as though they meant it.

And curiously the calamities that had befallen the villagers during the spring ceased. The chickens started laying again, better than ever some said, their eggs big, brown things and more than half of them double-yoked. And the cows swaggered into the milking parlours, their udders fit to burst, and the milk they gave was creamy and gorgeous, and there was more of it than anyone could remember, so butter was churned and salted and stored, and cheese was made, great ungainly rounds of it wrapped in muslin and hung from the ceilings in wire safes out of reach of the mice and voles. Even, mysteriously, little Eamonn Shortt's rash cleared up, leaving his tiny body smooth and pockless and without a trace of the ordeal he'd been through. And Seamus Goff said the pain had all gone from his thigh where his dog had bitten him, but he still winced a bit if anyone came too close to him so he could have been lying, just pretending he was all right so he wouldn't be out of step with everything else that was going on. Patrick Farrel's two best breeding cows didn't come back to life though, and Hannah O'Mahony wasn't in good shape either, given now to acting demented, and jumping at shadows, and wandering about in a daze like she didn't know where she was exactly, talking to herself, arguing away, even slapping herself from time to time as if chastising herself, or someone she thought she was, for being naughty.

But Father Cunningham, seduced by the balmy days, forgot about hell for the time being, maybe thinking it was hot enough on earth anyway, and his Sunday sermons took on a more kindly tone. He talked about the love of God, and about love among men which made the young bucks at the back of the church snigger since they knew all about that only they wouldn't have called it love, and about things that didn't seem to have much relevance, like good-will, and about letting bygones be bygones, and about forgiveness. He stressed that for some reason: forgiveness. But it didn't stop him handing out whole rosaries as penance for fatuous sins like dirty thoughts which a lot of the young men confessed to just to get him going. And another thing the villagers noticed: when stressing forgiveness he kept his eyes fixed on Johnsey as if his words were directed specifically at him. But if they were, Johnsey made no sign that he was aware of it. He sat, isolated, at one side of the church and to the rear in the darkest part near the statue of Saint Anthony, his eyes riveted to the priest's face but static and unemotional, staring until Father Cunningham looked away, finished with forgiveness and on to something else like the dire state of the church's finances.

And one Sunday after Mass Mr Biddlecomb mentioned this to Patrick Farrel as the two of them took a stroll from the church back to Biddlecomb's store, taking the long way round by the river so they could be alone. 'You notice that too?' Patrick Farrel observed, more than asked.

Mr Biddlecomb nodded.

'Mean anything, d'you think?'

'Like what?'

'I'm asking you.'

Mr Biddlecomb paused to light his pipe, and give the matter his full consideration. He blew a lungful of smoke into the morning air and watched it drift away from him in the warm stillness. 'Maybe Father Cunningham knows something we don't,' he observed finally.

Patrick Farrel frowned. 'You think?'

'Could be,' Mr Biddlecomb said solemnly. 'Priests have a way of knowing things.'

'They do?'

'Bound to, aren't they? Being all close up to God and the like. Or maybe – maybe,' Mr Biddlecomb paused to wave an invisible insect from before his eyes, 'or maybe he *recognises* something in that Johnsey fella.'

Patrick Farrel planted himself in the pathway as if he was stunned. 'You mean – ' he began.

But Mr Biddlecomb interrupted quickly, 'I don't know *what* I mean, Patrick.'

Patrick Farrel folded his arms across his chest and stared hard at Mr Biddlecomb with a small slyness in his eye. 'You know what you mean all right,' he said.

'I don't,' Mr Biddlecomb protested, and started to walk on.

'Hang on, hang on,' Patrick Farrel said, trotting to catch up. 'You mean we was right, don't you? You're meaning that Father Cunningham sees evilness in him, don't you? That's what you mean, isn't it?'

Whether Mr Biddlecomb meant it or not when he said it no one will ever know, but as the potential of the idea grew on him he quite seemed to like it. 'Could be, could be,' was what he told Patrick Farrel. And then, glancing up at the sky, 'Better get a shift on,' he said. 'Got to get the store open before the men start thinking – ' he stopped and looked puzzled, perhaps forgetting what he was about to say. 'You coming, Patrick?' he then asked after a moment.

But Patrick Farrel stayed where he was. He shook his head slowly. 'No. But I'll be along later.'

'Have it your own way,' Mr Biddlecomb told him.

Of course Patrick Farrel told Davey Shortt what he thought Mr Biddlecomb had said, and Davey Shortt told Connor Neill, and Connor Neill told Billy Maken. But, as is the way with gossip, each teller garnished what he had heard, spicing it up and making it ever a little more sinister, embellishing Mr Biddlecomb's thoughts with monstrous suppositions of their own. So, before the day was over everyone knew for certain that Mr Biddlecomb had heard direct from Father Cunningham that the Johnsey fella was probably possessed and that he, Father Cunningham that is, was shortly to perform an exorcism on him, with or without his permission. And because of the kudos it gave him – the ear of the priest was not to be sneezed at – Mr Biddlecomb didn't deny it: when tackled he just frowned and pursed his lips, and let the men go on thinking whatever they wanted. And when Billy Maken persisted Mr Biddlecomb gave him a benign smile and pointed significantly to the ceiling, and somehow conveyed that his silence was on strict instructions from the Almighty Himself.

'Mam?'

'Yes, son?'

'Why's everyone pickin' on Johnsey, saying he's a devil and all?'

'Because,' Mam said, like she always said if she didn't have an answer, or when she had one but didn't want to let on.

'Because why?' I asked.

'Just because,' Mam said and started pounding the dough she was kneading with her tight little fists.

My Mam always made her bread of an evening, liking it to settle, as she put it, overnight, believing that bread which was too fresh was bad for you, giving you collywobbles. So she'd make it, and when it was baked she'd wrap the loaves in slightly damp cloths, and put them high up on the shelf in the pantry off the kitchen. Wrapping them in those cloths stopped them going stale, she said. Keep them moist. She also had the belief that the smell of fresh baking helped you to sleep, and maybe she was right about that. And it was an evening when I asked her why everyone was picking on Johnsey. One of the warmest evenings I can remember. The windows were all open but covered in some netting to keep the flies and midges out.

I waited until she'd put the last batch of bread in the oven before saying, 'Just because isn't no answer, Mam.'

Mam straightened up and stretched her back like she had a crick in it, putting her hands on her hips and leaning sideways and then back. 'It's all the answer you're getting,' she said without looking at me, and starting to wipe the flour from the table with a wet rag.

'It's just stupid,' I told her.

'Stupid or not, it's the way it is,' Mam said, keeping up her wiping, cupping one hand at the edge of the table and catching the flour. And then, still without looking at me, she added sharply, 'And it's not something for you to be sticking your nose into either.'

'Well, *I* like him,' I told her.

'You don't know him.'

'Yes, I do.'

'You don't.'

'Spoken to him lots of times, I have.'

And that was true. Well, almost. I'd *met* him lots of times but we didn't speak every time we met. Sometimes it didn't seem like we needed to speak, like it wasn't *right* to speak, so we'd just sit beside one another and think our thoughts, and sort of knowing what the other was thinking, or thinking we did. And it was funny: just having Johnsey there with me was sort of comforting, in a way making up for my Dad being dead. It was as if by not speaking he was telling me he'd always be there if I did want to talk to him. About anything. But maybe that was because when we did chat he'd ask me lots of things about my Dad – what sort of man he'd been mostly.

'And what would you two have to talk about?' Mam asked, glancing at me from the corner of her eye.

'Men's talk,' I told her pompously.

'Ha!' Mam snorted like she didn't have much time for what men talked about.

'Talked about Dad, too,' I said, thinking that might catch her interest.

It caught Mam's interest all right. It was like I'd hit her. First she turned slowly on her heel and faced me, and said, pausing between each single word almost, 'You – talked – about – your – father – to – that – man?' Then, without waiting even for a reply, she came towards me, almost running. She grabbed me by the shoulders and started shaking me, the queerest look I'd ever seen in her eyes. 'What did you tell him about your poor father?' she demanded, and, 'What did he ask you about Thomas?' and, 'What did he want to know? Tell me, tell me, tell me!' and the words were coming out of her mouth so quickly she was sort of spitting at me.

'Get off me, Mam,' I said, trying to struggle free. But Mam wouldn't relax her hold. If anything she gripped me tighter and kept on asking me what Johnsey had wanted to know about my Dad. 'Nothing, Mam,' I told her. 'Nothing.'

'Don't you dare lie to me, Aiden. You said he asked you about – '

'Just what sort of man Dad was. That's all,' I said, ducking and wriggling from her grasp at last. I stood back from her, just staring at her, and I was panting.

And then, suddenly, Mam was crying, standing there with her arms outstretched like the statue of the Virgin in the church has, and the sobs were heaving out of her and the tears were rolling down her face. And she kept repeating, 'I'm sorry, Aiden. I'm sorry. I'm sorry,' her voice rising with each cry until in the end she was near enough to screaming.

'Mam, Mam,' I said quietly and went to move round the table to try and comfort her, take her in my arms, maybe, and give her a hug the way I'd seen Dad do when he wanted to comfort her. But it was as if she didn't know who I was. She backed away from me, her eyes, still wet and teary, taking on a wild, terrified look. I'd seen that look, but only in the eyes of animals: in rabbits caught in snares and not yet dead when you went to get them, in cattle when they got their first whiff of the abattoir. I'd seen it in a collie dog I had once. *My* dog. Born on the same day I was and given to me when both of us were three months old. He went missing one evening when he was just ten, and the next morning I found him at the bottom of the cliff, still alive but in a terrible state with probably every bone in his body broken. All I could do was cradle him and watch the life shiver out of him, his little black and white head pressed against my chest and the gaspy sort of breath making its way through the blood and onto my face like pleas of help. And his big sad eyes just gazing at me so sure I was going to save him, but he must have known I couldn't because it was a helpless, hopeless look and filled with fear of the unknown. That was the look Mam had when she finally ran out of the room, and raced upstairs and into her bedroom, slamming the door.

And all through that night she sobbed and whimpered and muttered to herself. It was the most awful night, Mam in that state and me not knowing what I could do about it, if anything.

Eleven

No one ever knew what time the fire started exactly, but by three in the morning it was raging, filling the sky with a great red glow like one of those spectacular sunsets that sometimes got lost on their way to Africa and burst over the valley, leaving everyone standing there, gasping at the wondrous colour of it all and a bit awed too since they seldom saw anything so beautiful. By the time the alarm was raised and people had hurried to the scene the fire was well out of control, so everyone just watched as Johnsey's house crackled and toppled in upon itself sending sparks shooting upwards and sideways and making the women shield their eyes and pull their shawls tighter over their hair.

Mr Biddlecomb, one of the first to arrive and looking comic in his underwear and an oilskin coat, sucked in his breath too quickly and started to splutter. Patrick Farrel slapped him on the back. Mr Biddlecomb bent himself double and coughed and coughed. Then he spat a glob of smoke-stained mucus onto the ground. 'Jesus!' he swore. Then, 'That's a fire and a half,' he managed to say.

'Sure is,' Patrick Farrel agreed.

'Sure is,' Davey Shortt agreed.

'A fire and a half, like you say, Mr Biddlecomb,' Connor Neill said.

'Never seen a fire to beat this one,' Davey Shortt confessed, almost as if he was quite enjoying the spectacle.

'Wonder how it started,' Patrick Farrel wondered.

Mr Biddlecomb shrugged. 'God knows.'

'Must have been one of them electrical gadgets he had put in,' Connor Neill said. 'I hear them things can start fires like nobody's business. Send out sparks, they do.'

'Could have been something like that all right,' Patrick Farrel agreed.

'*Could* have been,' Davey Shortt said, but there was a strange side to his voice that made the other three men look at him.

'You got another idea?' Connor Neill asked.

'Could have been lots of things,' Davey Shortt answered. 'Doesn't take a lot to set them old houses off in flames.'

'That's what I'm saying,' Connor Neill said. 'One of them electrical things – that'd do it and no mistake.'

'Or a bit of turf rolling out of the fire,' Mr Biddlecomb said.

'Or falling asleep with your pipe still alight,' Patrick Farrel suggested.

'Or one of them electrical things,' Connor Neill insisted.

'Or someone just tossing a match onto the thatch by mistake,' Davy Shortt said, again with a curious hint in his voice.

'Just tossing a match onto the thatch wouldn't set it off,' Connor Neill said in a scoffing tone.

'No,' Mr Biddlecomb agreed. 'Of course, if someone *wanted* to set the thatch alight it wouldn't be all that hard, would it?'

'Easiest thing in the world,' Davey Shortt agreed.

Patrick Farrel gave Davey an odd look. 'Tried it then, have you?'

'Tried lots of things, I have,' Davey Shortt said enigmatically and with his usual sly sort of grin.

But Mr Biddlecomb wiped the grin from Davey's face by saying, 'Well, there'll be a right lot of trouble over this, what with Johnsey being burned alive and all.'

And it was as though Mr Biddlecomb's words made the men realise for the first time that Johnsey might have been burned alive, made them realise, too, the consequences of that.

'It'd be murder, wouldn't it?' Connor Neill asked.
'Sure would.'
'Only if someone *did* light the place on purpose,' Davey Shortt was now quick to point out.
'They'll find that out soon enough,' Mr Biddlecomb told him. 'Have all sorts of ways about finding that sort of thing out now, they do.'
'Well, I was in my bed,' Patrick Farrel said.
'Me too,' Connor Neill added. 'With the wife too.'
'And me,' Mr Biddlecomb said.
Only Davey Shortt said nothing. He'd gone a curious greeny-white colour and was scratching his crotch, which was a sure sign he was worried. Mr Biddlecomb, perhaps maliciously, decided to add to his worry. 'You in bed too, Davey?'
'Sure was.'
'Prove that, can you?' Mr Biddlecomb probed.
'Can't prove it, but I was there all right.'
'Sure hope you can – after all you've been saying about how easy it is to start something like this,' Patrick Farrel said, waving an arm towards the burning cottage.
But, it appeared, Davey Shortt wouldn't be called upon to prove his whereabouts, not to prove his innocence of murder at any rate, for suddenly one of the women gave a little yelp out of her, and the men turned, and saw Johnsey standing a little way off, in a terrible state. All the hair had gone from his head and his face, giving him a look of a man already dead. And his clothes were in tatters, blackened and smouldering. And his hands, which he held away from his sides, had the skin all peeling off of them, strips of it, hanging down and making his fingers look absurdly long. His eyes were the worst thing though, red as the fire itself, and sunken into his scorched face.
'Christ,' Mr Biddlecomb said in a whisper.
And the woman who'd given the yelp, Betty Cannard, made a move towards Johnsey, wanting to help probably. But he was having none of that. He turned his dreadful gaze on her and kept it on her until she recoiled beneath it.
Then someone shouted, 'Get the doctor over here quick, someone.'
And Johnsey spun round in the direction of the voice, and

he roared, 'No! Just leave me,' and his roar was such that people obeyed him without protest, and backed off, and started to drift away, looking back of course and seeing Johnsey just standing there before his gutted cottage like his flesh had melted and glued him to the ground.

Mr Biddlecomb opened the store so the men could have a drink, and some of the women gathered in Mrs Biddlecomb's kitchen so they could give her their versions of the tragedy and take sips of tea to steady their nerves. And while the women chattered the men were remarkably silent, none of them seeming to have anything to say, although there was a fair amount of sighing and shaking of heads, and there was a bit of shivering too since the stove had gone out and most of them were only half dressed, and the summer fret was blowing in from the sea making the dawn quite chilly, the damp of it seeping into their bones.

Patrick Farrel at last looked as though he was about to break the silence, had even cleared his throat and opened his mouth, when the door from the back kitchen to the store flew open and banged back against the wall with a crash that set the bottles chiming, and Mrs Biddlecomb lumbered in like a thunder clap, launching herself at her husband. 'You left the man standing there?' she accused.

Mr Biddlecomb looked about him for help, but the men all lowered their heads. 'He told us to. Said to leave him. Just did what he asked,' he said, his voice trailing off as if he recognised the enormity of his omission.

'So you just left him there?' Mrs Biddlecomb demanded.

'That's what he wanted,' Mr Biddlecomb insisted. 'Didn't he?' he asked, looking about him at the bent heads, hoping for a nod at least.

'God, but you're a stupid man,' Mrs Biddlecomb told him. 'What would you expect him to say in the state he was.'

Wisely, Mr Biddlecomb kept his mouth tight shut.

'I'll tell you this, Larry Biddlecomb, if you don't get your fat backside back to that house and see that the man is all right I'll be skinning you alive before the sun gets six inches into the sky.'

But even his wife's dire threats wouldn't shift Mr Biddlecomb. 'I'm not going near him,' he said adamantly. 'You didn't see the look he had in his eyes, woman. Like he'd eat anyone who went within a yard of him. Oh, no. *I'm* not going back near him.'

'Just going to leave him there to die, are you?' Mrs Biddlecomb demanded.

'He's not going to die,' Mr Biddlecomb told her.

'Might,' Connor Neill said suddenly.

Mr Biddlecomb looked like a man betrayed. 'What d'you mean, *might*?' he demanded.

'Might die,' Connor Neill said. 'Looked pretty close to it to me,' he added.

'Well, *you* go and see what you can do for him then,' Mr Biddlecomb half shouted.

But that was a different kettle of fish, and Connor Neill had no intention of going to see what he could do for Johnsey. 'Oh, yeah?' he said. 'And maybe find him already dead and then the Gardai having a great time saying I did it. No, thank you very much.'

'I'll go,' Kevin Keogh said, but quietly.

'What was that you said, Kevin?' Mr Biddlecomb asked.

Kevin Keogh looked about him as though now seeking escape. But seeing none he repeated, 'I'll go.'

'Well, go on then,' Patrick Farrel told him, giving him no time to change his mind.

'Right,' Kevin Keogh said, and left the bar, pausing only to tighten the cord of his pyjama bottoms.

'Satisfied?' Mr Biddlecomb demanded of his wife.

'God, but it's good to know I can depend on you in a crisis,' Mrs Biddlecomb answered with a terrible sneer.

'Whisht up, woman,' Mr Biddlecomb said. 'And get back in there with the women where you belong.'

If looks could kill, Mr Biddlecomb was dead as a doornail, but they couldn't and Mr Biddlecomb survived a bit longer although you could all but see the men thinking how glad they were not to be in his shoes, not to have to face the wrath of Mrs Biddlecomb if the look she was giving was anything to go by, a look that would shrivel a stone. Nevertheless, she did as she was bid and headed towards the kitchen, muttering to herself like a witch-doctor.

But she never made the kitchen. She'd reached the door all right, was about to leave without a backward glance, when Kevin Keogh came back into the store at a trot, and went straight to the bar and downed the drink he had left behind, almost choking himself in his hurry. And when he tried to speak the stammer got the better of him and all he could do was make clucking noises like a broody hen.

'For God's sake calm down, Kevin,' Mr Biddlecomb ordered. He poured a stiff whisky and shoved it along the bar. 'Drink that and calm down.'

Kevin Keogh swallowed the drink in a single gulp, and it seemed to do the trick. He didn't calm down but he managed to speak which was all Mr Biddlecomb wanted. 'You're not going to like this,' Kevin said, turning the empty glass round and round in his fingers.

'Not going to like what?' Mr Biddlecomb asked, but quietly, as though fearful of what the answer might be.

Kevin Keogh pushed his glass across the bar. Mr Biddlecomb eyed it.

'Give him another one,' Patrick Farrel said. Mr Biddlecomb didn't seem to care for that idea. 'I'll pay,' Patrick Farrel said.

'Ah,' said Mr Biddlecomb, and gave Kevin another drink, or rather he poured Kevin another drink but held onto the glass, not passing it over directly, sort of dangling it in front of Kevin like a sop.

'Give it to him,' Patrick Farrel said.

Mr Biddlecomb handed Kevin the drink, and watched as he swallowed that one too.

'Now tell us, Kevin,' Patrick Farrel said.

Kevin Keogh took a deep breath. 'You're not going to like it,' he said. 'Hannah O'Mahony's got him.'

It was as if, for a moment, the significance of Kevin's words didn't register. There was a slight buzz in the store as some of the men muttered to themselves, disappointed, and thinking what an idiot that Kevin Keogh could be when he wanted. Then Mr Biddlecomb said, 'Oh, Christ!' and everyone froze, and Patrick Farrel said, 'Jesus!' and Davey Shortt said, 'Shit!' and Mrs Biddlecomb let out a wilful cackle and went into the kitchen to tell the women what was going on.

'What you mean, Kevin – Hannah O'Mahony's got him?' Connor Neill asked, being the first to recover.

'Just what I said. She's got him. Got down there and there she was with her arm about him leading him into her house and talking to him like she'd known him all her life.'

'Oh, Jesus!' Mr Biddlecomb said, truly making it sound like a prayer. 'She'll tell him everything.'

'Just got to stop her doing that,' Davey Shortt said.

'Hah! Too late for that now. Make things worse if we –'

'Oh, Jesus!' Mr Biddlecomb said again.

'You think she *did* know him – from before, I mean?' Matt Gillsenon asked.

'How could she?' Patrick Farrel demanded. 'Never set one foot outside the village, has she? If *she* knew him *we'd* know him, wouldn't we?'

A group of the men nodded readily.

'Funny woman, that Hannah,' Harry Copter said.

'Gone funny, you mean,' Davey Shortt corrected.

'Whatever,' Harry Copter said. 'Still a funny woman.'

'Only been funny since little May –'

'Doesn't matter since when – still funny,' Harry Copter persisted.

'Shut up you two, for Christ's sake,' Mr Biddlecomb exploded, sounding angrier than any of them could ever remember him being, except maybe the day Olly Carver had accused him of trying to have it off with his second-oldest daughter, Heather, and Mrs Biddlecomb thinking that was the biggest joke she ever heard and laughing her wicked head off and telling Olly not to worry about it since Mr Biddlecomb wouldn't know where to find his thing and wouldn't know what to do with it anyway – if it hadn't dropped off, that was.

'Being funny maybe she *thinks* she knows him,' Willie Little said pensively.

'That could be it, you know.'

'Could be indeed,' Harry Copter agreed.

'Happens,' Willie Little concluded.

'Doesn't matter, does it, whether she thinks she knows him or not.' Davey Shortt said sharply. 'What we going to do about it, that's what I want to know.'

That set them all thinking, and they could all have fallen asleep for all the noise they made.

'Nothing we can do, is there?' Patrick Farrel asked finally. 'Just have to wait and see, wait and see what comes of it.'

So, they settled their minds down to wait. They went about their work in their orderly way, but there was a watchfulness about them as though half expecting some malicious spectre to appear from the soil and point an accusatory finger in their direction. And they were jumpy and snappy, and the women complained, and that made them jump and snap all the more.

And nobody saw sight nor sign of Johnsey, which seemed to make their nervousness worse, like his invisibility gave him a hold over them. They tried to see him, of course, going round to Hannah O'Mahony's cottage and banging on the door, but she never opened it to them and kept the curtains tight drawn across the windows every moment of the day and night. They did see Hannah herself all right since she'd come to the store every couple of days for a bit of shopping, but Mr Biddlecomb's attempts to cajole information from her led to nothing, nothing except her lopsided loony smile and a few demented words that made no sense and put a curious look on her face as if she was really pleased with herself about something.

'That damn woman's driving me mad,' Mr Biddlecomb told Patrick Farrel after a few days. 'Can't get any sense out of her at all. All she does is grin at me.'

And there didn't seem to be much sense either in Willie Little saying one evening, 'Maybe Johnsey's dead and she's just hanging onto his body for a bit of company,' but in a way that left the rest of them wondering if he was being serious or just poking fun at them.

'Maybe they're –' Davey Shortt began, but stopped abruptly and wiped the leer off of his face when Patrick Farrel gave him a warning look since he knew Davey well and knew, too, what he was about to suggest, and the suggestion that a burned up man and a crazy woman might be doing it was – well, like tempting some dreadful calamity to befall them, Patrick Farrel felt.

'Just saying – ' Davey Shortt tried again.

'Well, don't,' Patrick Farrel told him.

And that was the way of it through the hottest part of the summer, all of them on edge, all of them wondering what was going to happen, all of them starting to feel uneasy with each other again.

Twelve

In Ifreann August was recognised as the last month of summer. It used to be September, but something had gone awry with the weather in recent years what with all those spiky, bleeping things the big countries were shooting into the heavens, upsetting the balance of God's creation, playing havoc with the natural cycle of things. 'Bloody stupid, I call it,' Mr Biddlecomb called it.

'What's that, Mr Biddlecomb?'

'Sending all that stuff up there,' Mr Biddlecomb replied, pointing vaguely upwards with his bottlewasher.

'Oh, that.'

'Yes, that.'

'Got to try and learn things, don't they?' Kevin Keogh said, getting into it.

'Don't see why,' Mr Biddlecomb said. 'Nothing up there, is there? So what's the point in learning about nothing?'

'Don't *know* that though, do we?' Kevin Keogh persisted. '*Might* be all sorts of things up there.'

'Nothing that can't wait till we turn up our toes and get up there to find out for our own good selves.'

There seemed to be some sort of logic in that, and most of the men agreed with Mr Biddlecomb, nodding and looking quite smug as if they'd come up with the statement themselves. But Kevin Keogh, with the bit between his teeth, wasn't about to be fobbed off like that. 'No point in knowing things when you're dead, Mr Biddlecomb,' he pointed out. And there appeared to be an ounce of logic in that too, which confused the men, so the subject was changed, and they got back to talking about things they could all understand without wracking their brains.

And if it was to be the last month of summer, it was a glorious one that year, and the whole valley was scented with new-mown hay and the salty smell of the reeds brought in for thatching and left in long lines to dry. And if you passed Kitty Mercer's cottage you'd be knocked over by the scent of her sweetpeas which she grew every year and used to decorate the church, getting her toe in the door, people said, and who, though only sixty, believed herself to be within a whisper of filling her plot in the graveyard. And there was the smell, too, of Mrs Finch's lavender, cut by now and hung in bunches, ready to be distributed about the houses she visited since she believed it made child-labour less painful, and sent the dying off with something nice to remember; it kept the flies out too, which was useful.

And the women took time off from their household chores to sit in their gardens, basking as though filling their bodies with a warmth that would have to sustain them through the harsh winter ahead. And the children played by the river, swimming in its cool waters, and leaping into it from the bank with great whoops of delight, pretending they were plunging down from great heights, impossible heights, and being wonderfully brave so to do, their joyous cries making the old people look wistful, and turn their eyes in upon themselves, yearning to recall the happiness of their own childhood before it was too late and their reason left them or they died. And men walked their fields at a slow pace, perhaps believing that if they hurried time would hurry by also, and this lovely time would be snatched from them before they had a chance to enjoy it to the full. Often they sucked blades of long, sweet grass, tasting the goodness of the earth and giving themselves something nice to remember before the ground went cold and unfriendly, hard and harsh as the season ahead of them. Even the animals had that contented look about them, and the wild ones seemed less afraid as if they knew they were safe as long as the men were content. The foxes sunned themselves, their coats as shiny and red as Molly Pickard's hair, and that was very red, and barely opened their eyes if someone passed close. And in the warm evenings the owls shrieked less, their calling muted as if they too were reluctant to disturb the remaining tranquillity.

True, the thunderstorm that struck in the second week shattered the peace of it all but only overnight, and when the rumblings had rolled themselves away over the mountains, and the rain ceased, the quiet returned, and the whole valley lapped at the moisture as though grateful to be this cooled.

Two nights after the storm, late, I went for a walk up to the spinney field because I couldn't sleep. Mam was still being odd with me, more so since the fire that had destroyed Johnsey's house, and I was upset since it wasn't like her. So, I went up to the spinney field thinking I might see some badgers since I knew they had a sett in the circle of trees. I squatted on the ground, and pulled my legs up under me, hugging my knees.

I don't know how long I'd been there: half an hour at a guess, when I heard this little crack behind me like a twig snapping although it sounded pretty loud in the stillness of the night, and there was Johnsey standing behind me. 'Hey, Johnsey!' I said. 'How you doing?' I asked trying to be cheerful.

He looked awful, and the white light of the moon probably made him look worse. His hair had grown back but in patches, tufts of it sticking out in all directions, a bit like that of an abused doll. And his face was distorted. It had healed all right but was badly scarred, and in the healing the skin must have tightened, misshaping his eyes and dragging his mouth into something approaching a permanent lopsided manic leer. His hands, too, had suffered, and his fingers were hooked like talons and he held them away from his side as if they still pained, or maybe just the memory of the pain made him do this. And his arms were mottled, red and blue and white. He wore boots and trousers and that was all.

'Good to see you out again,' I said. 'I missed you,' I added without really knowing why. 'Been thinking about you a lot,' I went on, not wanting to keep talking but not knowing what else to do. 'How you doing?' I asked again.

Johnsey made a little face as best he could. 'Okay,' he said. 'Doing okay.'

'Good. That's good.'

Slowly, laboriously, he sat down on the ground beside me. He smelled of liniment. 'Missed you too,' he said after a while.

'I wanted to go and see you but – '

'I know,' he interrupted.

'No, really – '

'I know.'

'Anyway, here you are.'

That made him smile, although it wasn't something that looked like a smile except in his eyes. 'Here I am.'

Something moved in the spinney, but almost immediately it was silent again, the air filled with that curiously expectant silence that tells you you're being watched but you can't see what's watching you.

'*You* all right?' Johnsey asked suddenly.

'Me? Yeah. I'm fine,' I told him. 'Why?'

'Just wondered. Being out here at this time of night – morning now.'

'Couldn't sleep. Not tired, I suppose. Just couldn't sleep.'

Johnsey nodded at that as if he understood. In the distance the sea crashed against the rocks in its methodical way, a steady warning that it could wreck ships, and lives and dreams, although from where we sat it sounded melancholy more than anything else, a woe-filled noise as if mourning all the damage it had done.

'Aiden –' Johnsey began, his voice hoarse as though still filled with the smoke from the fire, and sounding very serious too. But whatever he was about to say was put to one side. 'There's your badger,' he said instead, and sure enough an old brock had come from the spinney, snuffling its way towards us. Then it raised its head and sniffed and saw us. It stared at us with puzzled eyes for a while, not afraid it seemed, but curious as to what we were doing there at that hour of the morning, intruding, albeit without malice, on its privacy. It gave three little snorts and turned and waddled back into the spinney, being quiet about it for all its bulk and awkwardness.

I waited for Johnsey to speak, to say whatever it was he had been about to say when the badger distracted him. But he wasn't ready to go back to that again, not for a while anyway, so we sat there in silence and watched the moon go off to some other part of the world in a ship of haze, and watched the dawn ease itself onto the valley slowly, the new light filtering through gossamer veils of fret that drifted in from the ocean as though carrying the dawn in with them or, at least, escorting it.

'I'd better go,' Johnsey said suddenly, easing himself to his feet, twisting onto his side first and getting up that way. His back was all scabby but the scabs were in lines like he'd been scourged.

'Oh,' was all I could think of to say. 'See you again.'

Johnsey, standing now and looking down at me, nodded. 'Yes.' He walked away from me. Then he turned and stared at me hard. 'Aiden?'

'Hmm?'

'Hannah told me about her daughter.'

'Oh,' I said, and waited.

But that was it. Johnsey had nothing more to say to me for the moment. I watched him walk off across the field with long, cumbersome strides, and then the mist enveloped him, and he just sort of vanished from my sight. Suddenly I was cold. I stood up and shook myself, flapping my arms a few times, and then set off home, taking the path through the woods for some reason.

There is something about woods that makes you feel you should walk quietly in them like you were going into a great cathedral or something, like you should tiptoe and not disturb the sanctity of the place with noise. So I did almost tiptoe and went quietly, so quietly that even the sentry-crow, guarding the flock on that side, failed to notice me, and the old and greying leader-crow himself had to give the raucous two-tone caw of alarm. At his signal the flock rose and scattered, then gathered high in the air above the trees, riding the rising column of warm air, waiting for me, the intruder, to withdraw. Only the unfortunate sentry-crow who failed in his duty didn't join the wheeling flock: each time it approached the furious leader banked sharply and drove it off. I felt great sorrow for the outcast, morose and all alone, bewildered by the terrible fate that had overtaken him so suddenly.

Connor Neill was breathless, his chest heaving and the sweat pouring off his face like it did off a horse's flanks after a hard day's ploughing, and it was all he could do to summon up the strength to bang his fist on the back door of Patrick Farrel's house. And exhausted though he was, he didn't seem able to stop his thumping, and kept on and on until Patrick himself opened the door. 'Jesus Christ, Connor,' was his greeting, and then he saw the state of Connor, white as a sheet and still gasping for breath, and added, 'Christ, man, you better come in.'

'Seen him,' Connor said when he'd recovered a bit, recovered his breath at any rate.

They were in the kitchen and both of them with mugs of strong black sweet tea in their hands, sitting opposite each other across the scrubbed table.

'Seen who?'

'Him. Johnsey,' Connor explained, and then took off, the words tumbling from his mouth as though if he didn't get rid of them they'd choke him entirely. 'Coming up along the river I was when I saw him. Didn't see him at first. *Heard* him first. Heard that awful hollow voice talking. Hollow. Like something from the grave. Honest, Patrick. Like something right out of the grave. Heard it saying, now don't you worry, little May, you'll be vin – vin something. Don't know what. I – '

'Vindicated,' Patrick suggested.

'Yeah. Yeah. That was it – what did you say?'

'Vindicated.'

'Yeah. That was it. What does it mean, Patrick, vindicated?'

But Patrick Farrel was in no fit mood to explain. 'Go on, will you, for Christ's sake.'

'Oh. Right. Well, I heard this voice saying that and it really made me shit myself it did, I can tell you. Terrible, terrible. And then before I knew it or where I was I was on top of him. Looming out at me he came, out of the mist. You know the way the mist hangs about over the river of a morning? Well, that's how it was, and out he loomed. Jesus! Loomed out at me just where we'd found little May all frozen stiff as a board, and stood there blocking my way, and staring at me with those eyes of his, and a kind of smile on his face, at least I think it was a kind of smile, maybe now that I think of it it wasn't, but it was something. God Almighty, that face of his, Patrick!'

'Never mind that face of his,' Patrick Farrel said quickly. 'Did he say anything to *you*?'

'Didn't give him the chance, did I? Wasn't about to hang about down there and have him do me a mischief, I can tell you. Took to my heels and came straight here.'

'But you *did* hear him say – heard him talking as if to little May?'

'Too bloody right I did. Clear as I can hear you talking to me now.'

'You didn't just – well, imagine it, Connor? I mean, you'd been pretty startled by finding him there and all.'

'Startled? Is that what you call it? I was frightened out of my bloody skin, I was. But I heard it all right. Heard it before I even seen him like I told you. Heard his voice like it was coming out of the grave – out of – '

'All right. All right, Connor.'

And with all that off his chest, and worn out by the telling of it, Connor Neill was glad enough to be quiet for a while, and used the time to finish his tea, throwing back his head and all but pouring the sticky liquid down his throat.

'Hannah must have told him,' Patrick Farrel said but more to himself than to Connor.

'And what else did she tell him then?' Connor wanted to know.

'God alone knows,' Patrick Farrel said gloomily. And then, 'Look, you'd better get yourself away home. Keep this to yourself for now, though. Don't you go blabbing it all over the place, hear?'

'Won't tell a soul,' Connor promised.

'Just make sure you don't,' Patrick Farrel warned, knowing Connor liked to be the centre of things and tell everyone everything he knew.

'I won't. Honest to God I won't.'

'We'll all meet later at Biddlecomb's and talk it out.'

'Good idea.'

'And you just think about it. Make sure you tell us everything that went on.'

'I just did, Patrick. There was nothing else.'

'Think about it,' Patrick Farrel ordered.

'All right. I'll think about it.'

'That's all I'm asking.'

But when the men met later in Biddlecomb's, Connor Neill was asked a lot more. Everyone seemed to have a question for him, although sometimes the same question was asked over and over, and each time Connor would say, 'I told you all that,' and whoever had asked would say, 'Well, tell us again,' and Connor did, being careful and not elaborating too much, maybe making the appearance of Johnsey in the mist sound more like an apparition than it actually had been but only because, by now, he was feeling ashamed at being so frightened. But when he'd finished his answering the rest of the men were, in truth, as frightened as he'd been, and all they could do was fire more questions into the air, letting the replies come from anyone who felt like it.

'What'll happen to us if he tells the Gardai?'

'Maybe he won't tell the Gardai.'

'What'll he do then?'

'How the hell do I know? Maybe nothing.'

'Nothing? 'Course he'll do something.'

'You think Hannah told him about Christy too?'

'Why should she?'

'Did she know?'

'Sure she knew.'

'Oh, Jesus!'

'You think she told him about it?'

And that was the question all of them wanted answered, and they were still worrying about it when Mr Biddlecomb decided it was time to close up for the night, giving Patrick Farrel a knowing nod as he bustled about clearing away the glasses and standing by the door, watching the men leave, nodding to each one the way Kevin Keogh did when he was counting his sheep coming out of the dip. 'Right bloody mess,' he commented to Patrick Farrel as he locked the door with the huge bolt that went right across the whole door.

'Pity he didn't die in that fire,' Patrick commented.

'Well, he didn't, so there's no point wishing it.'

'Pity though.'

'Shouldn't be thinking like that,' Mr Biddlecomb said, calling up a rare burst of morality from somewhere.

'Maybe shouldn't, but you think it too, don't you?'

But Mr Biddlecomb wasn't about to admit to any such thing. He checked the stove, and gave the embers a bit of a rake, and then sat down in front of it, sticking his thumbs in his braces. 'You thinking what I'm thinking, Patrick?' he asked.

'Don't know what you're thinking, do I?'

Mr Biddlecomb waited a while before replying. Then he gave his braces a snap and stood up. 'No,' he admitted. 'Best thing we can do is sleep on it. Things might look better in the morning.'

'Hah,' snorted Patrick Farrel, but he didn't pursue the matter for the time being, and left the store, giving Mr Biddlecomb a tired sort of pat on the shoulder as he went out the door.

'Mam,' I said. 'Johnsey's better.'

Mam was darning, wearing her spectacles on the end of her nose. 'How do you know that?' she asked without looking up.

'Seen him.'

'When?'

'This morning. Early this morning before you were up.'

'And where was that?'

'Up in the spinney field.'

Mam gave me a glance now. 'What were you doing in the spinney field before I was up?'

'Just sitting and thinking.'

'You think too much, Aiden. More than is good for you.'

'Mam, Hannah O'Mahony told Johnsey about May.'

Mam put her darning down on her lap and stared at it. Then she pulled her hand out of the sock, rolled the wool and stuck the needle into the ball. Her hands were shaking as she did this. 'I see,' she said, putting the wool and all into her darning basket, closing it with a snap and placing it on the floor beside her. Then she took to staring into the glow in the range. Since my Dad's death she had taken to wearing her nice long hair in a tight bun with a net holding it close to her neck. It made her look older, and she looked very old and tired now sitting there. And then her shoulders started to shudder, and I knew she was sobbing again.

'What's the matter, Mam?'

Mam shook her head.

'Why don't you tell me?'

Mam kept shaking her head. So I left her there since I couldn't stand seeing her like that, and me not knowing how to comfort her. It was like she didn't really want to be comforted, like it would be wrong for her to find any comfort from me or anyone else, like she was punishing herself but for something she couldn't quite understand, or understood and had undertaken to do the penance for somebody else.

Thirteen

Just to fool them summer did lengthen itself and spilled over into September, but they'd been bamboozled before and the villagers weren't about to let a freaky thing like the weather pull a fast one on them again. So they kept a close eye on Olly Carver's chimney, waiting for the smoke to come up out of it, just so they wouldn't be caught on the hop. The women all started their gathering, as they called it, getting in the fruit ready for bottling and pickling so they'd have some sweetness to take away the sourness from the cold days ahead. It was a particularly trying time for Enid Mulligan, Frank Mulligan's widow, who lived about the same distance from the village as Olly Carver but in the opposite direction. It was Enid who specialised in growing marrows, and wonderful marrows they were too, but she was funny about them, giving each and every one of them a name, and talking to them, scolding them if they didn't swell, praising them for all she was worth when they ripened. Two years earlier she'd gone berserk when she caught Gleb Fennessy doing something terrible, cutting a hole in the end of the marrows that had gone a bit overripe, and rutting away with a daft grin on his face and grunting like a pig. Bad enough, it was, that one of her children had been violated, so to speak, but the marrow and ginger jam for which she was famed didn't sell all that well in the village since no one wanted the jar with Gleb's white bits in it, did they now? All of which meant Enid had to take herself and her pots of jam off to the town which was tiresome and cut down on her profits. And although Gleb had long since gone off to Australia and was doing well enough for himself, people said, helping to keep those kangaroo things under control, and nobody else was all that likely to try out their passion on her vegetables, Enid stood guard over them with old Frank's shotgun, and woe betide anyone who came within ten feet of her plot, well intentioned or not. But it was an incident no one forgot, and every year it was dragged up again, and set all the men laughing, giving them a chance to be lewd, not that they needed the chance, and Gleb and his marrow became part of the folklore. And when a man's wife was really heavy with child he was told, 'Ah, sure, there's always Enid's marrows for you to be going on with,' and the stock reply was, ''Course there is, and a lot less trouble than a wife they are too!' and that got a great annual laugh also.

And when the fruit was all safely tucked up in jars, and labelled, and stored, the women started getting the wool ready for spinning and carding, but waiting until autumn was definitely upon them before actually starting either operation since they vowed the summer was the wrong time because of the heat, and the winter no better because of the cold, both heat and cold doing something to the make-up of the wool that rendered it brittle, made it snap all the time on the wheel, and gave them endless grief instead of the whole thing being a pleasure.

And then there were the hams to be cured, and wrapped in muslin, and hung from the rafters. And fish to be salted and packed into barrels, and children who didn't behave themselves to be told they, too, would be strung up by their necks alongside the bacon, or sealed in the barrels and not let out again until spring if they didn't start behaving themselves and doing what they were told. And winter bedding and clothes had to be taken from drawers and chests, and shaken, and aired, and the holes the little moths had made there were to be repaired. A busy time, but a not altogether happy time since it all gave promise of a bitter season just around the corner.

For the fishermen, though, it was a good time with seas that were calm and nets that were full, and it was the time the men chose to give thanks for those wonderful catches, and for them having survived the whims and hazards of the ocean. 'Fish is curious things,' Denny Mackel used to say, and what he didn't know wasn't worth knowing, and him with a face a bit like a carp too. 'They's holy things, you know. Special to God, they are, so He gave them spirits just like humans, He did,' he maintained. 'Got to show your gratitude to them fish, and thank them, or they'll be up to all sorts of wicked tricks on you.' And so, on a chosen day, when the boats sailed in, the eldest son of the youngest fisherman in the first boat home would take the body of the largest fish they'd caught back to the shore, and offer it back to the sea, and say, 'Go safely and become a living creature again, fish. And return next year so our bellies may be filled with your sweet flesh and our hearts filled with your holy spirit.' And if someone was foolish enough to ask Denny Mackel why all this palaver was necessary, he would, being a mild and patient man, explain, 'They *own* the waters, you see, the fish do. The sea and the rivers and streams and all,' as if that clarified everything.

And for those men who got their living from the land there was a mellowness about the time. The hay was in, and the straw, and beets were stacked high in the farmyards. What cattle and lambs were for the selling had been sold, and the money counted and put away, to be taken out from time to time through the cold months of winter and counted again, and little bits of it peeled off to buy the things they needed to see them through until spring.

And Father Cunningham said a special Mass that he liked to call his harvest Mass, giving thanks to God Almighty for His great bounty which was easy enough for him to do since he didn't have to lift a finger except for going through the coins in the collection-plate. And he had the women bake loaves and bring them to the church, and the fishermen bring fish, and the farmers bring sheaves of hay since they didn't grow wheat, and he'd place them on the altar and bellow his way through the offering-up of them like someone who wasn't all that convinced God was listening to him but was going to get the Almighty's attention at any cost, or maybe he'd heeded what Father Reynolds had said that time he came back from the missions in Fiji about what the Aborigines or Maoris or whatever they were out there said about God not really wanting to be bothered with us at all, but it being up to *us* to attract *His* attention by maybe whistling or dancing or roaring as Father Cunningham was doing at his harvest Mass.

Anyway, it was probably the best time of the year in the valley. Or should have been. Only now they all had Johnsey to contend with.

Not that Johnsey deliberately set out to disrupt the calm, or didn't seem to at least. But he was there, always there, stalking about, a soulless creature it seemed, and one in a horribly mutilated body which made matters worse.

'Just can't seem to go anywhere nowadays without him being there,' Davey Shortt complained.

'Like there was half a dozen of him,' Kevin Keogh observed. 'See him somewhere and when you get to the next place he's there too, before you.'

'Weird,' Willie Little said.

'Not natural at all,' Kevin Keogh agreed.

'It's that awful face of his that's getting to me,' Davey Shortt admitted.

'It's his not talking that gets to me,' Patrick Farrel said. 'Not heard a word out of him since the fire, have we?'

'Maybe lost his voice – burned out of him, you think?' Harry Copter wondered.

'Naw,' Davey Shortt quashed that one. 'Me wife says Hannah told her she'd been having great talks with him,' he said, and immediately regretted saying it.

'That's worse,' Patrick Farrel pointed out. 'God alone knows what she's telling him.'

'*And* what he'll make of it,' Willie Little put in.

'You mean what he'll *do* about it, don't you?' Harry Copter said.

But if Hannah O'Mahony had been having great talks with Johnsey and telling him things the villagers would have wanted kept quiet, Johnsey wasn't doing anything about it it seemed, not for the moment at any rate, although what the men expected him to do was anyone's guess. And anyway, his being there, a visible and emaciated avenging angel, as they started to regard him, was enough to be going on with, and as Davey Shortt said, he was everywhere, silent and staring and accusing.

'Like he's got eyes in the back of his head,' Patrick Farrel said. 'When you face him he's looking at you, and when you pass him you can feel those eyes of his still cutting into the small of your back and him not having turned round at all.'

Mr Biddlecomb, who had taken to lapsing into unusually long, pensive silences of late, saying only that his bile was at him, nodded. 'Doesn't have to be anywhere near you and you can feel him staring at you,' he said.

Mrs Biddlecomb gave her buttocks a little twist and settled herself more comfortably on her stool before giving a great humph at that. 'Doing just what he wants,' she said under her breath.

'Huh?' her husband grunted.

'Doing just what he wants,' Mrs Biddlecomb repeated aloud. 'Haven't any of you got the sense to see what he's up to?'

'What's that, Mrs Biddlecomb?' Willie Little asked.

Mrs Biddlecomb gave one of her tolerant sighs. 'He knows the lot of you are stupid and he's just letting you all give yourselves away.'

Mr Biddlecomb rounded on her. 'What's that supposed to mean, woman?'

'Means he knows what you've done but doesn't know who done it, so he's just letting you all make fools of yourselves and give yourselves away,' Mrs Biddlecomb said and, noting something akin to consternation in the faces of the men, pressed on, 'And when he finds *that* out, you all better start looking out for your hides.'

'We don't *know* he knows anything,' Mr Biddlecomb protested but with little conviction, and wilted quickly under Mrs Biddlecomb's scornful gaze.

And after closing time that night Patrick Farrel put his hand on Mr Biddlecomb's shoulder in a small gesture of despair, and said, 'She's right, you know, that wife of yours.'

'I know,' Mr Biddlecomb admitted reluctantly. 'Not a lot

we can do about it, though, is there?' although his tone sought just a glimmer of hope which was dashed when Patrick shook his head, and agreed.

'Not a damn thing.'

'So, what *do* we do?'

Patrick Farrel shrugged. 'Wait?'

'Wait for what, though?' Mr Biddlecomb asked.

'Your guess is as good as mine.'

So, that was all they could do: wait, without knowing exactly what they were waiting for, which made the waiting all the more menacing.

The leaves on the trees just started to change colour now, the lush green paling a little, getting ready for the yellows and golds they would wear as soon as autumn came. And small birds took to resting a lot, and keeping their songs to a minimum, and preening themselves with extra care as they prepared for their long journeys to warmer more hospitable climates, and doing nothing that might impede their flight.

Scarlet hips swelled on the wild roses that entwined themselves through the hedges that bordered the lanes, and the women picked them to make the best possible cure against wheezy chests and noses that wouldn't stop running. They gathered blackberries, too, for jam and tarts, and kept an eye on the sloes which wouldn't be collected until the first frost coated them since that was when they were at their best, the crisp frost sealing in their goodness.

In the woods pheasants gathered, absconders from that big estate on the other side of the hills, and they quarked loudly among themselves, their strident voices mocking as though aware they had escaped the slaughter that would shortly come under way. And the fox cubs of the spring were young adults now but none too wily yet, and they sat in circles round their mothers and listened attentively as the cruelty of winter was explained to them, looking serious and heeding the advice.

There was a lot of hammering going on too as barns were repaired, and fencing-posts replaced, and a fair bit of swearing also as the men, clumsy with their big, hard hands, missed nails and whacked their thumbs. And Father Cunningham had a gang of the men up on the church roof repairing the leak that had surfaced in the spring of that year, and none of them all that happy about undertaking the job since they hated heights and got giddy, even if they were doing God's work, as Father Cunningham cleverly put it, and making it sound like they'd be guilty of some sort of obscure sin if they refused to co-operate. 'You look after your own houses, don't you?' he asked. 'Keep them warm and watertight and habitable? Well, surely you can do as much for the house of God?' was how he put it. Mind you, by way of compensation, Father Cunningham was known to be more lenient on anyone who helped him out when they came to confess their sins, cutting down from a whole decade to just three Hail Marys, which was a fair enough bargain, wasn't it, when you took into consideration the time of year that was in it, and how important it was to get your soul all polished up what with winter just up the road bringing its possibility of death.

And Father Cunningham took the hearing of confessions very seriously, being appropriately solemn and melancholy about the ceremony as befitted a sacrament wherein people were asked to lay bare their souls and implore the Almighty to save them from eternal damnation. He only allowed one light to be lit in the church, keeping the area of the confessional in gloom as though suspecting sins might become visible in the light. He didn't slam back the little sliding door the way some priests did: he opened it quietly, and gave his blessing, and listened attentively before pronouncing the penance, so everyone really felt they'd been shriven. Not everyone went to confession, though. Most of the women did, but they wouldn't have that much to tell, nothing that would frighten the priest or God anyway. But only a few of the old men bothered, the younger ones keeping their sins a secret for the time being, telling themselves that what God didn't know wouldn't hurt Him, which said a lot for what they understood about the Almighty. And anyway, what was the point in bothering Him when He'd plenty to be going on with; time enough for that when illness struck and death became a probability. Still, there were certain days when everyone went to the church and made a clean breast of it. The first Saturday in September was one of those days for some obscure reason: people just did it, and that was an end to it and reason enough.

So, that year, on the first Saturday in September, the little church was packed, and the young men waited outside, smoking surreptitiously, and making lewd comments to the girls who went in, their pretty heads bowed as befitted genuine penitents, rosaries clasped in their fingers. All the boys wanted Betty Midgen, of course. By far the prettiest girl the village had ever produced, she was. Gorgeous. But none of them could get near her. Those huge black eyes of hers like polished coal would flash and strip the young men of their budding potency, turning them into floundering boys under her gaze, making them hugely awkward and fumbling despite their adolescent promises of what pleasures they would bestow on her if she could agree to step out with them.

'God,' one of the lads would sigh, eyeing Betty's fine big, upstanding breasts. 'If only I could get my teeth into her.'

'It's not my teeth I want to get into her,' someone was sure to respond, and they'd all whittle away at their frustration with a laugh.

But wishing and longing was as far as any of them ever got, since Betty wouldn't give them the time of day. Betty had plans to marry someone special so she could better herself and get away from the drudgery of the village. Of course, *all* the girls had plans to better themselves and get away from Ifreann, but Betty was the one most likely to achieve that. So, making her way into church that evening and hearing the bawdy chat that the boys directed at her, she bridled, and rounded on a bunch of them. 'Grow up, you lot,' she snorted. 'None of youse even know how to use what you've got, and what you've got wouldn't bring a smile to a pixie's face anyway.'

And even if any of the young bucks could have thought of a reply to that one, the chance of their saying it was choked. Rounding the corner of the church came Johnsey looking for all the world like some creature from the pages of one of those horror magazines the boys sometimes got their hands on and gloated over, terrifying themselves into the bargain. And they looked just about terrified now. Their jaws dropped and they stepped back, almost tripping over each other, their eyes narrowing as if they believed looking at Johnsey with their eyes wide open would affect their eyesight, maybe make them blind like gazing at an eclipse. But Johnsey only gave them the briefest glance, enough to put the heart across them though, and went into the church.

'Jesus!' young Pat Farrel said, looking like he'd seen a ghost. 'Did you see *that*!'

'Like one of them mummy things, ain't he?'

'Without the bandages.'

'Like – what's the name of that one?'

'What one?'

'The one that comes back to life when they fuck about with his coffin?'

'Dunno.'

'Yeah, you do.'

'Don't.'

'The one we saw in – remember – *Return of the Mummy*?'

'That's what *I* said – like a mummy without the bandages.'

'Frightens the shit out of you, don't he?'

'Sure does.'

'Wouldn't want to meet him in the dark and me alone.'

'No bloody fear.'

'My Dad says he's some kind of devil,' young Pat Farrel said, and like most of the young ones reported what their Dads said as gospel.

'What's he doing goin' into a church then?' Muiris Cavanagh wanted to know.

'What do you mean, Muiris?' young Pat Farrel demanded, suspecting a slur on his Dad.

'Devils can't go into churches. Kills them stone dead. The way crosses kill vampires. That's what churches do to devils, so what's *he* doin' going into a church?'

'Yeah, well, I said me Dad said *some* sort of devil, didn't I?'

'Oh. Not a *real* one?'

'Yeah, a real one, but –' young Pat Farrel was getting confused and was none too happy about it.

'Either he's a real one or he's not,' Muiris Cavanagh insisted.

'I'm only tellin' you what me Dad said,' young Pat Farrel replied, already trying to think of some way to get his own back on that smart Muiris Cavanagh.

However, some sort of devil or not, Johnsey was inside the church and suffering no ill effects, it seemed. The men, gathered at the door, leaving the pews for the women, moved aside to let him in, averting their eyes like their sons, and the women, having prepared their lists of sins and having them neatly collected on the tips of their tongues, turned their heads and eyed Johnsey, following him as he made his way along the aisle and came to a halt directly by the confessional.

'What you s'pose he thinks he's doing?' Davey Shortt asked in a tight whisper. 'Barging his way in front of all the women,' he added by way of explanation.

'Looks like he's listening, don't it?' Willie Little said, trying in vain to scratch his nose with his stump of an arm.

'Probably wouldn't *have* to listen, that fella. Probably *knows* what all of us are going to confess,' Kevin Keogh said.

'Or keep back. Not tell for the time being,' Willie Little said.

'Whatever,' Davey Shortt said.

And it did look a bit as if Johnsey was listening. His head was certainly inclined towards the confessional, and his eyes had a keen enough look to them, but it could just as easily have been the way the burned skin had healed and tightened and dragged his head to one side, making it for ever cocked.

'Who's in there now anyway?' Willie Little asked.

'Mrs Finch,' Davey Shortt told him since he liked to keep an eye on all the comings and goings.

Willie tittered. 'She's going to be jumping out of her knickers when she comes out and finds *him* standing there.'

'Jesus, you're right,' Davey Shortt agreed, and the rest of them nodded too, and craned their necks for a better view.

Mrs Finch was taken aback certainly, but she did no jumping at all. Swamped in the grace of God and her soul as white as the driven snow, she stopped in her tracks briefly to stare at Johnsey, but then smiled at him, a bit tentatively it was true, but then there might have been something tentative about her forgiveness which would account for that. Then off she went towards the sanctuary to say her penance under the glowing red of the oil-lamp.

Kitty Mercer was next in the queue, but she didn't go into the confessional. She half stood up, took a good stare at Johnsey, and then sat down again pretending she'd only raised herself to settle her skirt more comfortable under her backside. But Johnsey made no attempt to go in either. He stood there by the door, moving his head slowly so he could take in all the congregation with his gaze. And suddenly the church was silent as a grave. Even the curious little hum of people just being together died out, and the flame in the sanctuary lamp stopped flickering. It only lasted a minute or two, but it seemed like an hour, and then Father Cunningham started stamping his feet like an old cow, and coughing, signalling the penitents to get on with it. And when, still, none of the women moved, Johnsey went in and closed the door behind him.

The villagers had just got it settled in their minds that, ah well, he wasn't the terrible creature after all but just an ordinary man about to tell his sins, and not such awful sins either if the silence was anything to go by, when all hell seemed to break loose. There was a kind of strangled roar from Father Cunningham and he slammed the little dividing screen shut so hard it bounded open again and he had to slam it shut a second time. Then Johnsey came out, and without even a genuflection to Jesus in the tabernacle, stormed out of the church, pushing his way through the gaping men in the porch. He'd only just got out when Father Cunningham also left the confessional. He seemed to stagger a bit, and rested for a second, leaning his shoulder against one of the ornate pillars that surrounded his cubicle. He looked awful: his face as white as the surplice he wore and with a couple of violent purple patches on it that matched the stole he had hanging about his neck. And he was talking to himself, saying, 'No, no, no,' over and over in a bewildered, frightened kind of way.

Kitty Mercer, her penance interrupted or maybe said, came bustling back down the church to see what on earth was the matter with the priest. But God alone knows what Father Cunningham saw coming towards him. It certainly wasn't the inoffensive Kitty Mercer, that was for sure. As soon as she got within a dozen feet of him he started to back off, holding both hands out in front of him as though to ward off some incredible foe, some spectre witnessed only in nightmares, all the while muttering, 'No, oh, my God, no. No.'

'Father?' Kitty tried, using her special voice, the one she used on Jesus when she'd done a particularly nice arrangement with her sweetpeas and felt He should be made aware of it. And, for a moment, it seemed to work. Father Cunningham ceased his mumbling and gave her a puzzled look, and said, 'Ah,' and he stopped backing off, and put his hands down. Then he took to staring about him but in a vague way as if he was lost. But he wasn't calm for long. Suddenly, there was a terrible cry that came out of him, a scream of terror that sent shivers down everyone's spine and made the bristles on the back of their neck tingle. Then he was running out of the church like someone demented, his eyes wide and a little line of bubbly saliva coating his lips. Out of the church and down the path he raced, leaping into his old Standard motorcar, and driving off at a terrific rate towards the town as if Beelzebub himself was after him.

'Well, I never,' Kitty Mercer said to Mrs Finch who happened to be closest to her.

'Jesus fucking Christ,' Davey Shortt said to any of the men who could hear.

'What do we *do*?' Kitty Mercer asked.

'Go home,' Mrs Finch said in her practical way.

'What about Father?'

'Gone, isn't he?'

'But – '

'No buts, Kitty,' Mrs Finch said, anxious herself to get out of the church now. 'Just go home.'

And that's what they did, most of them anyway. And they locked their doors securely that night, and made sure the windows were bolted, and they pulled the curtains across them tightly for good measure.

And Mr Biddlecomb closed the store dead on time, shooing everyone out, and even depriving himself of the little after-hours chat in front of the stove that he enjoyed so much; shooing them out brusquely and locking the doors behind them, putting on the big double bolt that he never used and which was now unoiled and difficult to shove into its socket.

Alone, he pulled up a chair and sat down on it as he raked the embers in the stove, staring at them as if they might give him some enlightenment. They didn't, of course, and he sat back with a great sigh, swinging the poker between his legs, his eyes closed.

He was still there when Mrs Biddlecomb came down to see what was keeping him. 'You staying there all night?' she asked, but with a rare gentle tone to her voice.

'Just thinking,' Mr Biddlecomb told her, and Mrs Biddlecomb was quiet for a while, letting him think on.

Only when he gave another big sigh did she say, 'Come on to bed. You can do your thinking lying down just as well.'

Mr Biddlecomb heaved himself to his feet and followed his wife out of the store. 'I just don't understand what's *happening*,' he admitted as they made their way upstairs.

'No one does rightly,' Mrs Biddlecomb said, which was as near as she'd ever got to consoling him.

'It's like – like –' Mr Biddlecomb started but just couldn't think what it was like.

'Get yourself a good night's sleep,' Mrs Biddlecomb advised, 'and then when you've a clearer head you can think about it in the morning.'

'Never seen *anything* like it,' Mr Biddlecomb told her.

'The priest?'

Mr Biddlecomb nodded.

'I heard,' Mrs Biddlecomb replied, as though that made matters worse.

'What *could* Johnsey have said to make him go running off like that, do you think?' Mr Biddlecomb asked.

But if Mrs Biddlecomb had any idea what Johnsey might have said that made the priest go running off like that she wasn't about to divulge it for now. She lowered her fat body onto the bed, setting the springs screaming in protest, and toppled over onto her side, and within a minute she was asleep, snoring fit to waken the dead. Mr Biddlecomb stared at her for a while, vaguely wondering what had become of the nicely plump, handsome woman he had married all those years ago, and then got in beside her, pulling the eiderdown over his head.

My Mam had this little tune she used to hum when she was upset or annoyed, and she was humming it that night. Oddly, it was a jolly tune, not the sort of ditty you'd expect someone to choose if they were unhappy or angry. I think she hummed it just to stop herself saying anything, maybe because she knew if she did speak she'd be likely to start an argument.

'What's the matter, Mam?' I asked.

Mam gave me a quick glance but just went on humming.

'You upset because of what happened?' I asked, and when she didn't reply, I added, 'in the church, I mean?'

Mam spun round and looked hard into my eyes. It was a curious look, not one I'd seen before. There was a lot of things in it, like love, I think, and worry, and fear – mostly fear. 'No,' she snapped, and then went back to her humming again.

'Well, what is it then? I know you.'

'Oh, do you now?'

'Yep. Know when you start that humming there's something on your mind,' I pointed out, remembering a day when my Dad said that to her and made her smile.

Mam stopped humming and smiled. A very sad sort of smile it was too. 'Come here to me,' she said kindly.

I got up and went to her, and she put her arms around me, holding me very tight, and rocking me, holding me and rocking me in the way women held and rocked their men before seeing them off to seek work abroad, kind of as if they half suspected they'd never see each other again, the way my Mam and Dad used to every night before Dad went out onto the grey sea and neither of them knowing what might be out there in the way of danger. 'Tell me, Mam,' I said into her ear, and instantly regretted speaking because Mam released me, and without a word left the room and went upstairs, leaving me standing there none the wiser, and starting to worry myself now.

I don't know how long I stood there just looking at the door Mam had gone through, but it was quite a while. I don't know *why* I stood there either, doing nothing. Maybe I was waiting for Mam to settle down but without really thinking that. Finally I went out of the house, taking my worries with me, and headed out across the fields the way I always did when I wanted to think. 'That boy thinks too much,' my Dad used to say. 'Better than not thinking at all – like some,' Mam always answered, giving my Dad one of her kindly, critical looks. 'Sometimes better not to think at all,' Dad would answer. 'Only if you're stupid,' Mam would say then. But then they'd laugh, and I'd know they were just teasing each other.

The first dew had spread itself over the valley. It glistened in the moonlight, and sort of kept the hedgerows awake so that they gave off their scent the way they did in daytime. And the cattle stayed awake too, grazing heavily, enjoying the luxury of the moist grass, better by far than when the wind and the sun dried it and made it coarse to the taste and took a lot of chewing. Only a few of them raised their heads and stared at me as I made my way towards the spinney, their big brown eyes winking in the moonlight as they blinked.

When I got to the spinney I was surprised to find Johnsey sitting there. He looked round and nodded to me. 'I knew you'd come,' he said.

'Oh?'

'Yes.'

'How'd you know that?'

Johnsey shrugged. 'Just knew it.'

'Couldn't have *known* it,' I said. 'Guessed it maybe. Not known it.'

Johnsey gave a little grunt of a laugh. 'All right. I guessed it,' he conceded, and waited for me to sit down beside him.

We sat there in silence for a while. Johnsey rolled himself a cigarette. He did it with one hand which I thought was clever. Only when he had lit it and taken a couple of puffs did I say, 'Well, you certainly stirred things up, didn't you?'

Johnsey nodded. 'Suppose I did.'

'What'd you want to go and do that for?'

'Had to be done,' Johnsey said, and made that sound like a good enough reason.

We went back to sitting in silence again. I picked a blade of grass, and lay back, sucking on it, letting the juice seep into my mouth, sweet as honey. Then, 'Johnsey?' I said, after a bit.

'Hmm?'

'Can I ask you something?'

'You can ask.'

'Who are you? I mean, really who are you?'

'Really who am I,' Johnsey said as if he was trying to puzzle that one out for himself. 'Who am I?' he asked aloud. 'Does it matter?'

'Doesn't matter. I'd like to know, though.'

'So would I. So would I,' Johnsey told me, and I knew I wasn't going to find out any more.

An owl whooshed low over us, so low I fancied I could feel the wind beneath its wings. 'Johnsey?' I tried a different tack.

'Another question?'

'What you doing here?'

Johnsey didn't move for a moment, but then he turned his head and gazed down at me. 'Looking for something,' he said, and looked away again.

'For what?'

'The truth.'

'The truth? About what?'

'Better you don't ask too many questions, boy. What you don't know can't hurt you.'

'Hurts more when you don't know things sometimes.'

Johnsey gave a wry bit of a smile at that. But then he nodded and said, 'You're a wise man, Aiden Meehan. That's what you are: a wise man.' He stood up and stretched. I thought he was going to leave so I put in quickly, 'Everyone's talking about what happened in the church.'

Johnsey let his arms fall slowly to his side, and I thought how very like wings they seemed, like those of the owl that flew back from foraging now, a small, wriggling rodent in its talons, and I wondered if Johnsey mightn't some day just fly off to wherever he'd come from.

'They're saying it must have been something really awful you said to Father Cunningham to make him act the way he did, running off out of the church like that, as if the Devil was after him. That's what they're saying.'

Johnsey nodded. 'It was something awful,' he said.

'Why'd you say it then?'

'It needed to be said,' Johnsey told me simply.

'You're not making it easy on yourself, you know, doing things like that.'

'Easy?'

'You know.'

'Tell me, Aiden.'

'You know. Don't like people prying, they don't.'

'Only 'cause they've got things to hide.'

'Maybe so, but doesn't make them like you prying.'

'And maybe finding out the truth? That what you mean?'

'Don't know what I mean. I just don't want to see anything more happen to you. That's all.'

'Like what, Aiden?'

'Like anything.'

'Like my being killed? Is that it? The way Christy Codd and his mother were killed? Is that what you're saying?'

'They wasn't killed. I mean, Christy did it all himself.'

Johnsey shook his head sadly. 'Christy and his mother were killed, Aiden. I know they were.'

'You shouldn't be saying things like that. Christy was crazy. He'd done something wicked too.'

'Oh, and what was that?'

'Did something wicked to May O'Mahony and then strangled her, didn't he?'

'That's what they said, was it?'

'It happened like that. Everyone knows it happened like that.'

For what seemed a very long time Johnsey just looked down at me. I couldn't see his eyes but something told me they were filled with sadness. Maybe it was just the way his shoulders sagged and the small movement he made with his hands, turning them palm upwards like he was pleading. 'Oh, Aiden, Aiden,' he said in a voice that told me I'd been right about the sadness in his eyes. 'I don't want to hurt *you*,' he added. 'Not you.' And then he left me, striding away. A cloud swept across the moon, plunging everything into darkness, and when it became brighter again, Johnsey was nowhere in sight.

Autumn

Fourteen

Because summer had stretched itself way beyond its normal span, autumn that year was to be short, making everything in the valley wrap itself up and snuggle down in a hurry, and the air was filled with that humming noise that bees and other small insects make when they're not too far from panic.

The villagers knew that autumn had definitely arrived when the rooks started to pair off, doing their frolics high above the tree-tops, and making a lot of noise about it, but being careful in their choice of partner since, for many, it was a choice that would last their lifetime. Of course, mistakes were made and when, in early spring, it was time for them to mate, some changed their minds, and this caused ructions, but it gave the younger single birds a chance to nip in, which was lucky for them.

From early dawn until dusk then, the rooks cawed and wheeled, the older males landing briefly on high branches from time to time to fan out their tails, and bob like courteous suitors, and announce what fine fellows they were, while the females pretended to be coy and unwilling, gliding by with gaze averted, sometimes two of them together and seeming to natter like old widows mischievously enjoying the antics of a younger generation.

Rooks, like starlings, had a curious reputation among the villagers. Harbingers of death, some people called them, but this was probably because they only called attention to themselves when winter was just round the corner. And while crows were shot, the rooks were left in peace, just in case by killing one the wrath of the others was invoked, and life was difficult enough without that. And sometimes in spring, when the gales came in from the sea, and whipped the tallest branches of the trees to a frenzy, sending nests and the chicks within them thudding to the ground, everyone became concerned lest the birds blame them for the misfortune. Once, someone staying at the big house over the hill had dared to open fire on the rookery on the edge of the wood that marked the boundary of the estate, and for days the villagers waited to hear of what terrible retribution might befall him.

'Well, just goes to show you, doesn't it,' Clem McLoughlin said.

'What's that, Clem?'

'Tripped up, didn't he, and just about shot his arm off,' Clem told them.

'That's the rooks for you,' Mr Biddlecomb said knowingly.

'Certainly is.'

'Be a long time before *he* takes a shot at them again.'

'Be a long time before he's even able to hold a gun again.'

'Teach him.'

'Aye,' Mr Biddlecomb agreed with smugness in his voice as though the event proved he wasn't all that stupid to believe in the power of the rooks.

Of course, it didn't help matters any that Johnsey seemed to have a strange affinity with the rooks, making it appear that he was, in some mysterious way, in league with them. Tom O'Shaughnessy was the first to notice it and bring it to the attention of the rest of the men. Tom worked for the owners of the big house, a kind of odd-job man for which he lived rent-free in a small cabin that had been used by the shepherd in the days when the estate could boast over two thousand sheep. And maybe it was living alone in that isolated dwelling that made something of the shepherd's traits rub off on Tom, making him quiet, and soft-spoken, and patient like most men who have anything to do with sheep seem to be.

'Very strange, it was,' Tom said, and all the men turned and peered at him since it wasn't often Tom had anything very strange to report. Nobody asked Tom what was so very strange since they knew that such a question would probably fluster him, making him curl up within himself and say nothing. They also knew that left to his own devices and to his own time he'd soon enough come up with an explanation.

'Very strange, indeed,' Tom said eventually. 'Had to be seen to be believed. Just standing there, he was, and the rooks circling round and round him, and not a sound out of them. Never seen that before, I haven't – rooks circling in silence. They don't do that, do they? Not as far as I've known them. Always cawing, they are, when they're circling. But not with him standing there. Round and round they went. Low over his head, like they were – dunno – sort of talking to him, but in whispers so only he could hear what they had to say.'

'That'd be Johnsey you're talking about, I suppose,' Connor Neill supposed, and was put in his place when several of the men rounded on him and said, 'Hush up, will you, Connor.'

But Tom didn't seem to mind the interruption. 'That's it. Johnsey. Him just standing there, his head kind of cocked. Then I think he must have said something. Can't be sure. Couldn't hear anything myself. But all of a sudden the rooks were off again, flying away up high and making a terrible racket again, worse than usual, I'd say, and that Johnsey sort of chuckling to himself like they'd told him something funny, and then walking away from them with a wave of his hand.'

That flummoxed the men for a while. They forgot about drinking and just stared at Tom, wondering if there was more to come, and probably hoping there wasn't.

'You sure you weren't imagining it, Tom?' Mr Biddlecomb asked. 'Not meaning to be rude or anything, but, like, well, you know how it is, we all imagine things from time to time, don't we?' he asked, and most of the men nodded.

But Tom shook his head vehemently. 'No imagining, I can tell you. Tell you something else,' he went on. 'Them birds, they followed him right across the field. Very strange sight that was. Right up until he climbed over the wall. You know something? I'd swear they were sort of seeing to it that he got out of the field safely. Sort of protecting him. Don't ask me why I thought that. Just a feeling. Looked like that to me, anyway.' And then, without another word, Tom swallowed what was left of his drink, pulled his cap down firmly on his head, and left the store.

Patrick Farrel was the first to speak. 'What do you make of all that, then?' he asked, the words coming out strained.

Mr Biddlecomb grimaced but said nothing.

'Must have gone soft in the head living up there on his own all the time. Tom, I mean,' Davey Shortt said.

Patrick Farrel shook his head. 'There's nothing wrong with Tom O'Shaughnessy's head. If he says he saw what he said, then he saw it all right.'

'Saw *something* maybe. Not what he said he saw though,' Davey Shortt insisted, mostly because, like everyone else in the store, he didn't dare believe that Johnsey had the ear of the rooks. 'Probably just feeding them or something. That'd be it most likely. That Johnsey feeding the birds. That'd be the explanation.'

'Could be,' Mr Biddlecomb agreed.

'Tom didn't say nothing about no food,' Connor Neill pointed out. 'Just said Johnsey was standing there talking to them. If he'd been feeding them Tom would have said so.'

'All right. So he wasn't feeding them,' Davey Shortt snapped. 'Maybe just standing there the rooks got curious and came down for a look. He's funny-looking enough for them to want to take a peek.'

'You ever tried that?' Mr Biddlecomb asked. 'Stood in the field when the rooks is pairing? Wouldn't come within a mile of you, they wouldn't. No matter how bloody funny you looked.'

'Well, me for one isn't about to believe it,' Davey Shortt announced. 'You lot can believe what you like.'

It didn't take too long though – two days only – for Davey Shortt to change his mind. Coming home with a pole slung over his shoulder and a couple of rabbits he'd snared swinging from it, he spotted Johnsey in the field with, sure enough, the rooks circling low over his head and not a sound out of them. Davey put the pole down and crouched behind the stone wall that surrounded the field, peering over the top. But then curiosity got the better of him, and he decided to creep closer, maybe hear what Johnsey was saying to the birds. Down on all fours, like an Indian, he crept across the field, keeping as low as he could and pausing every now and then and cocking his head trying to pick up any trace of talk. Suddenly there was a single, warning cry from the sentry-rook, and then all hell broke loose. Before he knew what was happening Davey was swamped by angry birds, diving at him, their fiercesome talons extended, their beaks half open, their beady eyes livid with anger, and all of them cawing and screaming at him with a vehemence the likes of which he had never heard. He was up on his feet in a hurry and racing back the way he had come, the sweat pouring off him, and every bone in his body shaking in fear. Only when he vaulted the wall and raced up the lane did the birds abandon their attack, wheeling away, their calls now sounding like manic laughter to Davey's ears.

'Set them on me, I swear to God. Set those bloody birds on me,' he later said in the store, still looking pretty shaken.

'Now who's imagining things?' Mr Biddlecomb asked, happy enough to have a go at Davey Shortt.

'Jesus God, I take everything back,' Davey admitted. 'I'm telling you that's just what he did. Didn't *see* him do it or *hear* him say anything but all of a sudden they were on me, the whole bloody flock of them and I'm telling you if I hadn't got out of there pretty damn quickly they'd have torn me to shreds and no mistake.'

'You been making that beer of yours again, Davey?' Leonard Midden wanted to know.

Davey Shortt reddened and glared at him. 'No I bloody haven't,' he half shouted. 'And 'twasn't beer any how.' And that was true enough. Davey Shortt had, for a brief time, tried his hand at distilling a brew of his own devising, and during that time had reeled about the village in a state of permanent intoxication, and while under its influence had done many a strange thing. He had, for example, knelt under Kitty Mercer's window, roaring for all the village to hear that she was the most lovely woman he had ever set eyes on, and had broken into song, the words fumbled and sodden. Only when his wife grabbed him by both ears and dragged him home did he stop his yowling, and took to laughing instead, finding the whole thing funny beyond belief. And he had seen St Patrick too, wearing a mitre and cope and carrying a crook, he was, and telling Davey that there were one or two snakes he had overlooked, and would he, Davey, kindly see to it that the place was rid of them? Which probably started Davey's nightmares about serpents, nightmares and daymares too, Mrs Shortt said, seeing them everywhere along his path, and in his hair and beard, and even curled up on a slice of fried bread Mrs Shortt had set in front of him in an attempt to dry the alcohol out of him. Only when the batch ran out did Davey return to his normal self, but the men never let him forget it, ridiculing him, principally because he hadn't offered to share his concoction with them.

'Been taking something, though?' Leonard Midden insisted.

'Not a bloody thing. I swear on my mother's grave. Sober as I've never been.'

Now, Patrick Farrel seemed to take him seriously. 'You mean Johnsey really did set them birds on you?'

'Sure as I'm standing here,' Davey said, and then corrected himself. 'Sure as I'm sitting here,' he said just in case some wag took him to task.

'You heard him do it?' Patrick Farrel persisted.

Davey rubbed his chin. 'Well, no. No, I didn't *hear* him tell them to go for me. But it must have been – I mean, he must have told them to. They wouldn't have gone for me just like that off of their own bat, would they now?'

'Could have done.'

'Naw. Never heard of that happening.'

'First time for everything,' Leonard Midden said.

Davey rounded on him. 'You're just trying to get me going, aren't you?' he asked, clenching his fists and getting ready for a fight.

'Uh-huh,' Leonard assured him. 'Got yourself going all by yourself.'

That made the rest of the men laugh, and Davey didn't like that. He stood up and sent his stool scudding across the store floor. 'Well, fuck the lot of youse,' he swore. 'Just you wait till he does something on you, then we'll see who's got the smile on his face.' And with that off he went in a great huff.

'I think you believed Davey, didn't you?' Mr Biddlecomb asked when the store was closed for the night and just himself and Patrick Farrel were left inside.

Patrick Farrel shrugged. 'Could be true,' he said, sounding reluctant.

Mr Biddlecomb blew out a stream of breath.

'Just said *could* be,' Patrick Farrel reminded him.

'I know you, Patrick Farrel. When you say *could be*, you mean *is*.'

Patrick Farrel gave a wry laugh. He leaned forward and warmed his hands on the glowing embers. 'Just let's say it wouldn't surprise me if it was true,' he said, leaning back in his chair again. 'There's so much that's queer about Johnsey.'

Mr Biddlecomb gave him a funny look. 'You know something? That's the first time you sounded as though you felt sorry for him.'

'Sorry?' Patrick Farrel shook his head. 'Wouldn't say that. Well, maybe a bit, after that fire disfiguring him and everything.'

'Well, I'm not sorry for him, I can tell you. If you want the truth I'm bloody scared of him, Patrick. Something in my water tells me he's going to be the death of us all.'

Patrick Farrel gave another laugh. 'You're as bad as that Davey Shortt for exaggerating,' he said. 'There's more of us than there is him if the worst comes to the worst. We can take care of ourselves.'

'I didn't rightly mean it like that,' Mr Biddlecomb said, taking his turn at warming his hands. 'Didn't mean anything physical. It's what he's doing to all of us up here,' he explained, tapping his head. '*That's* what I mean.'

'Dare say we can deal with that too.'

'Not so sure, I'm not. Tell you what it is – it's not knowing what *he* knows. That's what's making us all of a jitter.'

'Maybe he knows nothing,' Patrick Farrel said hopefully.

'Oh, don't you make no mistake. He *knows* something all right. Got to. What would he have been doing up at the O'Mahony girl's grave if he didn't know something? And didn't Willie Little hear him talking to her like she was alive and well and standing not a foot away from him?'

'Could be reasons,' Patrick Farrel said, sounding as if he was trying to convince himself this was true.

'Tell me one. Go on, tell me one.'

But Patrick Farrel couldn't. He couldn't think of anything else to say either it seemed, so he rose and stretched and scratched the back of his neck. 'Bed,' he said. 'That's where I'm heading. Have a good sleep and put that Johnsey out of my mind.'

'If you *can* sleep,' Mr Biddlecomb said. 'Haven't slept a wink in weeks, I haven't.'

'That's the one thing I can always do – sleep. Not hell or high water will ever keep me awake.'

'It's neither hell nor high water I'm bothered about,' Mr Biddlecomb said, standing also and standing the two wooden chairs on the table in the room, leaving the floor nice and clear for cleaning in the morning. ''Night Patrick.'

''Night to you.'

Fifteen

It wasn't all that long though before Mr Biddlecomb and Patrick Farrel learned that Johnsey *did* know things, although the information came to them in a roundabout way. Perhaps inevitably it was Davey Shortt who told them, but he got it from his wife who got it from Kitty Mercer who'd been told by Mrs Finch, and *she'd* been the one who heard it at first hand.

Mrs Finch had a christening to attend. As a midwife she had a lot of christenings to attend since many people believed that by omitting her from the guest-list they might make her feel slighted and, who knows, maybe put some sort of hex on their child. She was a very good midwife and was in some demand, often travelling up to fifty miles to drag some infant into the world. And this christening was twenty miles away, in the town, and Mrs Finch liked to look her best on such occasions, for her own sake and for the sake of the village. 'Don't want them thinking we don't know how to dress or behave ourselves, do we?' she liked to say. Anyway, she'd just washed the pretty lace-edged blouse she intended to wear, and was hanging it out on the line with a towel under it so it wouldn't get creased, when Hannah O'Mahony came by.

'Oh,' she said, 'that's a pretty blouse,' which was unusual since Hannah was never one known to be pass-remarkable.

'Why, thank you, Hannah,' Mrs Finch said, somewhat taken aback.

'Very pretty indeed,' Hannah added.

'It is, isn't it?' Mrs Finch asked, standing back and taking a good look at the garment. 'It's very old. *Very* old.'

'I can see that,' Hannah said. 'They don't make things like that anymore, do they? Not with such fine delicate lace-work.'

'They don't indeed, do they? More's the pity. Everything's that nylon stuff now. Makes a body itch something terrible and doesn't give the skin a chance to breathe. Unhealthy. Very unhealthy.'

Hannah gave no sign that she agreed with all this. She stared at the blouse and smiled a silly smile to herself. 'I have one something like that,' she volunteered. 'Somewhere,' she added vaguely.

'Really?' Mrs Finch asked, slightly irked.

'Somewhere,' Hannah said again.

'You should get it out and wear it, Hannah. Do you the world of good to get yourself dressed up sometimes.'

Hannah brightened and let a huge smile slide across her face. 'Oh, I will, Mrs Finch. Indeed I will. There's a special day just coming down the hill and that's the day I'll wear my pretty blouse like that.'

Something about the way Hannah emphasised the special day alerted Mrs Finch, or maybe just roused her curiosity. 'And what special day would that be, Hannah?'

Suddenly Hannah became furtive. She kept the smile on her face, perhaps not knowing it was there, and looked quickly up and down the lane. Then she motioned for Mrs Finch to come closer. 'When little May comes back,' she said in a whisper.

Mrs Finch was stuck for words. 'When little May –' she began, and then let her face sink into those lines she adopted when speaking to some young and frightened mother-to-be, but held her tongue for the moment.

'That's right,' Hannah went on, however, getting more secretive and holding onto Mrs Finch's hand. 'When little May gets back.'

'Hannah, dear –' Mrs Finch tried but was quickly interrupted.

'You remember how she was took? Well, Johnsey who's staying with me for a while says he knows who took her,'

Hannah announced triumphantly. Then her face clouded for a second. 'No. He says he *thinks* he knows who took her but that it won't be all that long before he knows for sure. Well, well, Mrs Finch, when he does find out he'll be able to bring her back and that's when I'll wear my pretty blouse.'

'I see,' Mrs Finch said.

Hannah was warming to her task. 'And there's something else,' she said, gripping Mrs Finch's hand so tightly now it made her wince. 'You'll remember that poor Christy Codd and his mother?'

Mrs Finch didn't trust herself to speak, so she just nodded, and eased her aching hand from Hannah's grasp.

'Well, Johnsey says it wasn't like it seemed at all. Not at all like what it seemed.' Hannah frowned, and then added. 'He seemed very *sad* that it wasn't like the way it seemed. Very, *very* sad.'

And then Hannah seemed to lose the thread of things, and looked bemused as though wondering what she was doing there at all, and shuffled off, stopping once to look back briefly as if undecided which way to go.

'That's what the wife told me anyway,' Davey Shortt said later in the store.

There was only himself and Mr Biddlecomb and Patrick Farrel and Connor Neill there, which was something of a disappointment to him. Still, the reaction he got from the other three was some small consolation.

'But Jesus, *we* don't even know who –' Connor Neill began, but quickly frightened himself into silence.

But Davey Shortt wasn't going to let his moment be whittled away like that. 'What you say is right, Connor. *We* can't even be sure who killed little May. I mean –' and then he, too, realised the enormity of what he was saying, and took to supping his drink, not lifting his glass but leaving it on the bar and lowering his head to it.

Patrick Farrel took a deep breath. 'It's not who killed May I'm thinking about so much,' he said slowly. 'It's Christy and his mother. That's our problem. I mean, if it's true he thinks there's something funny about that, and starts digging, and – well, all our heads are in the noose for that one.'

'But none of *us* knows who did that either,' Connor Neill put in. 'That was the whole point of it, wasn't it?'

Patrick Farrel nodded. 'That was the point of it all right. But just 'cause *we* don't know doesn't mean *he* won't find out.'

'How can he?' Mr Biddlecomb, clearly more frightened than the others, asked.

'Patrick Farrel shrugged. 'Knows enough already, doesn't he.'

'If you can believe Hannah,' Mr Biddlecomb pointed out.

'Couldn't make up a thing like that,' Patrick Farrel answered. 'Not something that would just skidaddle into your head. No, he must have told her what she said.'

It was then that Mr Biddlecomb voiced what they were all thinking. 'Well,' he said. 'If that's the case we'll just have to stop him finding out any more, won't we?'

'And how do we do that?' Connor Neill asked without thinking, and then he saw the looks they gave, and gazed back at them, his mouth still hanging open.

'Only way,' Mr Biddlecomb said. Nobody answered. 'Any of you any better ideas?' Mr Biddlecomb demanded, getting angry now as if he felt they were accusing him of being the only villain. He poured himself a drink and swallowed it in one enormous gulp. 'Well?' he asked, fortified. '*Have* any of you a better idea?'

One by one the others shook their heads.

'Well, there you are then,' Mr Biddlecomb said, for some reason feeling vindicated.

'I don't like it,' Connor Neill said eventually.

'None of us bloody *likes* it,' Mr Biddlecomb said. 'It's not a question of liking it or disliking it. It's our necks we've got to be thinking about.'

'Still don't like it,' Connor insisted.

'Christ Almighty,' Mr Biddlecomb exploded. 'Will one of you hit him before I come round and murder him with my bare hands?'

No sooner were the words out of his mouth than Mr Biddlecomb realised what he had said. For some reason he spread his hands on the bar and stared at them, but quickly pulled them off the counter and put them behind his back when he saw the others staring at them also.

'You going to do it then?' Connor Neill asked.

'Me?' Mr Biddlecomb sounded appalled.

'Your idea,' Connor pointed out.

'Yes, but –'

'Would you two stop it?' Patrick Farrel said, making it an order rather than a question. 'It all needs thinking about. A lot of thinking,' he said seriously. 'And another thing – it's got to be only us four who know anything about it. Not another soul, mind. Just us four.'

Mr Biddlecomb and Davey Shortt nodded their agreement, but Connor Neill still looked unhappy.

'Connor?' Patrick Farrel asked.

'Don't know if I want to be involved,' Connor admitted.

'You *are* involved,' Mr Biddlecomb pointed out. 'Just as much as we are. Just as much as every man in the village is.'

'That's different,' Connor protested. 'Yeah, sure, I'm involved in the other thing, but this – ' He shook his head.

'Well, if you're not with us we can't just let you walk out there and blab all about it, can we, now?' Davey Shortt asked, only half joking.

'Meaning?' Connor asked.

'Shut *up*, you two,' Patrick Farrel said. 'Connor's got the right to – well, not to be one of us if he wants,' he added, knowing that was the best way to get Connor to come round to their way of thinking.

And sure enough, after another mouthful of stout and a little think to himself, Connor nodded, and said, 'Okay. I'm with you.'

'Good,' Patrick Farrel said. 'And who knows, maybe something will happen so we don't have to do anything at all.'

'Yeah, maybe,' Connor agreed, and brightened a little although he knew full well that it was a forlorn enough hope.

Of course, what Hannah had said to Mrs Finch was all over the village in no time at all, and whenever two people met, you could be sure they were talking about it. 'You hear what Mrs O'Mahony's supposed to have said?' I asked my Mam just for something to say since she wasn't really talking much to me again.

'Yes,' Mam said, and made it clear that was an end of the matter.

Then I noticed the photograph of my Dad was gone from the mantelpiece. 'Mam, where's Dad's picture gone?'

'Upstairs. I've taken it upstairs.'

'What'd you do that for?'

'Because I wanted to.'

'I can't see it if you have it upstairs.'

Mam said nothing.

'I liked it where it was so I could look at him sometimes.'

Still Mam said nothing.

'Say something, Mam.'

Mam looked as if she was going to say one thing and then decided to say another. 'You can remember quite well what your father looked like.'

'I know I can.'

'Well, you don't need any old picture of him then.'

'But it's like he's not part of the house anymore. Up there he kept an eye on us, didn't he?'

'That's being silly, Aiden.'

'No, it's not. It's the way I felt anyway.'

'Well, you just have to stop feeling that way. Simple as that. Now go and feed the dogs and get some turnip in if you want to eat yourself.'

I thought I'd cheer her up by making a joke of what she'd just said. 'I'm not going to eat myself, Mam,' I said with a smile.

But Mam didn't think that was funny. 'Aiden,' she snapped. 'If you don't stop once and for all trying to make me look like a fool I'll – '

'I was just joking, Mam.'

'Well, kindly don't. It's no time to be joking.'

'What's that mean? No time to be joking? What's so different about *this* time?' I wanted to know.

But Mam didn't answer that. She started slicing the liver, hacking angrily at it, and tossing the slivers of meat into a bowl of flour. She still remained quiet as she added salt and a bit of pepper, and then got down the big heavy pan that for years had been too heavy for me to lift. 'Be a real man when you can lift that, Aiden,' Dad used to say, and the day I did manage to lift it all by myself he gave me a great hug, and was proud as anything of me.

'What's wrong, Mam?'

'Nothing's wrong.'

'You never used to be like this, all snappy and everything, biting my head off for nothing.'

Once again Mam looked as if she was going to tell me something, but again she changed her mind. Instead she stoked up the range to get a good heat into it, and then swung round. 'Are you going to do as I asked and feed those dogs of yours and bring in a turnip?'

'Yes, Mam.'

'Well, do it then, and stop asking all those questions. There's nothing wrong and that's an end to it.'

I went out to feed the dogs, muttering.

'And we can do without that muttering to yourself as well,' Mam called after me.

'I was praying,' I lied.

'Huh,' I heard Mam grunt.

At least the dogs were in a good mood, wagging their shaggy tails and leaping all over me, pink tongues lolling in excitement. And from the windowsill the old tom cat mewed, looking for food too, but that wasn't my job. Mam fed the cat, and confided in him, the way I told my secrets and troubles to my dogs.

They gulped their food, sharing the same bowl and never quarrelling, and when they'd licked the dish clean they looked up expectantly, wanting more. Always wanting more no matter how much I gave them. 'Greedy gannets,' I said to them, and then knelt down and cuddled them both, letting them lick my face – something Mam didn't like, but Dad had always let them so I did too. That's the way I was then, always doing things my Dad had done and trying to be like him, and that's why it hurt me with Mam taking the photograph away like he wasn't someone to copy any more.

Sixteen

Father Cunningham didn't come to the village for a couple of weeks. A replacement was sent, a Father Doherty, a young man, just out of the seminary by the look of him, and very zealous and still chummy with God. He didn't think much of the state of the church, and said so, which didn't get him off to the best of starts since who was he, a whippersnapper albeit a priestly one, to criticise? He even got Kitty Mercer's back up which was a difficult thing to do since Kitty believed all priests were fine men, and made great allowances for them. But Father Doherty wasn't all that keen on flowers and ordered Kitty to remove her arrangements from the altar. True, they were dried flowers with the time of year that was in it, and she had gone overboard a bit leaving little space for the priest to manoeuvre as he got on with the business of transubstantiation, but he could have been kinder about it, couldn't he? Not just say, 'Mrs Mercer, would you kindly get that ridiculous concoction of flora off of the altar. It's God's table, not a vegetable patch.'

Well, Kitty Mercer wasn't standing for that. In a rare fit of temper she went to the altar and swept the flowers off it, sending the vases and chunks of driftwood in which they were artistically set hurtling onto the sanctuary floor, one of the vases, a cheap and gaudy Indian confection in brass and enamel that her son, Seamus, a merchant seaman, had given her after a trip to Bombay, tumbling down the steps and ending up at Father Doherty's feet with a rattle. 'There you are, Father,'

Kitty said. 'They're off God's table,' and stormed out of the church leaving Father Doherty bewildered since, clearly, he hadn't come across this sort of temperament before, and probably wouldn't again in a hurry.

And to teach him a lesson, and to show him no young upstart with the fluff still on his face was going to come into the village and push his weight about, they boycotted the Saturday confessions, leaving Father Doherty to sit there and wait, and maybe reflect, and wonder what the hell was going on. They went to Mass though, because that was something they *had* to do, but donned blatantly glum faces during the sermon, and coughed a lot, and sighed loudly. And only the women went to communion, snapping in the host as though wishing to take the unfortunate priest's fingers off too, the women and Arthur Hayes but that was understandable because Arthur was a very sick man, and would be dying soon, and it wouldn't be prudent for him to get God's back up just at the moment.

So, there was relief as well as expectant excitement when Father Cunningham returned, and Kitty Mercer came into her own again, decking the altar with a profusion of leaves and twigs and pretty dried pink and blue flowers, and making something of a rainforest of it. She hovered over Father Cunningham like he was the prodigal son himself, helping him dress for confessions, holding the surplice for him so he could slip into it without tossing his fine head of grey hair, and holding the stole so he could kiss the cross on it before wrapping it round his neck. And on Sunday morning she got out the good chasuble, the white one with the gold thread that the Carmelite nuns in Tranquilla Convent had woven into it, the one kept for really special occasions, and made Father Cunningham look quite splendid for his return.

Johnsey didn't appear at either confession or Mass. Indeed, no one had seen him for a while.

'Maybe he's flown off with them birds he gets on so well with,' Davey Shortt said facetiously.

'Fat chance of that,' Mr Biddlecomb retorted.

'Could be sick,' Connor Neill suggested. 'Maybe them

burns have got to him at last.'

That was certainly more plausible, and the men considered this possibility for a while. But Patrick Farrel put the dampers on it by saying, 'Hannah would have said something.'

Then Willie Little said, 'Amazing how he got over those burns, isn't it, though? Have killed most men, they would.' He shook his head at his amazement. 'Never did find out how that fire started, did we?' he asked, giving Davey Shortt a sidelong sliver of a glance.

'No we didn't,' Davey said with a kind of a smirk on his face. 'Did we now?'

Riled a bit by the smirk, Willie Little pursed his lips for a second, and then rubbed the side of his nose. 'Could make a guess, though, if pushed to it,' he said.

Mr Biddlecomb interrupted. 'Plenty of guesses been made already, Willie. No point in guessing. Guessing gets no one anywhere.'

'Got to guess,' Willie Little insisted. 'If you don't know the truth you've got to guess. Nothing else you can do, is there?'

'Well, go guess somewhere else,' Davey Shortt told him.

'For the love of God, you two. Would youse ever stop your squabbling,' Patrick Farrel said, clearly with something on his mind and trying to think.

'Oh, I'll stop all right,' Willie Little said. 'Don't need to guess none, I don't. Not about that fire anyway. Know all about that, I do. Just like Davey there. He knows all about it too, don't you, Davey?'

Davey Shortt was off his stool in a flash and stood there, squaring up, ready for a fight.

'Hoy,' Mr Biddlecomb shouted. 'I'll have none of that in here. If you want to act like hooligans, do it outside.'

'Sit down, Davey,' Patrick Farrel said, his voice filled with that weary tolerance that parents use on loved but recalcitrant children. And Davey sat down again. 'And you,' Patrick Farrel said to Willie Little.

'I'm going,' Willie announced. 'Can't have a civilized talk in this store any more without some yahoo making –'

'Goodnight, then, Willie,' Mr Biddlecomb said pointedly.

When Willie had gone Mr Biddlecomb rested his elbows

on the counter, and asked, 'So what do you think?'

'About what?' Connor Neill asked.

Mr Biddlecomb gave a sigh. 'About Johnsey, of course.'

'Oh, him,' Connor said.

'Yes. Him.'

'Maybe he's just lying low for a bit,' Davey Shortt suggested.

'And why would he do that?' Patrick Farrel asked. 'Unless – ' He stopped abruptly and frowned.

'Unless what?' Connor Neill asked.

'Yes. What are you getting at, Patrick?' Mr Biddlecomb asked too. 'Unless what?'

'It's stupid,' Patrick Farrel admitted, looking bashful and a bit ashamed.

'Tell us anyway,' Mr Biddlecomb urged.

'Yeah. Go on. Tell us,' Connor Neill all but pleaded, keen enough to witness Patrick Farrel make a fool of himself.

'We'll tell you if it's stupid or not,' Davey Shortt promised, and you could almost see him readying himself to pooh-pooh whatever Patrick was about to say.

None of them had ever known Patrick Farrel to be so reluctant to express his views, or seen him so nervous. He kept glancing over his shoulder at the door as though expecting some malevolent ghost to come flying in and grab him. His palms were sweating and he kept rubbing them on his trousers, up and down, up and down.

'Here,' Mr Biddlecomb said, pouring a small whisky and putting the glass under Patrick Farrel's nose, waiting for him to drink it. When he'd swallowed the drink, Mr Biddlecomb said, '*Now* will you tell us what's on your mind, for heaven's sake.'

Patrick Farrel took a deep breath, letting it out slowly as he spoke so that the words had a strange, eerie, menacing edge to them. 'You know what we were talking about the other night? About Johnsey and –' he stopped as the three other men nodded quickly as though they, too, were reluctant to have that conversation voiced again. 'Well,' Patrick went on, 'ever since that night, even on the way home after us speaking, I've had this feeling that I'm being watched. Followed and watched, only I've never seen no one. And I've had another feeling. I know it's crazy so you don't need to tell me, but I just feel – it's more than that really, it's like I *know* that Johnsey somehow knows what we've been talking about. About him. About how –' Patrick Farrel lowered his head, and shook it, then buried it in his arms.

It was as though Mr Biddlecomb, Davey Shortt and Connor Neill had been turned to stone. None of them moved. None of them even blinked, and it seemed, too, as though none of them were even breathing. There wasn't a sound in the store, and it stayed that way for several minutes. Then, outside, the wind blew into a sudden gust and rattled the window Mr Biddlecomb had been promising his wife to repair for the past fortnight. A log snapped in the stove. A bluebottle, late to hibernate or do whatever bluebottles do with their time through the late autumn and winter, flew haphazardly across the store.

'Patrick, Patrick,' Mr Biddlecomb said quietly. 'He *can't* know.'

Patrick Farrel looked up. 'I *know* he can't. I keep telling myself he can't. But it doesn't change anything. I'm telling you he *does* know.'

'You *think* he knows,' Mr Biddlecomb corrected.

Connor Neill said, 'Patrick could be right, you know. We've always said there was something funny about that Johnsey. That he had some sort of power and things. Maybe he can know things he can't know.'

'Don't you start,' Mr Biddlecomb warned testily.

'Just saying,' Connor Neill said.

'Look,' Mr Biddlecomb said. 'Tell you what. How about we all have a drink on the house and stop all this nonsensical talk?' and knowing none of them was likely to refuse a free drink he set out the glasses and filled them generously. 'There we go,' he said magnanimously.

But when they'd drunk their drink and gone home for the night, Mr Biddlecomb settled himself in his chair by the stove, and thought about Patrick Farrel's strange premonitions. And although he hadn't admitted it, would not have dared to admit it, he had himself had uneasy feelings since the night they had spoken about the possibility of ridding themselves and the village of Johnsey. He had, however, succeeded in dismissing them, telling himself he was being a silly old fool to even think those feelings had anything to do with what he and the others had discussed. But now, but now . . . Mr Biddlecomb gave an involuntary shiver. He leaned forward and stoked the fire.

'Mr Biddlecomb?' his wife called from upstairs.

'Yes?'

'Are you coming to bed?'

'Yes, yes, yes,' Mr Biddlecomb said to himself. 'Yes, in a minute,' he called back.

'Well, would you hurry up about it?'

Mr Biddlecomb ignored that. He stood up and spread his arms, easing the stiffness in his back. Then he walked to the door and checked that it was properly locked. He checked the windows too. And it was as he was about to turn from the window that he saw, or thought he saw, the ugsome, distorted face of Johnsey staring in at him. Mr Biddlecomb clutched at his chest and gave a horrible gurgle. He thought, for a moment, that he was about to die. Then he screamed without really knowing why.

Mrs Biddlecomb came tumbling down the stairs as fast as her dodgy hips would allow her. 'What in the name of God – ' she started and then saw her husband standing there, white as a sheet, and every bone in his body shaking, staring at the window.

'It's him,' he managed to say.

'Him? Who?' Mrs Biddlecomb wanted to know.

'Him. Look.'

Mrs Biddlecomb looked. She went closer to the window and peered out. Then she turned and eyed her husband. 'You have had a drink more than you should, haven't you?' she demanded.

'He's out there. Watching,' Mr Biddlecomb told her.

'There's no one at all out there, you old fool.'

Mr Biddlecomb looked bewildered. Slowly he let his hands fall and turned to face his wife. 'No one out there?'

''Course not. Sensible people are all in their beds by now. And that's where I should be, and you,' and off she went, muttering to herself about how it was her bad luck to end up with a husband who saw things that weren't there and kept her out of her nice warm bed of a night that had a rawness to it fit to give a body pneumonia. 'Now, come *on*,' she ordered when she reached the door to the kitchen.

'Coming,' Mr Biddlecomb answered meekly.

And as Mr Biddlecomb followed his wife upstairs, Connor Neill said goodnight to Patrick Farrel and Davey Shortt, hurrying up the little path to his cottage and making sure he was safely inside before his two companions were out of sight.

Davey Shortt gave a short cackle. 'Scared him plenty, you did, Patrick,' he remarked as if he himself hadn't been frightened at all.

'Connor's all right,' Patrick Farrel observed, meaning, as far as he was concerned, Connor Neill was a good sort of man.

'Oh, yes. He's all right,' Davey Shortt said, but somehow got a different slant to his words, expressing the opinion that Connor was no great shakes as a man, just all right.

'And maybe right to be scared,' Patrick went on. 'I can tell you *I* bloody well am.'

That left Davey Shortt in something of a quandary. His habit was to agree with Patrick Farrel – he, Patrick, having that kudos relative wealth can bring despite his reputation for tight-fistedness. But Davey Shortt was stupid enough to believe that if he admitted he was scared again, as he had unwillingly confessed to being frightened half to death when the rooks attacked him (if, indeed, that tale was entirely true), he would be seen as a coward, and lose what little credence he held within the community. So, 'Can't see why you should be,' he said now. 'Nothing that Johnsey can do to you, is there? What could he do? Nothing. Not a thing he can do to you. Nothing,' he insisted perhaps a bit too vehemently.

'That's what scares me,' Patrick Farrel admitted. 'I don't *know* what he might do. Could have all sorts of tricks up his sleeve that I wouldn't know about.'

'God, Patrick, I never thought I'd hear *you* saying you was scared of a creature like Johnsey.'

'Never come across a creature like him before, have we?'

'No, but – '

'Well, then, I've every right to be scared of him. Don't know what way he's going to jump.'

'No, but – '

'So he's got the advantage over us. He's the one calling the bloody tune. All we can do is wait, and it's the waiting for the unknown and unexpected to happen that's giving me the jitters.'

There wasn't a lot that Davey could say to that, and with Patrick so clearly shaken, and happy enough to admit it, Davey found himself getting nervous, and the longish walk home after Patrick had left him loomed out in front of him now, dark and gloom-laden, and filled with possible spectral hazards.

And when Patrick did take his leave, saying, 'You take care now, Davey, hear?', his simple wish sounded strangely ominous, and Davey Shortt set out for his own home at a good clip.

The wind was in a cantankerous mood just now: blowing up and then dying down again in fits and starts, chasing thin clouds across the face of the moon and making it disappear and reappear by turn as though it were playing some outrageous game of peek-a-boo with the world below it. When it was covered and the world dark Davey Shortt didn't mind it too much, but in the occasional flashes of light, when shadows appeared and created monstrous shapes that seemed to leap out at him, he got the willies. And perhaps with reason.

He was only a couple of hundred yards from his home when it happened. During a dark spell Davey was sure something cold and damp touched his cheek. He jumped and gave a small squeak, but when he made to brush the object away there was nothing there. Then the clouds scudded away from the face of the moon and Davey Shortt just about shit himself. For one brief second he could have sworn he saw Johnsey standing right in his path, and in his hands one of those wire snares Davey himself used to trap rabbits, and him pulling on the ends of it, snapping it open and closed, and grinning at Davey in the most terrible way. Then darkness returned, but much as he wanted to run and get away from the dreadful place, Davey found he simply could not move. For what seemed an age he was forced to stand there, frozen, knowing that if Johnsey did attack him and try to throttle him, he would be powerless to defend himself. And then it was mercifully light again, and there was nothing standing in the path. Davey gave a yelp and raced the rest of the way home, slamming the door behind him and leaning back against it, puffing, and saying, 'Oh, my God, oh, my God,' over and over, until his knees gave way and he slid to the floor.

Seventeen

Everyone thought that finally Olly Carver had slipped up and got his timing wrong, and it was as though one of the great tenets of their faith had been shattered. But there it was, plain for all to see, the grey-brown smoke rising from Olly's chimney, signalling the first frost, and it being the balmiest evening anyone could remember for that time of year.

'Just goes to show, don't it, that you can't trust *anything* no more,' Kitty Mercer said, and Mrs Finch agreed, nodding her head and setting the velvet poppy on the side of her beret bobbing.

'If we can't count on Olly, what can we count on?' she asked, and this time Kitty Mercer agreed, nodding also, and up and down the village people mourned the tragic loss of Olly Carter's acumen.

So, they were overjoyed when they woke the next morning and found the valley crisp and white, and stiff as any alb Kitty Mercer herself bleached and starched for Father Cunningham, and this despite the fact that Olly's fire signalled the approach of winter which they dreaded. 'Ah,' people sighed. 'Just knew Olly wouldn't let us down,' and conveniently overlooked the doubts they'd proclaimed.

And when Heather and Myrtle Carver came down from the hill to do the monthly shopping, Mrs Biddlecomb was generous with the rations, letting the scales go a bit over the mark for sugar and tea, and throwing in a few extra slices of salted bacon. And Mr Biddlecomb sent Olly up a small bottle of whiskey, just to say thank you for getting it right again. And Mrs Bannagher sent a goose, and Mrs O'Toole sent a big jar of pickled beetroot, and Kitty Mercer sent a bunch of her dried flowers, although what Olly was going to do with those was anyone's guess.

'Want a hand then?' one of the young bucks asked as the Carver girls set off for home with their goods, struggling a bit since they hadn't expected to be quite so loaded.

Heather and Myrtle hung their heads and said nothing.

'Go on, let us give you a hand. Carry them all the way home for you, I will if you want.'

'No,' Heather said.

'Always say no, don't you? All you Carver girls say no to everything.'

'Yeah,' Dougie Neill, Connor's eldest, said. 'End up right old spinsters if you keep saying no to everything like that.'

'Our Dad says we're to say no,' Myrtle said, and Heather gave her a bit of a dig in the ribs since being the young one she was supposed to let Heather do all the talking.

'Your Dad's not here though, is he?' Dougie pointed out.

'Makes no difference,' Heather told him.

'Makes a lot of difference,' Dougie insisted. 'What he don't know won't hurt him, will it?'

'Might hurt you a bit though,' Sam Cotter said. 'If it's the first time you've had it.' That set all the boys laughing, set them rocking back on their heels too.

'You're *disgusting*, Sam Cotter,' Heather Carver said.

'No, I'm not,' Sam protested. 'Am I, lads?' he asked his pals, and they all agreed that he wasn't disgusting, saying, 'Naw,' in chorus, and heaving themselves from their slouched positions and following the girls.

'Yes, you are,' Heather insisted.

'Time all you Carver girls were broke anyway,' Sam went on. 'Not natural the lot of you living up there like bloody nuns, and us down here just waiting to give you the time of your lives.'

'Come on, Myrtle,' Heather said, making her sister hurry.

And maybe it was that hurrying that made things get out

of hand. As Heather and Myrtle trotted down the winding lane that led towards the track which would take them home, the boys ran after them, quite excited now.

'Maybe your Daddy's giving you all you want,' Dougie shouted.

'Yeah,' Sam Cotter said.

'Yeah,' said Eamonn Finch, who should have known better.

'That'll be it all right,' young Pat Farrel said.

The girls started to run.

'Come on,' Sam Cotter said, and the boys chased after them.

By now Myrtle was in tears, and she dropped the jar of beetroot, and it splashed all over her little dress and that made her cry even more.

'Look what you did,' Heather said, rounding on the boys.

'Didn't do nothing,' young Pat Farrel said. '*She* dropped it.'

'*You* made her,' Heather said. 'Just you wait till our Dad hears about this.'

That made the boys falter in their step for Olly Carver was known to have the fiercest temper, and had once thrashed a lad to within an inch of his life for just accidentally licking his lips while his eyes happened to be resting on one of Olly's daughters. And he made no apology for the whipping either, Olly didn't. 'They're *my* daughters,' he said. 'And no one so much as looks at them without my say so.' And there was no arguing with that.

But now the four boys were roused and even the dire threat of Olly Carver's vengeance didn't cool them down. Not for long anyway. Sam Cotter and Eamonn Finch grabbed a hold of Heather, and young Pat Farrel and Dougie Neill caught little Myrtle in a vicious grip. And before any of them knew it they were all in a heap on the wide grassy verge, the boys groping, the girls struggling like mad. Myrtle was screaming her head off too by this stage, so young Pat Farrel put his hard hand over her mouth. Myrtle bit it, making Pat yelp and give her a slap. Heather got her knee up quickly and caught Sam Cotter where it hurt him most, and sent him reeling back into the lane. 'Christ,' he swore, holding himself and bent double. 'Christ.' The pain made him angry, and when Sam Cotter got angry he could be mean as a weasel. 'I'll teach you, bitch,' he said between his teeth, and lunged at Heather, getting on top of her and pulling away at her underclothes, his thick-lipped mouth slobbering as it sought out hers. 'Hold her fucking legs, will you, Eamonn, for Christ's sake,' he said, and Eamonn did, sitting on one and holding onto the other with both hands, his eyes fixed on little Myrtle who was by now just about naked and looking as if she might be paralysed since there was barely a move out of her as young Pat and Dougie ran their tongues all over her like hounds lapping water.

There can be no doubt that rape would have taken place had not Eamonn and Sam suddenly found themselves grabbed by the scruff of the neck, lifted well off the ground and hurled over the stone wall that ran the length of the lane, to land with a thud so terrible that it knocked all the wind out of them, and made each of them believe his back had been broken. But they didn't even have that much time to think about their possible crippling because they were soon joined by young Pat and Dougie who shot over the wall as though launched from a cannon, landing some ten yards further to the right which was unlucky for them because that was where the bed of nettles and brambles were, and them with their pants down and the stinging and scratching and ripping all the worse and the sorer for that.

'What the fuck happened?' Sam Cotter managed to ask, still lying flat on his back, and not daring to move.

Young Pat and Dougie ignored him, busy as they were trying to extricate themselves from the brambles without doing their manhood irreparable damage, trying to pick the thorny tendrils off their balls with the delicacy of lace-makers but their thick fingers making this futile, and every so often one or both of them would throw back their heads and yowl in agony.

But Eamonn had eased himself up onto one elbow albeit gingerly. 'Wish to Christ I knew,' he said.

'You see nothing?' Sam demanded, and seeing Eamonn up on one elbow got himself into the same position, wincing.

'Not a bloody thing. Only thing I know is I was sailing

through the air and landing here nearly on top of yourself.'

'Same as us,' Dougie shouted across. 'Youse were lucky, though. Look where we bloody landed.'

'It wasn't Olly, was it?' Sam Cotter now asked.

'Not likely. If it was Olly we wouldn't be lying here alive. We'd be lying down all right. But stiff and dead, that's for certain.'

'Them girls still there?'

'Dunno.'

'Well, go look.'

'You go look.'

'Can't bloody move, I can't. Not yet.'

'Neither can I,' Eamonn protested.

'Yes you can. Look at you – you're moving now, aren't you? Go on, for the love of God.'

Eamonn crawled to the wall and peered over it as if half expecting to be faced with some fantastic ogre. He glanced about for a while, and then made his way back to Sam Cotter, staying low and on his hands and knees. 'Nothing,' he reported.

'They've gone?'

'Yep.'

'And there's no one else there?'

'Nope.'

'Jesus. What the hell happened to us then?'

Eamonn shrugged. 'Dunno, do I?'

'You feel nothing?'

'Felt someone grab a hold of me and throw me,' Eamonn said, and then added, 'I think.'

'Yeah,' Sam agreed, but with awe in his voice. 'Didn't rightly feel like some*one* though, did it? More like some*thing*.'

Eamonn got very agitated. 'That's what I was thinking,' he admitted. 'Didn't feel like no hands that took hold of me. Like claws they were, digging into me and all.'

'Yeah,' said Sam. 'Just like claws.'

'Give us a hand over here, will you?' young Pat Farrel pleaded.

Eamonn went to young Pat's aid, and Sam followed, not wanting to be left alone. 'Jesus,' he swore. 'Be a long time before you'll be able to get that thing up without excruciating yourself,' he said with a certain glee.

'Don't I fucking know it. Pull them brambles back a bit.'

Eamonn pulled the brambles back a bit, and swore gently to himself as the nettles stung his arm.

'That's better,' young Pat said, and eased himself out of the brambles, and then just standing there and watching Dougie struggle to do the same. Indeed, the three of them just stood there and watched Dougie.

'Hey, Pat,' Sam Cotter asked quietly. 'You see anything?'

'Nothing.'

'Feel anything?'

'Now?'

'No, dope. When you was thrown.'

Young Pat thought for a while. 'Felt something grab me by the back of the neck and the seat of me arse and throw me,' he said finally.

'What you mean – something?' Sam Cotter wanted to know.

'Just something.'

'You mean someone, don't you?' Sam Cotter asked hopefully.

'Suppose I do. Didn't rightly feel like a person, though. Not like hands. Like –' Patrick paused and flexed his fingers, staring at them as they grappled. 'Like claws, I think,' he added, which was just what Sam Cotter didn't want to hear.

But by then Dougie had freed himself and was sitting on the grass carefully examining his injuries. 'Bloody in shreds, I am,' he complained.

'Better get the hell out of here,' Sam Cotter said, standing erect now and seeming to have forgotten his terrible pain.

'That's for sure,' young Pat agreed, doing up his buttons and wincing as he did so.

'What we going to say?' Eamonn asked.

'About what?'

'About – you know – us flying through the air like that, and no good reason for it.'

Sam Cotter rounded on him. 'Nothing. That's what we're going to say. Nothing. Not a single word,' he ordered. 'Want to have everyone laughing at us, is that what you want?' he asked, believing that was certainly a good enough reason for keeping silent.

'Them Carver girls will talk,' Dougie pointed out, also getting his pants back up with a lot of grimacing.

'Maybe they won't.'

'Oh, they will, and then we're for it.'

But Sam Cotter was proved right. None of them wanted to be laughed at, so they kept the whole incident secret, and when any of the Carver girls came to the village the four of them made a point of it to stay well out of the way.

And, oddly, the girls, Heather and Myrtle, said nothing about the affair either, but that was probably because they were terrified of what their father, Olly, might do, not only to the boys but to themselves since he was sure to think they had led the lads on: that was the way his mind worked, wasn't it? But Heather and Myrtle were as puzzled as Sam and Pat and Dougie had been about the method of their rescue. 'I seen nothing,' Myrtle said. 'Had me eyes closed.'

'Me too,' Heather said.

And so, unable to fathom it, they put it down to Jesus, or maybe His Virgin Mother Mary, or maybe even some saint they didn't know about but whose job it was to protect young girls coming home with the shopping from louts like Sam Cotter and his friends. And that started them thinking that maybe they were a bit special, like that Saint Bernadette they'd been told about in school, and look at the trouble she'd landed herself in by reporting her visions, no one believing her, and being hauled up in front of all those bishops and people, and everyone saying she was cracked in the head and talking about taking her away from her home and locking her up in a big house filled with mad people, and some of them wanting her burned at the stake the way they'd done it to that other poor saint somewhere in a savage-like country. And neither Heather nor Myrtle wanted anything like that to happen to them, the very thought of being set alight and their bones crackling away like kindling even giving them nightmares, so they kept it all to themselves, talking about it only when they were alone. And in a secret place they had, a place they'd go to and pick wild raspberries when the time was right, they constructed a little altar of stone, and put a picture of Saint Philomena on it since she was the only saint they happened to have a likeness of, although they didn't know it was Saint Philomena so it didn't matter all that much, and said an occasional prayer there, covering their heads respectfully with hankies the way they believed little girls should when in conversation with saints, thanking Jesus for sending the saint to save them, and was there anything in particular He wanted them to do by way of showing their gratitude? There didn't seem to be. At least, Jesus never let them know that there was, but that was just like Him, doing all His kindnesses for nothing, the same as He wanted people to behave although He must have known there wasn't much chance of that since He knew everything. But they'd asked Him, and that was the important thing. He couldn't come back to them and say they had taken His benevolence for granted.

Besides, thinking that Jesus *might* one day come to them and ask for some favour added excitement to their dull lives, and if that happened, wow, wouldn't they be the ones who were the envy of everyone?

So, nothing of the incident would ever have been known had not Dougie Neill put his foot in it, shooting his mouth off, trying to show off to his father. True, it was his birthday, and his father, Connor, had taken him to Biddlecomb's store for a birthday drink. And it would have been fine if Dougie had taken just one drink. But the other men bought him drinks too, all of them thinking what a funny thing it would be to get the young whippersnapper reeling, show him he wasn't the man he thought he was, not yet at any rate. And by the end of the evening Dougie *was* reeling, and talking a lot of nonsense too, in a loud voice.

'Time you got that boy of yours home,' Mr Biddlecomb told Connor.

'I'm no *boy*,' Dougie shouted.

'Time you went home anyway,' Mr Biddlecomb said.

'Time to get your nappy changed,' Willie Little said, and

had everyone in fits of laughter at that.

And then someone, although no one could ever be sure who it was precisely, said, 'See he's tucked up safe and mind that Johnsey doesn't get his claws into him.'

Well, it was as if Dougie had been whacked over the head with a plank. He stopped his shouting instantly, and gazed about him in a dazed way, looking at everyone in turn as though to divine who had spoken. And although it was later mooted that no one in the store had uttered the words but that they had, in some mysterious way, just floated into the men's consciousness, Dougie decided it was his own father who had made the remark. 'Why d'you say that?' he demanded, slurring his words but trying desperately to soberise himself.

'Said nothing, I didn't,' Connor protested.

'Yes, you did,' Dougie insisted, lurching towards his father as if to attack him.

'Hold on now. Hold on,' Patrick Farrel said, grabbing Dougie and holding him back.

'Let go of me,' Dougie yelled.

'Not till you quiet yourself.'

'What's got into him?' Davey Shortt wanted to know.

Connor Neill shook his head. 'Dunno. Never seen him like this before.'

'He's your bloody son,' Patrick Farrel said, still hanging onto Dougie.

'It was him that did it,' Dougie suddenly shouted, adding to the confusion.

Mr Biddlecomb started to laugh. 'Him that did what?' he asked, chortling as he spoke.

'Him. Johnsey. It was him that did it.'

Suddenly Mr Biddlecomb stopped his laughing, and the rest of the men fell quiet the way they always did when anticipating bad news.

Still holding Dougie, Patrick Farrel asked, 'What did Johnsey do, boy?'

'Sent the four of us flying,' Dougie said, mumbling.

'What did he say?' Mr Biddlecomb asked.

'Said Johnsey sent the four of them flying,' Willie Little said with a bit of a snigger.

It could have been the use of the word claws that got to Dougie, but whatever it was he now was convinced that Johnsey had been behind his curious aerobatics. Yet, drunk as he was, he was careful to play the innocent, and now, haltingly, recounted a tale of how he and young Pat and Eamonn and Sam Cotter had been strolling along the lane when Johnsey hove into view and blocked their path. And then, as if it suddenly dawned on him that this didn't make much of a story, be began to fantasise, saying that Johnsey had waved his arms and uttered the strangest words and suddenly there they were, the four of them, hurtling over the wall and into the field, and leaving the path clear for Johnsey to go on his way.

'It's the drink talking,' Mr Biddlecomb announced, but the looks the other men gave him left him in little doubt that they weren't about to accept this by way of explanation.

Connor tried to get some sense out of his son. 'Can't just have waved his arms and got the four of you flying,' he said, but Dougie had passed out now, and was snoring his head off in Patrick Farrel's arms.

Patrick Farrel let him slide to the floor and stood looking over him for a while before saying, 'Adds up, what he says.'

'What d'you mean, adds up?' Mr Biddlecomb demanded, not about to have any such fantastic and frightening tale add up in his store. 'No man can do that sort of thing.'

'Seems Johnsey can,' Willie Little said.

'Well, I'm not about to believe any such thing,' Mr Biddlecomb said but in a half-hearted way, and when he spotted Willie Little grinning at him he went on, 'and Connor, get that boy of yours out of here. Would you look at him dribbling all over the floor. Get him out of here and home to bed where he should be,' hoping that this distraction would get him off the hook.

Connor Neill slouched off his stool and took a hold of one of Dougie's arms. 'Well, give us a hand then, some of you,' he said in a peeved way.

'I'm going home anyway,' Willie Little said. 'Give us his other arm.'

And then Sammy Burchill decided he was going home too, and took a leg, and Leonard Midden took a hold on the other one and off they went, hauling Dougie Neill home between them, and Sammy Burchill saying, 'Feeding this lad too well you are, Connor.'

'It's dead weight,' Willie Little explained seriously as if he considered the point important.

'I'll dead him when he wakes up in the morning,' Connor promised, and that was them out of the store and making a comic enough picture as they lugged him up the street.

'Fits,' Patrick Farrel said when they were gone from view.

'Johnsey, you mean?' Davey Shortt asked, still shaken by his encounter with the rooks and prepared to believe just about anything odd about Johnsey. Patrick Farrel nodded.

But Mr Biddlecomb wasn't going to give in that easily. 'Would you ever stop and think for a minute,' he suggested. 'It's just not *reasonable*,' he said, stressing the word as if reason was all that matters.

'Doesn't have to be reasonable,' Patrick Farrel said. 'Not when we're talking about the likes of him.'

'Patrick's right, Mr Biddlecomb,' Davey Shortt said. 'I can vouch for that,' he added.

'In that case we're all up to here in it,' Mr Biddlecomb told them, holding his hand up to his forehead.

'Unless we do something – and pretty damn quick,' Patrick Farrel said.

'Maybe we *can't* do anything,' Davey Shortt said. 'Maybe he's – ' he frowned and racked his brains.

'Indestructible?' Mr Biddlecomb suggested, hoping it would be taken as something of a joke.

But, 'That's the word,' Davey Shortt confirmed. 'Maybe he's indestructible,' he reiterated, taking his time over the word as if tasting the syllables.

'You'll be having us believe he's not even human next,' Mr Biddlecomb scoffed.

'Maybe he's not,' Patrick Farrel said gloomily.

'Would you not be so stupid,' Mr Biddlecomb said, getting nervous himself now.

'Nothing stupid about it if you think what he's been able to do.'

'Like setting them bloody birds on me,' Davey volunteered.

'And that visiting the graveyard and all,' Patrick Farrel said.

'And talking to little May O'Mahony and her long dead.'

'And surviving that fire that would surely have killed a man.'

'And now making people fly when he wants them to,' Davey Shortt said to end the litany.

'And that's not taking heed of what Hannah O'Mahony had to say,' Patrick Farrel added, having the last word. 'All about him knowing things.'

'All right. All right,' Mr Biddlecomb put in, having heard enough. 'So what do we do?'

'Nothing much we *can* do if he's – you know, that word you said,' Davey Shortt told them.

'Indestructible,' Patrick Farrel repeated to himself in a vague way.

'That's it. Nothing much we can do if he's that.'

'You're only supposing he's indestructible,' Mr Biddlecomb pointed out. 'Maybe he's not.'

Patrick Farrel took a deep sigh. 'Only one way to find out, I suppose,' he said. 'Got to stop him finding out everything.'

'If he hasn't already,' Davey Shortt added pessimistically.

'Got to stop him even more if he *has* found out,' Patrick Farrel pointed out in the tone of a man who had already made up his mind to accept the inevitable.

Mr Biddlecomb ran a rag over the counter, moving away from the two other men as he worked. When he reached the far end of the bar he asked, 'Who's going to do it then?' but when he got no answer, he came back to them. 'I asked who's going to do it?'

'Whoever of us gets the chance,' Patrick Farrel said.

Mr Biddlecomb looked happy enough about that since he, clearly, would have the least chance, and to share his relief he gave Patrick and Dougie another drink, and took one for himself to celebrate.

'If any of us is *able* to do it,' Davey Shortt said before drinking his drink.

'Can only try,' Patrick said. '*Got* to try,' he said to himself mostly, and swallowed his whiskey. 'Can't just do it either.

Got to make it so no questions get asked. Had enough of that.'

'Like an accident?' Mr Biddlecomb asked, sucking in his breath at the same time to announce his doubt about the possibility of that.

'Yes,' Patrick Farrel said.

'*That* won't be easy,' Mr Biddlecomb said.

'Nobody's talking about easy,' Patrick Farrel snapped. 'It's him or us, though, isn't it?' he asked, still a bit testy, and then quietly and again mostly to himself, he repeated, 'Him or us.'

Eighteen

Despite the crackling frost that covered the valley each morning now, and the fret and gloom that hung over it like a warning shroud, the villagers still clung to the illusion that winter had not yet come. And as though to verify this, or just tease them, the occasional bright day did occur, days when a watery, half-hearted sun sent weak and unwarming beams of yellow light down upon them, giving a curious majesty to the place, a painting almost, in hues of deepest blue and grey and milky white that shaded all that was ugsome and lit the fine, deep sweep of the valley with the mountains behind and to the north of it. And people accepted the meagre sun as a great gift, and nodded to each other, saying, 'See, there's still a ray or two of the sun left in the season yet.' And this knowledge warmed them a little, more than the sun itself did anyway.

It was a busy time too. Stock, though still in the fields, had to be fed since the grass was frozen and tasteless now, and at first light the men would shoulder great bales of hay and spread it out, and call, 'Come, come, come,' and the cattle would race across the field with stifled bellows, the steam pouring from their wide, moist nostrils, and the sheep, hampered by their soggy woollen coats would follow, bleating as though their life depended on the racket they made. It was a puzzling time for the dogs who found themselves redundant, and you could see in their eyes them wondering how it was the beasts came so willingly without having to be rounded up and encouraged.

They kept close to the men who owned them, always looking up with soulful eyes, waiting for the command that didn't come. And there was a slouch to their walk as they came home from the fields as if they believed they were in shame.

It was also the time that Peadar Taigh Donnelly disliked, because everyone avoided him, he being the coffin-maker, and he knew that even if he looked at someone in the friendliest way they would believe he was measuring them up in his mind's eye. So he either stayed at home or went for long and lonesome walks by himself, walks that he put to good use though, marking the trees that would be useful and could be purchased at a fair price from the big estate. He used to mark them with letters, but changed that to numbers when word got round that he was, in fact, putting people's initials on the tree-trunks, putting a hex on those people, too, which didn't go down very well. And on those days that he chose to work in the barn he used as a workshop he was careful not to hammer, using screws wherever possible so that no noise would emerge and echo about the place, and make his fellow villagers uneasy, making them wonder if he had inside knowledge and who he was getting a coffin ready for. He could, of course, have kept a stock of ready-made coffins, and often thought about doing just that. But he felt, somehow, that this might be encouraging death and, God knows, encouragement was the last thing it needed, coming as it did with its persistent wintry regularity, picking people off on a whim, and sometimes not even giving a hint of who it had chosen until it was too late to do anything about it.

And it was on one of the days without a hint of sunshine, a glowering day that pressed its broad bleak hand down firmly on everything, that Peadar Taigh Donnelly decided to take one of his lonely walks to the woods. He wrapped himself up well, and put a copper flask in his pocket, and a corned-beef sandwich too in case he got peckish. On his way out of the village he happened upon Kitty Mercer hurrying to the church, a woven basket filled with foliage on her arm. "Morning, Kitty,' Peadar Taigh said, politely raising his cap the way he always did when he spoke to one of the women and in a way proclaiming how he would politely treat them when it came to bury them. But Kitty Mercer pretended not to see him, and scurried on, turning her pinched face skyward as if assessing the likelihood of rain. Peadar Taigh sighed, and let his mind shrug off the insult although idly estimating that there were a few good years left in Kitty Mercer yet if things took their normal course.

As he crossed the field and came closer to the woods, to the place where the bracken and gorse grew abundantly as if it was a bastion and the woods beyond a fort to be defended, Peadar Taigh heard an odd sound that made him stop in his tracks and cock his pointed little head to listen. He heard it again, not quite a cry, nor a moan, nor a grunt, but a combination of all three and the likes of which he had never heard. But, probably because he was used to the eerie, plangeant noises mourners made as they gave vent to their grief, Peadar Taigh was in no way afeared, and moved towards the noise with some curiosity, stepping, with surprising daintiness, over the bracken and dodging the worst of the prickly gorse.

Nothing could have prepared Peadar Taigh for what he discovered. For several moments he stared, not knowing what to make of it. There, in that tiny clearing potted with rabbit burrows, was Davey Shortt, his head stuck down one of the burrows, his great fat buttocks swivelling from side to side at a great rate, the way Mr Biddlecomb's Airedale, with its docked tail, used to do before it got run over by someone's tractor. 'Well, well,' Peadar Taigh said to himself, and bent down. He patted Davey Shortt's rear end, and asked in his polite and courteous way, 'What you up to, Davey, eh?'

Davey Shortt gave a muffled answer, and waved his arms in a vague enough way. And Peadar Taigh, thinking he was stuck, caught a hold of his legs and gave a mighty tug. Davey didn't budge, but the roar he let out of him sounded as if it came from hell itself, or from the very bowels of the earth anyway. Peadar Taigh took a closer look. He clucked and pursed his lips and sucked in air as he noted the wire snare biting into Davey's neck. 'Oh, dear me,' he said. 'Very nasty, that is,' and took his knife from his pocket. He got the blade between the wire and Davey Shortt's skin, and started to saw, ignoring the gurgles and curses that came from the burrow. And it took him quite a while and a fair bit of sawing and twisting before the wire slackened, and fell away, and Davey could reverse himself out of the hole. He sat on the grass, his face bluish, his eyes popping, and not saying a word.

'I'd get me a ferret if I was you,' Peadar Taigh said, not meaning to lack compassion, just being practical.

Davey Shortt tried to answer but the words rasped in his throat and came out distorted and garbled.

'Don't try talking yet,' Peadar Taigh advised. 'Let the juices get back into that neck of yours first.'

So Davey Shortt waited for the juices to get back into his neck, and spent the time swabbing up the blood that oozed from the terrible weal that ran across his throat and all the way round to the back of his head.

After a while Peadar Taigh asked, 'Feeling better?'

'Yeah,' Davey Shortt managed to croak.

Peadar Taigh took the flask from his pocket and screwed off the cap, passing it to Davey. Davey shook his head but stopped that motion abruptly, maybe thinking his head would screw off too if he kept it up.

'Well, you better be getting yourself home and having that seen to,' Peadar Taigh counselled. 'You be able to get by yourself?'

'Yeah,' Davey said.

'Well, go on then.'

Peadar Taigh watched Davey Shortt make his way towards the village. Then he had a little chuckle to himself at the wonder of it all. Fancy any man in his right senses getting his head caught in a snare and stuck down a hole. Jesus God, them rabbits must be laughing their long-eared little heads off.

It hadn't been quite like that, though. It took Davey Shortt just under a week to get his voice back, leaving all the men wondering what the hell had happened to him. He stayed away from Biddlecomb's during that time, too, which didn't help their anxiety. And when he finally felt he was up to it, and came to the store, the men gathered round him, inspecting his wound, and asking whatever had he been up to getting his head nearly garrotted off him like that? But Davey wasn't saying anything. He was subdued and downright surly, and it wasn't until later that evening when only himself and Patrick Farrel and Mr Biddlecomb were alone that he explained, his voice, still croaky, adding to the mystery of it all. And even then he had to be prodded and encouraged.

Mr Biddlecomb did this by filling Davey's glass each time it was emptied: not for free, mind. He carefully noted each drink down in a little pad beneath the counter that he kept for just that purpose, knowing Davey would make good the debt when it was called in and that would depend more or less on what sort of humour Mr Biddlecomb was in, and how his relationship with Davey was at any given time. But the drinks didn't help. Davey got more and more sullen, his head drooping over the counter, his free hand running along the scabby scar on his neck like someone playing with a chain.

When Patrick Farrel could stand it no longer he said, 'Davey, are you going to tell us what happened to you or not?'

Davey nodded a little but said nothing.

'Well, get a move on then. Tell us.'

Davey Shortt straightened his back and opened his mouth tentatively as if it were a cage door, a cage from which some ferocious creature would rush out and over which Davey would have no control once it sensed freedom. He shut his mouth again quickly, and Mr Biddlecomb looked skyward in despair. 'For the Lord's sake tell us, Davey,' he said. 'Get it off your chest. Do you no end of good, that will.'

And maybe hoping for no end of good, Davey Shortt asked, 'You want to know the honest-to-God truth?'

'No point in telling us a pack of lies.'

'Well, the honest-to-God truth is – I don't know what happened.'

'Ah, will you come off of it, Davey,' Mr Biddlecomb said, getting tired with all this prevarication. 'You've got to know what happened. You were there, weren't you? And it happened to you, didn't it? Well, then.'

Davey Shortt took to shaking his head mournfully. 'I don't. I just don't. I was setting my snare and the next thing

I know my own neck is in the noose and my head being shoved down that rabbit hole, and the pegs being hammered in, and me stuck in there and not able to get out without strangling myself.'

'Yeah, but who – '

'That's what I don't know.'

'You must have seen – '

'Saw no one. Not a living soul.'

'Didn't you *feel* anything? I mean, you must have felt yourself getting shoved into the hole?'

Davey Shortt nodded pensively. 'Oh, I felt something all right.'

'What was that?'

'Someone shoving me into the hole, of course,' Davey said, cutting the words short and tight. And then, as Mr Biddlecomb stared at him, and Patrick Farrel looked away in disgust, he added, 'Mind you, come to think of it, didn't *seem* like someone human.'

'Goblins, I suppose,' Patrick Farrel said facetiously.

'Uh-huh,' Davey said, taking the suggestion seriously. 'Way too strong for that.'

There was something about the faltering way that Davey Shortt spoke which made Patrick Farrel eye him with some suspicion. 'You telling us everything, Davey?'

''Course I am,' Davey protested. ''Course I am.'

'Don't think you are, you know. *I* think you're keeping something back.'

'Why would I do that?' Davey wanted to know.

'You tell us why,' Patrick Farrel said.

'Know what I think?' Mr Biddlecomb asked. 'I think Davey Shortt there has had the pants frightened off of him and doesn't want to tell us why in case we take to laughing at him. That it, Davey?'

Obviously that had something to do with it anyway. Suddenly Davey Shortt was crying; not loudly, not even moving. He just sat at the counter, his chin in his hands and let the tears stream uncontrollably down his cheeks.

This was something very new as far as Davey Shortt was concerned, and Mr Biddlecomb looked at him askance. Then he leaned forward and asked, 'You all right, Davey?' and when Davey gave no reply, Mr Biddlecomb asked Patrick Farrel, 'You think he's all right?'

''Course he's not all right. He's crying his bloody eyes out, isn't he?' Patrick Farrel put an arm about Davey's shoulders and gave him a bit of a shake. 'What's up, Davey?' he asked gently.

Davey Shortt wiped away most of the tears with a swipe of the back of his hand. He sniffed a couple of times and then cleaned the dribbles on the end of his nose on his cuff. 'It was him,' he said finally, clearing his throat and saying again, 'It was him. Johnsey. Only he told me to say nothing.'

Patrick Farrel whipped his arm off of Davey's shoulder as if he'd been burned. 'You better tell us everything,' he said. 'Every bloody thing from beginning to end.'

'Came at me from behind, he did. Never saw him coming. Never saw him when he was there either, or saw him going. Just heard his voice, that was all. Like the way God's supposed to speak to people, out of the sky, and loud, oh, very loud and sort of angry.'

Davey paused and looked like he might start crying again until Patrick Farrel said, 'Go on,' in a sharp voice.

'Well,' Davey went on, 'he held me there with that snare about my neck and said, Who killed little May O'Mahony and started shaking me like I was one of them rabbits.'

'What did you tell him?'

'I said I didn't know – 'cause we don't know that, do we? And then he said, but you had young Christy Codd killed for doing it and his mother, and I told him, yes, we had Christy Codd killed but I told him his mother wasn't meant to be killed.' Davey was getting into quite a state again, and Patrick Farrel signalled with a toss of his head for Mr Biddlecomb to fill his glass for him. 'Thanks, Mr Biddlecomb,' Davey said.

'Pat's paying,' Mr Biddlecomb told him.

'Thanks, Pat,' Davey said.

'Now, go on,' Patrick Farrel ordered as if further information was part of the deal.

'Well, then he said *we*, you said *we*, he said, and I had to say, yes and then he wanted to know what I meant by we, and I told him it was all of us, and he said it couldn't have been all of us, there must have been just a few of us that made the decision, and I had to tell him he was right that it was just some of us that decided, and – '

'Did he ask who?' Mr Biddlecomb asked, wiping a trickle of saliva from his lips with a flick of his tongue.

Davey shook his head. 'Didn't have to. He reeled off the names like he'd been with us himself at the time.'

'*Our* names?' Mr Biddlecomb asked, getting very hot under the collar.

Davey nodded. 'All of our names. Willie's and Connor's and the others. All our names. Said them like he was knowing every bloody thing about us.'

'Oh, Jesus,' Mr Biddlecomb gasped.

'And after that?' Patrick Farrel asked, keeping remarkably cool under the circumstances.

'After that?' Davey took a little while to think. And then, when he finally started to speak, the words tumbled out of his mouth like there was no halting them, falling over each other, a garbled jumble. 'Well, he said you didn't *know* that Christy had done it, did you, and I heard myself saying, no we didn't *know* Christy had done it, and then he started shoving my head down that bloody hole and asking me all the time who I thought *did* kill May O'Mahony and I just kept shouting at him that I didn't bloody know who killed May O'Mahony, that none of us knew who killed May O'Mahony and that if we did know we wouldn't have blamed Christy Codd for it and I was still yelling my head off at him when he started tightening that snare about my neck and said, well I know and I know too what you and those pals of yours are planning for me so you can think again about it 'cause I'll have each and every one of you before you can lay as much as a finger on me. God!' Davey concluded like he'd just had to recall the most frightening thing in his life, and swallowed his drink.

Mr Biddlecomb swallowed what was left of his drink too, and eyed Patrick Farrel, waiting for him to say something constructive. He had to wait quite a while. Patrick Farrel was playing with a key, a large iron key, spinning it round and round on the counter as if hypnotising himself. 'That all?' he asked finally in a quiet voice and without looking up.

Davey nodded. 'Well, only that he told me not to say anything about what he asked or he *would* have my head off next time.'

'Could have killed you this time, leaving you there like that,' Mr Biddlecomb said.

Patrick Farrel looked up. '*Could* have, but didn't,' he said quietly. 'And told you not to say anything knowing you'd be the very first to say something,' he added.

Davey Shortt looked a bit affronted but said nothing.

'Never asked you if you knew who killed Christy, did he?'

Davey Shortt thought about that for a little while. Then he shook his head. 'No,' he admitted.

'Means he knows who did that too,' Patrick Farrel concluded.

Mr Biddlecomb wasn't having any of that. 'Means no such thing,' he said in a scoffing sort of way. 'Means he didn't *ask* who killed Christy, that's all.'

'Didn't ask so he knows,' Patrick Farrel insisted.

'Feel that myself,' Davey Shortt agreed.

'Even so,' Mr Biddlecomb went on. 'What difference does that make? None of us three killed Christy, did we?'

'Maybe not,' Patrick said.

'What you mean, *maybe* not. I didn't, and that's for sure.'

'So you say,' Davey Shortt said.

Mr Biddlecomb began to get flustered. He let a bellow out of him like a bull getting ready to charge, and God knows what he'd have done if Patrick Farrel hadn't said, 'Makes no difference that *we* didn't do it, he knows we was in on it.'

'Only because that moron sitting beside you told him,' Mr Biddlecomb pointed out.

'You'd have bloody told him and all if it had been your neck all wired up and your thick head stuffed down – '

'Shut up, Davey,' Patrick Farrel said, and Davey Shortt shut up.

'Time you shut that store and came to bed,' Mrs Biddlecomb yelled from upstairs.

'Christ!' Mr Biddlecomb swore under his breath. 'Still busy,' he called back.

'Busy!' Mrs Biddlecomb snorted and slammed a door.

'So,' Patrick Farrel went on as if he was unaware of the interruption. 'So, he knows who killed Christy and he admits he knows who done little May O'Mahony – '

He paused for a second, giving Davey Shortt the chance to add, '*And* he knows we've been, you know – '

'The question is,' Patrick Farrel went on, ignoring Davey's remark, 'what's he going to do about it?'

That set Mr Biddlecomb rocking back on his heels. 'Nothing much he *can* do, is there?' he asked hopefully.

'Did fucking plenty to me,' Davey Shortt said ruefully.

Patrick Farrel picked up the key he'd been fiddling with and stared at it as if it might open a chest filled with knowledge. Then he sighed and put it in his pocket. There was something very final about the way he did it, though. 'He can destroy us,' he said. 'Tear the whole village wide apart.'

'Maybe he's just bluffing about knowing,' Mr Biddlecomb said but with little conviction, coming round the counter and standing behind Patrick with his thumbs in his braces. 'Trying to make us panic or something.'

'Made me panic, I can tell you,' Davey Shortt said.

Patrick Farrel was shaking his head. 'Not bluffing. He *knows* all right. That's what frightens me most – him being able to know and us not having a clue.'

Something thumped on the floor upstairs, and Mrs Biddlecomb's voice rattled into the store like a bouncing metal cartwheel. 'Shut that store and get your fat backside up here, Mr Biddlecomb,' she called.

'Better shut the place and go up,' Mr Biddlecomb said, glad to have the chance to end the talk which was getting to him.

Patrick Farrel and Davey Shortt got down off their stools and made for the door. Then Patrick turned. 'Got to do *something*,' he said. '*Got* to,' he added.

'We'll talk about it,' Mr Biddlecomb said.

'That's all we're doing. Talking. Got to *do* something before he ruins us all.'

'Oh, yes. Absolutely. I agree,' Mr Biddlecomb agreed, just as he could have agreed to anything at that moment if only the whole subject could be dropped. 'But couldn't we just sleep on it and talk about it again in the morrow?'

'I suppose,' Patrick Farrel said with a weary sigh. 'I suppose.'

Alone, Mr Biddlecomb locked up the store, and threw half a bucket of slack into the stove to keep it ticking over until morning. Outside, a little breeze swelled up and set the flue humming, and Mr Biddlecomb took up the tune and hummed it himself to comfort him as he went upstairs in the manner of a child whistling in the face of awful darkness. And it was a feeling of awful darkness that swamped Mr Biddlecomb's consciousness now. A terrible premonition, he might have thought of it, had he known that word, but a premonition of what he could not be certain. It was as though in his mind's eye he could see everything disintegrating about him, dwellings collapsing, people running and screaming, and him alone in not understanding what all the fuss was about. Isolation. That was it, he thought, isolation. There would be a terrible isolation for every single man, woman and child in the village if Johnsey was allowed –

'Are you going to stand out there all the night long?' Mrs Biddlecomb called in a drowsy way.

But Mr Biddlecomb didn't answer. He stood quite still on the landing for a while, and then, as if making up his mind about something, he went down to the store again. He stocked up the stove and got it flaming nicely. He pulled a chair up close to it and sat down. He stuffed his pipe, lit it, and sucked. And he stayed there all night.

Nineteen

The hope that the men could keep everything a secret unto themselves was a forlorn one indeed. Well, Davey Shortt could hardly go waltzing home half decapitated and expect his wife to believe any old cock-and-bull story. To be fair, Davey did try to waylay her questions, pretending, to begin with, that he had less voice in him than he had, and then, later, saying it was all such a haze in his mind that he couldn't be sure about anything. But she kept at him, did Molly Shortt, kept at him – tenacious as a terrier, and finally, more for a bit of peace than anything else, Davey told her all about it. But he made her swear she'd keep this absolutely to herself, and Molly Shortt swore absolutely that she would. And probably she intended to, at the time she promised so to do at any rate. But, as everyone knows, the lives of every man, woman and child are strewn with broken promises, and Molly told Kitty Mercer (maybe thinking that since Kitty was a sort of sacristan she'd keep the secret like it was confessional), and Kitty Mercer told Maeve Neill, and telling Maeve Neill was like sticking it up on a noticeboard for everyone to see.

Who told Mam, I don't know, but someone did and got her into a terrible state. She nearly bit my head off when I asked, 'Mam, you heard what they're saying about Johnsey now?'
    'Yes,' she said, her lips slapping shut like a mousetrap.

'You think it's all true?'

'Don't ask stupid questions, Aiden. How should I know if it's all true or not.'

'Just asking.'

'Well, don't.'

'Oh, sorry,' I said, trying to be sarcastic but not making a great fist of it.

'You're always sorry.'

'No, I'm not.'

'Always *saying* your sorry then.'

Mam was making apple jelly in the big copper cauldron on the range, and she busied herself skimming the scum off the top with a wooden spoon. When she'd done that she started putting jam jars into the oven to heat so they wouldn't explode when she poured the boiling hot jelly into them. Then she put a spoonful of the liquid onto a saucer and put it to one side to cool and see if it set, holding the saucer sideways so the jelly would spread out and not be one big glob in the middle.

'Smells nice,' I said, trying to make peace, but Mam ignored me, and took some lids from a drawer and held them to the light like she was making sure they were clean. 'Want any help?'

'No,' Mam said, and then added, 'Thank you,' and went to look at the saucer.

The jelly must have set all right since Mam moved the cauldron off the heat and started taking the jars from the oven, putting them on a tray. Then she got what she called her jam jug (the only piece left from a tea-set her mother had given her for her wedding – at least I think it was her mother but it could have been someone else) and began filling the jars. She filled them right to the top so that there wouldn't be much room for the air to get in and turn the jelly mouldy. Then she put little bits of greaseproof paper on the jelly, and screwed down the lids. My Dad really loved that apple jelly and put it on just about everything, even sometimes eating spoonfuls of it without anything else.

'Pity Dad's not here,' I said. I wasn't even looking at her when I said it, so when she dropped the jar with a crash on the stone floor I fairly jumped out of my skin. When I did look across Mam was standing there, clenching her fists, and shaking. 'I'll clean it up,' I said.

Then Mam turned on me. 'Leave it,' she said, quietly at first. And then kept on repeating it, 'Leave it. Leave it. Leave it!' her voice getting shriller and more like a scream as she kept on. Then, without warning, she caught hold of the tray and hurled all the jars of jelly across the kitchen like she'd gone mad or something. And it sounded like she'd gone mad when she shouted at me, 'Just you be glad you father isn't here,' she screamed, and slumped into her darning chair and started to cry.

I went over to her and put my arm about her shoulder, but she shrugged it off. 'Go away,' she said very firmly, so I went away, went outside, went to my dogs and put my arms about them instead. 'It's okay,' I told them, stroking them, seeing they were a bit cringy since dogs get frightened by strange noises just like people do, and they'd never heard Mam hurling jampots round the place before. 'Too dark for a walk,' I explained since I guessed that's what they were hoping for, and they must have understood me because their tails drooped and their big eyes filled with disappointment. 'Oh, all right then. But just a short one. Not staying out all night just to please the likes of you two scoundrels,' I told them, and they seemed pleased enough with that, leaping about my feet and giving those little squeaks they gave when they were really delighted about something. 'Come on then,' I said, and the three of us set off in the direction of the river.

The villagers had a word for it: fitful. And that was exactly what that night was like. It meant that the wind blew up and down with no sort of rhythm to it, and the rain spittled down in a haphazard way, and the moon was in and out of the clouds at a great rate, just letting you get your eyes accustomed to the light before blindfolding you in darkness again, and making you wonder where you were. That's what fitful meant. And the river was that way too, flowing calmly enough until it met an obstruction, a boulder, a fallen tree that no one had got round to chopping up for firewood yet, a crazy dam the children had tried to make from bits of corrugated iron. Then it got itself into an angry way of thinking, and snarled its way round the hindrances, furious it couldn't move them, and letting them know its feelings.

We got to the willow where little May O'Mahony had been found, and the dogs started to whimper a bit, not a frightened whimper, a puzzled one more likely. So, I wasn't too surprised to find Johnsey standing there. 'Thought it might be you,' I told him.

'How's that?'

'Dogs. Started whimpering a way back.'

'Oh. Could have been anyone,' Johnsey pointed out and I knew he was sort of laughing at me.

'Uh-huh. They'd have growled at anyone else.'

'Oh,' Johnsey said again. And then, 'And what are you doing out?'

'Just out,' I said. 'Mam's upset about something so I thought I'd get out of her way.'

'Ah,' said Johnsey, as if he understood. 'Know what she's upset about?'

'Wish I did. Been funny for ages now,' I told him. 'Think it's got something to do with my Dad dying. Can't mention him at all but she gets all upset and starts acting strange.'

'Ah,' Johnsey said again.

We walked along the bank together, and Johnsey put his hand on my shoulder. He placed it there gently, and I liked the feel of it. It was as if I could feel something flowing from him into me, something good, something I required. It was something I'd always wanted my Dad to do, just touch me, but he nearly never did. Only when he was playing and fooling around, but not in the comforting way Johnsey was doing now.

'Got everyone really steamed up, you have,' I told him.

'I know.'

'You wanted to, didn't you?'

'Yes.'

'Better be careful then,' I warned.

'I'll be careful.'

'*Really* careful.'

'I'll be really careful. Anyway, I'm more worried about you than about me.'

'Why so? What's there to worry about me?'

Johnsey stopped walking and faced me, putting both his hands on my shoulders now. I could see his face quite clearly: the reflection of the moon in the river and it sending the light bouncing back made it easy to see Johnsey's face. And his eyes mostly. Grey eyes once, but reddened about the edges. And very sad, so sad they looked as if maybe they'd never smiled at all.

'Aiden,' Johnsey said and his voice matched the sorrow in his eyes. 'Aiden, there's something I have to tell you. I've got to warn you. There's a terrible pain waiting for you, something that will hurt you more than anything's ever hurt you in your young life, a pain I hope you'll never have to feel again.'

And although I had no idea what he was on about, I knew he was telling the truth. 'How do you know about this if I don't?' was all I could think of to ask.

'Because, in a way, I'll be the cause of it.'

'Well, why do it then?'

Johnsey gave a huge sigh. 'Because it has to be done.'

'You mean I'm going to be really sick?'

'Oh, no. No. Worse than that,' Johnsey told me in a far-off kind of voice.

'Can't be much worse than that,' I said.

'It can. It can. And it will, Aiden.'

'Can't you tell me what it is then?'

'Not yet.'

'A hint even?'

Johnsey smiled kindly. 'Not even a hint even.'

One of the dogs came close to me and licked my hand. 'Will I get over it?' I asked.

'The pain? Oh, yes.'

'Well, that's all right then,' I said and walked on a bit by myself. 'When – ' I began and turned round. But Johnsey had gone. No sign of him anywhere although there wasn't anywhere that I could see for him to hide. 'Must be going off my head,' I told the dogs. 'Going off my head, I am,' I said to them, and then we all raced back down the riverbank like we hadn't a care in the world, and hadn't met Johnsey at all either.

Patrick Farrel had no doubts whatever about seeing Johnsey, and the sight of his misshapen face looming out at him from the dark made him quake. Mind you, Patrick was at a disadvantage having only his longjohns on, and a pair of boots, and the woolly bedjacket his wife liked to use slung about his shoulders, but it was his own fault. Mrs Farrel had warned him to get himself properly wrapped up if he insisted on going outside at that time of night, but he had ignored her. 'Be all right,' he said. 'Won't be more than a minute.'

'Can't see why you have to go out anyway,' Mrs Farrel grumbled.

'Something not right out there. Cattle shouldn't be bawling at this hour. Be back in a minute. Probably nothing.'

'Well, if it's probably nothing, what are you going out for?' Mrs Farrel asked logically.

But Patrick went out anyway. He hadn't bothered to lace his boots, and one of them stayed behind when he made a step. His bare foot landed on a sharp little stone, and Patrick swore, but he learned his lesson and bent down, and tied both boots neatly. It was when he straightened up that he saw Johnsey, and he felt the blood freeze in his veins, as he put it later. 'Blood just froze in my veins,' he said.

'Not surprised,' Mr Biddlecomb sympathised. 'What did he want?'

'Would you believe it – nothing?'

'Nothing?' Mr Biddlecomb found it difficult to believe.

'Nothing 'cept to put the frighteners on you,' Davey Shortt said.

'Bloody succeeded too,' Patrick Farrel admitted.

'Yeah, but what did he *say*?' Mr Biddlecomb wanted to know.

'I told you – nothing,' Patrick Farrel repeated. 'He just stood there for a while with his eyes fixed on me, burning into me, you might say, and his head nodding a bit like he was telling me he knew everything there was to know about me, and then –' Patrick Farrel stopped abruptly, and looked suddenly puzzled.

'And then?' Mr Biddlecomb prodded.

'Then – then he just wasn't there. Gone like he'd melted away.'

'That's what I tried telling her the other week,' Mr Biddlecomb said, gesturing towards the kitchen with a nod. 'She wouldn't have it, of course.'

'So, what's he bloody well up to then?' Connor Neill, the only one who had not yet been approached in some way by Johnsey, wanted to know.

'You keep asking that, Connor,' Davey Shortt said.

'Yeah, 'cause no one answers me.'

''Cause we don't *know*,' Davey said.

'Well, why don't we ask him then?' Connor asked.

Davey Shortt gave a blustering, mocking snort, but Mr Biddlecomb and Patrick Farrel looked at each other, and then at Connor, both of them beaming as if the Holy Ghost Himself had come down in a flash and enlightened them. 'God, Connor, you may be a bit of an eejit at times but you might just have hit on something this time,' Mr Biddlecomb told him.

'Can't think why we never thought to do it before,' Patrick Farrel said.

Connor Neill had a grin the size of a rowboat across his face. 'Just thought it might work,' he said modestly, all the praise getting to him and making him suddenly self-conscious.

Davey Shortt was none too pleased, though, not at Connor being thought of as the wise one. 'Fat lot of good it'll do – talking to him,' he snorted. 'Bet what you like he won't give any of us the *chance* to talk to him.'

'We haven't asked him yet, have we?' Connor said.

'There's your answer, Davey,' Mr Biddlecomb said, pleased that Connor had put Davey Shortt in his place for once since it was usually the other way round.

'And who's going to ask him?' Davey now asked by way of retaliation. 'I'm not and that's for certain. Had enough of talking to that fella, I have. Christ knows what bit of me he'll try and take off this time if I go near him.'

'I'll ask him,' Connor volunteered, things going to his head. 'I don't mind asking him.'

'Good man, Connor,' Mr Biddlecomb said, delighted it wasn't himself who would have to approach Johnsey.

'Yeah. Good man, Connor,' Patrick Farrel agreed. 'What is it you're drinking then?' he went on, pointedly ignoring

Davey Shortt and enjoying the sulky look he put on his face.

But as it turned out Connor didn't have to ask Johnsey, not to meet and speak with them anyway. It was as if, once again, Johnsey knew what they'd been talking about and two evenings later when the four of them and Willie Little were in the store the door opened and in he walked – although later Mr Biddlecomb was to say the door never opened at all but that Johnsey just materialised out of the thin air, but this was utter nonsense; he also said that although Johnsey didn't speak at first he, Mr Biddlecomb, heard the words 'You wanted to speak to me' as clearly as if Johnsey had surely uttered them. Anyway, he certainly *thought* he heard them, and said, 'Eh, yes. We do. Emmm. A drink maybe?' he offered by way of a sop.

Johnsey shook his head, and edged away from the stove as if, still, proximity to any heat was painful. He moved to the end of the bar, away from the men, and leaned an elbow on it, cupping his chin in the palm of one hand.

Rebuffed, and unaccustomed to so being, Mr Biddlecomb looked totally lost, and stared in a baffled beseeching way at the others for some assistance. All he got was a small goading from Davey Shortt who rocked his torso back and forth as though heaving Mr Biddlecomb into a renewed attempt. All Mr Biddlecomb could manage now, though, was a silent opening of his mouth, and then a shutting of it, and a nervous pursing of his lips. And Patrick Farrel wasn't about to be of any help: the best he could do was simply to stare down the bar to Johnsey as if mesmerised.

'Well?' Johnsey suddenly demanded in a loud voice, making them jump.

It was as if the men were children again, wilting under the fiercesome gaze of Mr Ward who had been the teacher when they were all at school together, lowering their guilty heads to their desks as he demanded who was responsible for some harmless enough prank, waiting for one reluctant and shaking hand to be raised. And it was Willie Little, a bit on the sneaky side as, indeed, he had been in his schooldays, who finally landed them in it. 'They want to know,' he began before pausing to rephrase his statement, and say, '*They* want to know what it is you're up to,' he told Johnsey, carefully excluding himself from the desire for any such knowledge.

'Ah,' Johnsey said.

Emboldened, Mr Biddlecomb said, 'That's right. That's what we want to know.'

It looked, for a moment, as if Johnsey was going to ignore the question, as if, almost, he hadn't heard Mr Biddlecomb at all. He walked slowly to the window of the store and stared out into the gloom, and Mr Biddlecomb had, for some inexplicable reason, the uneasy feeling that Johnsey was a man more at ease in the darkness than in the light although, oddly, there didn't seem to be anything particularly sinister in that: just as many creatures, shy and timid, live their gentle lives under the shelter of night's protection, so Johnsey had that same haunted furtiveness about him. Or so it struck Mr Biddlecomb now. He didn't have much time to think about this, though, since barely had the thought entered his mind than it was jettisoned as Johnsey said, 'The truth. That's all I want. The truth,' without turning round, and making it appear he was talking to his own reflection in the window.

'Sure, God, isn't that what we all spend our lives looking for,' Willie Little said philosophically.

Johnsey turned and gave Willie a hard look. Then he shook his head. 'Some of us spend our lives trying to hide it,' he said.

Mr Biddlecomb didn't like the way things were going. He didn't like the obtuse. 'And the truth about what are you looking for?' he asked.

'Or hiding *from* it,' Johnsey added, as if Mr Biddlecomb hadn't spoken.

Davey Shortt, also, was getting unsettled. He ran his finger along the scar that crossed his throat. 'You seem to have all the answers already,' he said. 'Told me you knew everything anyway.'

Johnsey looked suddenly very sad, but he nodded anyway. 'Sometimes,' he said in a faraway voice, 'sometimes it's so awful, so *painful* –' he said and then stopped, turning back to the window. 'So often the innocent are made to suffer for the truth.'

Mr Biddlecomb gave a short cough as though clearing his throat would help clear his now befuddled mind. 'Look,' he said, trying to sound practical and bringing the conversation back to a level he could understand. 'All we're asking is why you keep sneaking up on us and trying to give us the jitters. We've done you no harm.'

Whatever reaction Mr Biddlecomb expected it certainly wasn't the one he got. Johnsey turned from the window again, only now there was a terrible fury in his eyes. 'You've done me no harm?' he asked in a voice so quiet Patrick Farrel didn't catch his words.

'What was that?' he asked.

'You've done me no harm?' Johnsey roared, and suddenly he was stripping himself to the waist, throwing the clothes from him in a frightening frenzy. 'Done me no harm?' he asked again and again, and then he was standing there in the middle of the store and the full horror of his burning plain for all the men to see. And it certainly was horrible. His flesh still had the aspect of rawness to it, red and tender. It hadn't moulded itself back to smoothness. It was in tatters, slivers of it hanging from his torso like grotesque baubles, pendants of living, misshapen tissue.

Davey Shortt and Patrick Farrel looked as if they were going to be sick, and Mr Biddlecomb made a gurgling sound, almost choking himself. And although clearly shaken, Connor Neill was the only one of them who could summon up words. 'We never done that to you,' he said. 'Tried to help you, we did, after the fire, but you wouldn't have any of it.'

Davey Shortt squirmed on his stool. He could feel, he thought, Johnsey's eyes boring into his mind, and he imagined, too, he could hear Johnsey's voice ordering him to 'Tell them. Tell them, tell them,' and he just about frightened the life out of Mr Biddlecomb when he screamed, 'All right, all right! I did set fire to that house of yours but you weren't supposed to be in it. Didn't mean *you* to get burned like that. Just wanted to frighten you the way you've been frightening us.'

There wasn't a sound in the store. Not a movement. Even the wind sucking the smoke from the stove up the flue ceased, and later Mr Biddlecomb was to swear the clock stopped its ticking as well. It was that impenetrable, malefic silence of men waiting for retribution. But revenge was not what Johnsey wanted, it seemed. Not for the moment anyway. Slowly, carefully, he started to dress himself again, and when he was fully clothed, in a tone that was almost friendly, he said, 'I'll have that drink now.'

Instantly Mr Biddlecomb leapt into action. He took a glass from the shelf behind him and gave it a right good polish with his cloth. He took a bottle of whiskey from the shelf too, opened it, and placed it on the counter beside the glass, watching as Johnsey poured himself a drink, watching as he swallowed it, watching as he refilled his glass.

'I didn't mean you –' Davey Shortt said suddenly in a sort of wail.

Patrick Farrel nudged him. 'Shut up, Davey,' he said.

Johnsey gave a wry smile.

Mr Biddlecomb hovered.

Connor Neil waited for Johnsey to have a sip of his drink and then supped his own.

Willie Little rubbed his stubbly chin on his stump of an arm.

And just when they thought the worst was over, Johnsey put his glass carefully on the counter, and said, 'Tell me about Christy. Christy Codd.'

'I never done that,' Davey Shortt howled, and suddenly took to weeping uncontrollably.

'And I didn't,' Willie Little was quick to say.

'None of us did,' Patrick Farrel said.

'Gardai said it was an accid . . .' Mr Biddlecomb started to protest but let his words peter out under the gaze that Johnsey threw at him.

'You all did it,' Johnsey told them. 'All of you,' he repeated. 'You killed an innocent,' he went on after a pause. 'And his mother.' Again he paused. 'And now the innocent continue to suffer,' he concluded with a huge sigh.

'You don't understand,' Mr Biddlecomb pleaded.

Johnsey gave him a tired smile. 'No,' he admitted.

'Had to put things to rest,' Patrick Farrel explained, but in a tone that signalled he was aware his excuse was lame.

'See, couldn't have everyone being torn apart wondering who had done for little May,' Connor Neill tried.

'So, you chose poor Christy.'

It was as if for the first time the men realised the full horror of their atrocity. They rounded their shoulders and dropped their heads, and Mr Biddlecomb felt the blood drain from his cheeks and turned his back to conceal it. Yet, foolishly, Davey Shortt, perhaps because of the terror that was in him, said, 'It *had* to be Christy who did it. It *had* to be,' he repeated as though any alternative was too appalling to consider.

Johnsey wrapped a great fist round the bottle of whiskey and looked as though he might hurl it across the store.

'Shut *up*, will you, Davey?' Patrick Farrel said through his teeth.

Johnsey put the bottle back on the counter, and stood up. 'It wasn't Christy,' he said coldly. All the men stared at him, their mouths open, small nerves twitching on their jaws. Johnsey turned on his heel and made for the door.

'Who was it?' Mr Biddlecomb and Patrick Farrel asked almost in unison. Johnsey kept heading for the door.

'For God's sake tell us who it was,' Mr Biddlecomb shouted, his voice high as a woman's. Johnsey opened the door.

And suddenly Davey Shortt was on his feet, trembling from head to foot like a man possessed. 'Who the hell *are* you?' he screamed, running to Johnsey and grabbing him by the coat, shaking him.

Very carefully Johnsey took Davey Shortt by the wrists and eased his hands from his coat. He straightened his arms and held Davey away from him. He let go, and watched as Davey's knees buckled and he fell in a heap on the floor. Then he left the store, leaving the wind to shut the door behind him.

Twenty

'You know,' Johnsey said, and I nodded through my misery.

On that Thursday Olly Carver sent down word that, as far as he could judge, winter would start in earnest on Saturday, and that we had all better prepare ourselves for the severest winter anyone had experienced and that included everyone, even Florry Corbison who was well over ninety. And if Thursday was anything to go by he clearly had a point: the sudden bitter coldness of it caught everyone by surprise, a dry and windless cold that froze the breath in your lungs if you chanced to swallow it, and left the cattle stiff-limbed and silent as though stricken with the rheum, and needing quite some prodding and goading to get them to shift and into the sheltering warmth of the barns, and even in there taking hours to thaw themselves out.

'Jesus!' I said, coming in from checking the sheep and putting my backside as close as I dared to the range, and saying, 'Sorry,' when Mam gave me her vexed look, the one she always gave me when I swore since she didn't like to hear me taking God's name in vain.

'If that's you in for a while, take your coat off and hang it up,' she said. 'No point keeping it on in the house and not having the benefit of it when you go outside again.'

Obediently I took my coat off and hung it up. It was a

grand coat, padded thickly and with a hood on it trimmed with fur. My Auntie Maeve in Gooseneck had sent it one Christmas, with a card saying, 'For the finest young man that ever was born', and it really annoyed me I hadn't been able to wear it for a while since it was far too big for me. But I kept it upstairs in my room and, quite often, I'd try it on, just to see how I was coming along, and a few times I fell asleep wearing it. Later, in a letter to Mam, Auntie Maeve had explained it was the sort of coat men wore when they 'made their little trips to the Arctic', and none of us ever disputed that. And the day my Dad had said, 'See you've grown into that coat of yours at last,' was the proudest day I could remember. And although I know it was stupid I even resolved to have myself buried in that coat.

'Shift,' Mam said, and I stood aside to let her check whatever it was she had in the oven.

And then, without warning, we were having that terrible row. As Mam stood up from the oven she winced, holding her side and sucking in her breath, and I stretched out my arms to try and help her. 'Don't – touch – me,' Mam said, the pain making her space the words and making them sound very cruel too.

'Just trying to help,' I told her.

'I don't *need* your help,' Mam snapped, sort of hobbling over to a chair and sitting herself down gingerly.

'Should see the doctor,' I tried.

'I don't *need* a doctor,' Mam said.

'You need *something*,' I told her, hurt and angry.

'All I need is to be left alone,' Mam told me.

'All right then. If that's what you want,' I said, almost shouting it, and took my coat off the hook.

And that was when Mam went really strange. 'Oh, that's it. That's it,' she said. 'Walk out on me. Just like your father did. Go on, then.'

'Dad didn't walk out on you, Mam.'

'Oh, didn't he? Didn't he, indeed. And what do you think he did then?' Mam was getting hysterical, her voice rising to a small scream.

I didn't know what to say. I opted for, 'Mam, Dad was drowned. You know that. He didn't leave you 'cause he wanted to.'

'Drowned,' Mam said, spitting the word. 'Oh, he drowned all right. Drowned in his own guilt,' Mam said, thumping the arm of the chair with her small clenched fist. 'High time you knew about that wonderful father of yours,' she added, swivelling towards me, her eyes blazing.

I didn't know what had got into her, and I didn't want to hear any more of this either. 'I'm going,' I said, and made for the door.

It was at that moment that Mam went completely berserk. Leaping to her feet she started to screech at me, the words hurtling from her like they couldn't wait to get out, like they were poison she had to spit out or die. 'So he didn't walk out on me, did he? So he just drowned, did he? So he was just washed overboard, was he? Well, let me tell you this, my lad, he walked out on me all right and he drowned because he wanted to be drowned. Taking the easy way out and leaving me to suffer the pain and the loneliness and the horror of it all. Oh, yes, that's what he did, so you needn't look at me like that. Killed *himself*, he did –'

'He didn't,' I yelled at her.

'Oh yes he did. And you want to know why? Want to know why that great father of yours killed himself?'

I clapped my hands over my ears and screamed, 'You're lying, you're lying!' I wanted to run from the room, but I honestly couldn't move. It was as if Mam had trapped me in her awful gaze, transfixing me, forcing me to heed her words, words filled with utter desperation as if, in some strange way, she had to say them to survive.

For a moment she was silent. She was standing there, weeping, hugging herself, watching me, her eyes, now, almost expressionless. I was crying too, and roughly I wiped the tears from my cheeks with my fist, and that seemed to set Mam off again. 'Oh, you can wipe your tears away, boy. I've done that this last many months. But the pain stays, I can tell you,' she told me. 'Nothing kills the pain,' she added as though making this sad observation to herself. 'Nothing whatever kills the pain.' She turned away for a second, and when she looked at me again it was as though she was staring at a stranger, as if she hadn't a clue who I was. And she was telling herself in a whisper, 'Drowning himself in the cold unfriendly water,' and shuddering, 'his lovely face all blue and his body battered on those rocks.' She took a strand of hair in her fingers and began twisting it. 'The sin of it all,' she said, and started rocking on her heels. 'The sin of it,' she said again, her voice rising to take on the semblance of the keening the women used at gravesides.

'Mam – ' I said, not knowing what else I was going to say.

But Mam didn't hear me. I don't know who she thought she was talking to, but it wasn't me. 'Glory, glory, glory,' she said, and then looked puzzled as though trying to recall where she'd heard those words before. And maybe she remembered it was my Dad who'd said them to her. She walked over to the chair my Dad had always sat in, and settled herself on the arm like I'd seen her do many a time, and started stroking the air in the way she used to stroke Dad's hair when he came home, tired and wet, from the sea. She was humming to herself now, too, soothing away the troubles from whoever occupied her mind. Then, with one finger, she traced the outline of someone's face. I knew it was Dad's. It was a little gesture she'd often used on him, and when she got to the bottom of his nose Dad would pretend to snap her finger off with a bite, and then she'd throw her arms around his neck and whisper into his ear, making Dad laugh.

And Mam started to whisper now. 'You shouldn't have left me all alone,' she said, and I felt a terrible hurt at those words. 'There was no need,' she went on. 'I wouldn't have told. I'd still have loved you like I always loved you from the first day I set eyes on you.' She had Dad's head in her arms now, cradling it to her breast. 'They made you do it,' she whispered. 'I know they did. You'd never have killed Christy and his mother if they hadn't made you.'

I couldn't control the great gulping sobs that ran out of me. I heard what Mam said, but they didn't make sense, maybe because I didn't want them to. I thought Mam was just – I didn't really know what had happened to Mam. 'Mam,' I called softly.

'Shush, Aiden,' Mam answered kindly. 'Your Daddy and me are talking.'

'Mam,' I called again.

But Mam wasn't listening. She was talking to Dad again, telling him not to worry, and then, without looking up, saying, 'We won't tell anyone, will we, Aiden?'

'No, Mam.'

'There you are,' Mam said. 'Only the three of us will ever know about poor Christy and his mother.'

Through my tears I heard myself say, 'Mam, Dad never killed Christy. He'd never do something like that,' I told her, I think trying to convince myself as much as Mam of Dad's innocence.

And if Mam had screamed at me then, if one of those spasms of anger and fury that had got into her so often since Dad was found dead had taken hold of her again, if she had rushed at me and thumped me and told me not to dare contradict her, it would, I believe, have made things easier to bear. But nothing like that happened. Very coolly and quietly, as if all her wits had returned and all the sadness left her, she nodded, and said, 'Yes, he did, Aiden. He told me all about it himself, didn't you, my darling?' she asked of the invisible head she nursed. 'Told Mammy all about it, and had me wipe the bloodstains from him too.' She studied her hands for a moment, and then, in the same quiet voice, she said to me, 'Run along now, Aiden. There's a good boy. Don't want you being late for school, do we?'

'Mam –'

'Shush, Aiden. You'll wake your Daddy.'

'You know,' Johnsey said, and I nodded through my misery.

I left Mam alone with my Dad, as she believed, and crept blindly out of the house and into the bright, brittle night, pulling my coat tightly about me to fend off the biting cold, and pulling the hood over my head too.

The dogs raced round the corner of the house, eager to go with me, giving their little yelps of delight; and in the field to my left the sheep, lying still as stone to conserve the warmth that was in them, all close together, making an eerie woollen hillock, raised their heads at the noise, wondering, probably, if they were about to be rounded up and puzzled by the timing. 'No!' I told the dogs. 'Go back!' And the two of them slumped to their bellies and crawled away from me, back to the shed where they slept. I knew they felt hurt, and I wanted them to be hurt. I wanted everyone and everything to be hurt, just as much as I was hurting anyway.

I leaned on the wall and stared at the sheep – passive and calm again now, their heads lowered, their eyes tight closed against the frost. Then Johnsey was beside me, leaning on the wall just like myself. I wasn't surprised. I hadn't heard him coming. He was just there. For a while we didn't speak, and then Johnsey said, 'You know,' and I nodded through my misery.

'I'm so sorry, Aiden.'

'You knew all along,' I told him. Johnsey made no reply. 'That's what you meant about the pain I'd have,' I said.

Johnsey nodded.

'Who else knows?' I asked.

'No one,' Johnsey told me. 'Hannah knows but she doesn't know she knows. Only your Mam and me and you, only us three know.'

'S'pose you'll have to tell – '

'Oh, no,' Johnsey interrupted. 'Oh, no.'

The dogs, perhaps thinking they'd done something wrong, had sneaked up to me, and one of them nuzzled my hand with its cold, cold nose. I stroked its muzzle, and that made me think of Mam stroking Dad's hair. 'You were wrong about the pain,' I told Johnsey. 'Don't feel any pain at all,' I lied.

Johnsey turned his head and looked down at me with a long, steady, disbelieving look.

The light in Mam's bedroom was switched on. We could see Mam in the window. She was standing, moving about a bit, like she was dancing close to someone. Then she disappeared.

'I hate him,' I told Johnsey. 'Serve him right to be in hell,' I added since that was the most awful punishment I could think of.

AUTUMN

And then Johnsey had me in his arms, rocking me. 'Aiden, Aiden, Aiden,' he was saying over and over. Nothing else. Just repeating my name as if it was some sort of prayer. And then I was crying again, and Johnsey was patting me, saying, 'That's right, that's right.'

I don't know for how long we stayed like that but it was quite a while. 'Better?' Johnsey asked, and held me away from him a little to look at my face.

I nodded, and used my coat sleeve to wipe up the tears.

Johnsey smiled and nodded. 'Good.'

'Better get inside,' I told him. 'Mam's –' I didn't know how to explain Mam's carry-on.

'You'll have to look after her.'

'Yes.'

'Aiden,' Johnsey said as I turned to go. 'Your Dad did love you, you know.'

'I suppose.'

'Things happen in life – things we can't do anything about,' Johnsey told me as if he knew about such things.

'I suppose,' I said again, and then something struck me. 'Johnsey, Dad didn't do that to May O'Mahony, did he?'

'Oh no, Aiden.'

'You sure?'

'I'm sure.'

'You know who did do it?'

'Yes, Aiden.'

'Who?'

But, 'Go tend your Mam,' Johnsey said, and walked away from me.

I watched him make his way down the lane, and for some reason something told me I'd never talk to him again. And when I went into the house and closed the door it was as if I was shutting Johnsey out of my life for ever.

Twenty-one

'God,' observed Willie Little. 'That Olly Carver's nothing short of a bloody genius. How he does it, I'd love to know. Bang on the nail every year.'

'Make himself a fortune if he could bottle it,' Mr Biddlecomb remarked absurdly.

'Wife says it's something to do with this feeling he gets in his bones,' Patrick Farrel told them.

'Whatever it's got to do with it's nothing but a miracle the way he can tell the whims of the weather even before God Himself knows,' Willie Little stated.

'Wonder if maybe it's God Himself that tells him,' Connor Neill wondered.

It certainly seemed as if the Almighy had whispered a quiet word to Olly Carver since his forecast couldn't have been any more precise: on Saturday winter descended on the village with a vengeance. From early dawn the snow fell, slowly at first and looking very pretty, but by late afternoon it was a blizzard, whipped up and blinding by the freezing gale coming in from the sea. 'Never known anything like *this*,' Mr Biddlecomb said.

'Last year was just as bad,' Billy Maken said solemnly.

'Not as bad as *this*,' Mr Biddlecomb insisted.

'Just as bad,' Billy Maken, who didn't like Mr Biddlecomb anyway, said again, and they'd probably have gone on contradicting each other until Christmas if Patrick Farrel hadn't put a stop to it.

'Doesn't matter if it was as bad or not. This one's bad enough and it's this one we've got to put up with.'

'Won't last,' Billy Maken now said.

'What makes you say that?' Connor Neill asked.

Billy Maken shrugged. 'Be gone in a day or two.'

'Oh,' said Mr Biddlecomb. 'Fancy yourself as knowing, do you?'

'Be like them Eskimos in their igloos if it don't,' Willie Little said with a grin.

'It'll go in a day or two,' Billy Maken insisted. 'Be all cleared up by Monday.'

'Huh,' Mr Biddlecomb grunted.

'Want to bet?' Billy Maken asked.

Mr Biddlecomb went very quiet all of a sudden. He'd been caught out so often in bets that he was reluctant to have one no matter how certain he was that he was in the right. 'I don't bet,' he told Billy.

'Since when?' Willie Little asked, glad to have a dig at Mr Biddlecomb.

'Since now,' Mr Biddlecomb said.

By evening it looked as if Mr Biddlecomb was right, since the weather showed no signs of improving, getting even worse if anything. Old trees cracked and snapped and tumbled to the ground under the unexpected weight of the snow. Sheep were hurriedly sought out and brought into pens before they suffocated. Women gave their thanks to God for having the foresight to stock up well, although what that had to do with God only they seemed to know. And Father Cunningham, in the village for confessions, got trapped, his old Standard motorcar skittering this way and that as the men pushed, its wheels spinning like crazy.

'Same thing happened last year, if you remember,' Billy Maken pointed out knowingly and with a cunning leer at Mr Biddlecomb who wasn't helping much with the pushing, just standing to one side and encouraging the other men with shouts of 'Right now, heave!'

'Never make it Father,' Patrick Farrel said.

'Kill yourself on them roads if you try,' Willie Little told the priest.

'Oh, dear,' Father Cunningham said, and then brightened. 'Ah, well. I can look forward to some of Kitty's fine fare, can't I?' he asked with a wide smile.

'Getting to be a regular thing this, Father,' Billy Maken said. 'You're getting stuck and having to stay with Kitty.'

'Hardly regular, Billy,' Father Cunningham corrected. 'Only once before, as I recall. Last year, wasn't it? Yes. Last year.'

'Two times makes it pretty regular in my book,' Billy said.

Father Cunningham gave Billy a small smile. 'In that case, Billy, yes, it's becoming a regular thing.'

Kitty Mercer, of course, was thrilled to have the priest to stay. Next best thing to Jesus Himself appearing in her cottage. It gave her a chance to do all the things she liked to do: cook, and bake, and take the lace-trimmed tablecloth from the chest, and the crocheted place-mats, and the napkins she'd embroidered herself, putting primroses and forget-me-nots in each corner. And the good china came out of the cupboard for an airing, and the fire was lit in the little parlour, and Father Cunningham was given the big bed with the feather eiderdown and the crisp linen sheets nicely heated with hot-water bottles. Last year, after Father Cunningham had stayed, Kitty Mercer had gone about the village with her nose in the air, like she was sniffing the odour of sanctity from under her armpits, Mrs Biddlecomb said, so everyone wondered what effect the priest's staying again would have on her this time.

'Oh, there'll be no stopping her,' Mrs Farrel said cattily since she would really have liked Father Cunningham to stay with her only her husband wouldn't hear of it.

'Be saying Mass for us in the end,' Mrs Biddlecomb stated.

'She thinks she's doing that already,' Mrs Farrel pointed out. 'Hopping about the altar like she owned it.'

'Not when Father's here,' Mrs Finch said, a bit shocked at the thought of Kitty Mercer saying Mass.

'No,' agreed Mrs Farrel. 'It's when he's *not* there I'm talking about. Never seen her prancing about when she's doing those flowers of hers?'

'Oh that,' said Mrs Finch.

'Yes, *that*,' said Mrs Farrel, as if *that* was quite bad enough.

'She does them so nicely,' Mrs Neill said, always one for keeping the peace.

'She has a talent,' Mrs Farrel allowed. 'Doesn't give the right to go getting on her high horse about it, though, does it? Thank you, Flora. Yes, I will take another cup of that pleasant tea,' she added to Flora Behan. 'You make a very good cup of tea, Flora,' she commented, almost as if this was a snub to Kitty Mercer's acclaimed cooking.

So, the women huddled in Flora Behan's kitchen and tore strips off the absent Kitty Mercer, and the men collected in Biddlecomb's store and had some pretty crude suggestions as to what might be going on of a night between Kitty Mercer and the priest. However, no hint of this was apparent when, later, almost everyone trooped to the church for confession, all of them looking as if butter wouldn't melt in their mouth, and you'd have been forgiven for wondering what they were doing going to confession at all, so innocent did they appear. But it was winter now, officially, wasn't it, and everyone knew what that could mean, so go they all did, the women bringing hot-water bottles (or bottles of hot water) with them, wrapped in cloth, cuddling them on their knees to keep their joints from stiffening in the cold of the church, and the men snuggled up close together inside the door, like the cattle most of them tended, none of them loitering outside in the wind, that was for sure, and a few of them daring to move up the church to get within warming distance of the paraffin-heater Kitty Mercer had strategically placed near the communion rail. And after every dozen or so penitents had been dealt with Father Cunningham would emerge from his curtained-off cubicle and go to the heater too, doing a slow pirouette, as though cooking himself carefully on all sides.

It was just after Father Cunningham had taken one of those warming sessions and returned to his cubicle that Johnsey and Hannah O'Mahony arrived. Kitty Mercer, ever vigilant, was the first to spot them from her vantage-point in the sanctuary where she'd been setting out the hand-embroidered hassock that Father Cunningham liked to kneel on when he had his little heart-to-heart chat with Jesus when confessions were over, and him usually exhausted with all that forgiving he had to do. Both of them probably, but Kitty's main concern was Father Cunningham. Now, as Johnsey and Hannah walked up the aisle, Kitty was through the little gilded gate that kept the congregation at bay like a flash, ready, it seemed, to defend her priest at the slightest sign of aggression. But since everyone was agog, wondering if there was going to be another incident, they shuffled their backsides along the pews, making room for Johnsey and Hannah to sit close to the confessional, and they were both seated before Kitty reached them. She gave a little snort through her nostrils, and doused them in a warning glare. But neither seemed to notice. Hannah was busy with her rosary, flicking the beads through her fingers at a great rate, and Johnsey was immobile, his head bowed, his eyes closed, and some of the men in the porch gave a bit of a giggle as Kitty retreated, but giving quick little glances back over her shoulder just to be on the safe side.

When Mrs Farrel came out of the confessional, looking as pious as a saint, and a bit smug too as if she'd given God a piece of her mind, nobody moved to take her place inside. Father Cunningham coughed. Still no one moved. 'Next,' called Father Cunningham. Mrs Brennan, Cahal's wife, leaned forward and touched Hannah on the shoulder making her jump. 'You're next, Hannah,' Mrs Brennan said in a devout whisper.

Hannah O'Mahony seemed to spend an inordinately long time at confession. But maybe people imagined that. Maybe it just *felt* like a very long time since they were all waiting for something extraordinary to happen, although why they should have expected poor Hannah to be at the root of any such happening was a bit of a mystery. When she did, finally, emerge, there was a curious sigh from the congregation, a sort of soughing as if some anticipated catastrophe had been averted, but there was a hint of disappointment in the sighing too, and then all eyes swivelled to fix their gaze on Johnsey. But, again, frustration was their lot. As soon as Hannah came out of the confessional Johnsey stood up. They had a little whisper together, and then they both left the church, Johnsey holding Hannah gently by the arm.

They'd only just left the church when Father Cunningham came out of the box. His face, people thought, was very grave, and he seemed a bit perplexed, staring about as if he wasn't quite certain where he was, or, if he did know where he was, what he was doing there. He blinked hard as though trying to wake himself up, and fiddled with the gold cross embroidered on the purple stole about his neck. He took a couple of steps in the direction of the heater, then stopped. He took a few more steps in the other direction, then stopped again. Only when Mrs Shortt (who had a pot roast in the oven and wanted to get her sins confessed and get back home) stood up did Father Cunningham appear to realise what was going on. He gave a small shiver, nodded to Mrs Shortt, and went back inside the confessional.

'Well!' said Mrs Farrel, her penance finished and God put in His place.

'Must be coming down with something,' Mrs Maken said charitably.

And at the back of the church Patrick Farrel said, 'Looked right funny to me.'

'You'd look right funny too if you had to spend the night with that Kitty Mercer,' Willie Little said, and that cheered up those that heard it, and they put Father Cunningham's queerness from their minds and started to try and keep themselves warm again.

Kitty Mercer moved the paraffin-heater closer to the hassock where Father Cunningham would kneel. The church was empty now, the front door locked and bolted, and, Kitty Mercer told herself, peaceful with the sanctity of shriven sins. She stood by the heater waiting for Father Cunningham to come out of the confessional. She waited quite a while. She got concerned: it wasn't at all like Father Cunningham to take so long. The idea that he might have died of a heart-attack had just started to take shape in her mind when Father Cunningham came out and walked very slowly towards her. There was something definitely awry with the priest, Kitty thought. His face was an unnatural grey, and his eyes looked like sightless things, or were turned inwards on himself, seeing only the state of his soul. That's what Kitty thought anyway. 'You all right, Father?' she asked.

Father Cunningham gave a wan smile, but nodded, and gave Kitty a little pat, like a benediction, on the cheek.

Kitty beamed. 'Ah, good,' she said. 'You had me worried there for a minute, Father. Not coming out for so long.'

'So long,' Father Cunningham said vaguely.

'You just kneel yourself down there and have your little talk to God,' Kitty instructed, helping Father Cunningham to his knees. 'Would you like me to stay?' she asked with concern, anxious not to intrude, knowing Father Cunningham usually liked his bit of privacy with the Almighty when confessions were over.

Father Cunningham shook his head.

'Right,' Kitty told him. 'I'll run along and get something nice and hot to go inside you.'

'Thank you, Kitty,' Father Cunningham said.

'And you'll remember to lock the sacristy door, won't you, Father?' Kitty warned, still, after thirty years, remembering the night the sacristy door wasn't locked and the cattle getting in and having a feast on the flowers she'd so carefully arranged for the Easter ceremony.

'I'll remember, Kitty.'

'And you'll put out that heater, won't you, Father.'

'I'll put out the heater, Kitty.'

'And the lights?'

Father Cunningham gazed up at Kitty Mercer, and Kitty was to say later that it was the saddest look she'd ever been given by any man. It was like, she said, as if, for Father Cunningham, the lights had gone out on him a very long time ago – if that wasn't being too fanciful.

'I'll be off then,' she told him.

Father Cunningham nodded, and put his head in his hands.

Kitty Mercer tiptoed out of the church, and left Father Cunningham alone with Jesus.

When eleven o'clock came and went, and Father Cunningham still hadn't shown up, Kitty Mercer got very anxious. The lovely casserole she had cooked specially for him, a wonderful concoction filled with carrots, leeks and parsnips to give it that sweetness she knew Father Cunningham liked, was drying out alarmingly, and that fine wedge of steak sitting in the middle of it all was disintegrating and soon it wouldn't be anything but part of the soggy mess she saw her meal becoming.

With a lot of tutting and shaking of her head, Kitty wrapped herself up again and headed for the church. She wasn't a fearful woman, but there was something about that night which frightened her. She was, of course, given to having the odd premonition, so maybe that was the reason for her being scared. Anyway, she decided to stick her head into Biddlecomb's store and get one of the men to go with her. Just in case. 'I'm sure there's nothing wrong whatever, but just in case – ' she explained to Patrick Farrel who had volunteered to accompany her.

'No harm in being prepared for the worst,' Patrick Farrel reassured her, sounding as if that was what he did all the time himself.

'That's what I thought,' Kitty told him, grabbing his arm as her feet nearly skated from under her. 'Ooops,' she said with a little laugh.

'Mind yourself,' Patrick warned. 'Can't have you breaking a leg and you with himself to look after overnight.'

The lights were still on in the church, but the paraffin-stove had run out of fuel and gone out. It was bitterly cold, the windows all fuzzy on the inside where the heat had been, and the little flame of the sanctuary lamp flickered crazily as if having to fight a losing battle to combat the raw chill.

At first neither Kitty nor Patrick could see the priest. He wasn't kneeling where Kitty had left him. Then they heard a low moan, and saw Father Cunningham stretched out face-down on the altar steps, his arms thrown out as though he was crucified there. They hurried over to him, bending down, both of them talking to him at once.

'Father?' Kitty called.

'Father Cunningham?' was what Patrick said.

Father Cunningham gave another low moan.

'Do you think he's had a stroke or something?' Kitty asked.

'Could have,' Patrick said.

'Should we move him? Turn him over onto his back, do you think?' Kitty wanted to know.

'Dunno. Maybe we better.'

So, they turned Father Cunningham over onto his back, and Kitty Mercer gave a shriek out of her and leapt back, clasping her hands to her cheeks.

'D'you know what it was like,' Patrick Farrel asked after he'd heaved the priest over his shoulder, got him back to Kitty's, seen him tucked up, and returned to the store.

'Tell us,' Mr Biddlecomb said agog.

'All them rips down his chest it was like he'd been trying to rip his own heart out with his bare hands.'

'Jesus!' Mr Biddlecomb said, and blessed himself quickly for good measure.

'What would he go and do that for?' Davey Shortt wanted to know.

'Not saying he *did* do it,' Patrick Farrel pointed out. 'Just saying that's the way it *looked*.'

'Must be some other explanation,' Mr Biddlecomb insisted hopefully.

'Won't know till he tells us,' Patrick said.

'*If* he tells us,' Davey Shortt said.

'Maybe 'twas the Devil that did it,' Willie Little suggested, keen enough to make matters worse.

For some inexplicable reason Patrick Farrel took the suggestion seriously. He gave it some thought, before saying, 'Could be,' and clearly meant it.

'Thought you said they were rips on his chest,' Davey said.

Patrick nodded.

'Can't have been the Devil then, can it?'

'Why not?' Mr Biddlecomb asked.

'Devil has hooves, don't he? Can't rip with hooves.'

'Nothing to stop him changing them into claws if he wanted to,' Willie Little told them.

'For God's sake, would the lot of you stop talking such fiddlesticks,' Mrs Biddlecomb snapped, whacking the counter with the cane she used to help her along. 'Be a perfectly reasonable explanation for it all when we hear it,' she added. 'Keep that stupid talk about the Devil to yourselves.'

So, they stopped talking about the Devil. Stopped talking altogether for a while, staring at their drinks and at one another until Billy Maken said, 'Means no Mass tomorrow, I suppose.'

'Got to be a Mass. Sunday, isn't it? Can't have a Sunday without a Mass,' Mr Biddlecomb said.

'You going to say it then?' Willie Little asked Mr Biddlecomb.

'Kitty'll do it,' Davey Shortt said, and they all had a laugh at that.

'They'll send that Father Doherty,' Mrs Biddlecomb pointed out.

'And how'll he get here in this weather?' Mr Biddlecomb asked, giving Patrick Farrel a wink so he could share in his pleasure at getting one over on his wife.

'If God wants us to have Mass He'll find a way for Father Doherty to get here,' Mrs Biddlecomb said, knocking the smile off Mr Biddlecomb's face.

'Maybe Father Cunningham will be better in the morning,' Connor Neill suggested.

'Maybe,' Patrick Farrel said.

'Yeah, maybe,' Davey Shortt agreed.

Kitty Mercer sat by the bed and patted iodine into Father Cunningham's wounds, the sting of it making him suck his breath in a bit. And as she patted she prayed, invoking the assistance of all her favourite saints. And when the priest fell asleep she still sat there, looking at him. She stopped praying though, maybe thinking that his falling asleep meant her prayers had been heard and answered. She sat there and thought about the lovely casserole that had gone to waste. And then she thought if she added more stock, and put the whole thing through a sieve, wouldn't it make a fine nourishing broth for Father Cunningham who probably wouldn't have been able to chew the meat anyway, after his experience. That's what she'd do, and quietly she went downstairs to do it.

Twenty-two

It was a good job Mr Biddlecomb hadn't pushed his luck and taken on Billy Maken's bet about the weather changing because, to everyone's surprise, over the Saturday night, an unexpected thaw set in – something to do with the Gulf Stream, Cahal Brennan said knowledgeably – turning the lying snow to an unpleasant slush, and leaving everything dripping as the ice melted, but making the road passable, which was a blessing.

'See?' Billy Maken, all dressed up in his blue serge suit and polished brown boots, asked, looking about him as the men stood in Biddlecomb's store waiting to hear if there was going to be a Mass or not.

'Just a respite,' Mr Biddlecomb said sourly, irked that the store was filled with customers he couldn't serve since Mrs Biddlecomb would have none of that. 'Drink before Mass?' she'd thundered when Mr Biddlecomb suggested a small, warming nip would do none of them, least of all God, any harm.

'Didn't say it would last,' Billy Maken pointed out.

'Any news of the priest?' Patrick Farrel asked, peering out of the window towards Kitty Mercer's cottage, and then up at the sky with a grimace.

'Nothing yet,' Mr Biddlecomb said, coming to join him, rubbing the window pane with a corner of his apron for a cleaner view.

It was a gloomy enough sight. All across the valley grey, snow-laden clouds rolled in from the ocean, bumping into each other, it seemed, the first assimilating the second and so on until the weight of the whole was more than the sky could stand and the heavy, glowering mass appeared to tumble earthwards right before Mr Biddlecomb's eyes. It was, he thought, as though some malevolent god was planning a mischief for the village and making sure no one from outside the valley knew about it, although quite why such a curious idea should cross his mind was beyond him. He gave a small shudder. 'Never seen it like this,' he said quietly so only Patrick Farrel could hear.

'Me neither,' Patrick Farrel agreed as though he, too, was filled with foreboding.

'Feels wrong,' Mr Biddlecomb said.

Patrick Farrel nodded.

'Like something bad was about to happen.'

Patrick Farrel nodded again.

'What you two whispering about?' Davey Shortt called.

'Mind your business,' Mr Biddlecomb told him.

He was about to turn from the window and return to his place behind the counter when Patrick Farrel said, 'There's Kitty.'

Suddenly there was a rush for the window as if the sight of Kitty Mercer was a phenomenon not to be missed. 'What's she doing?' asked Willie Little, who'd been slow off his mark and couldn't see out.

'Heading for the church, looks like.'

'What's she look like?'

'Like she always does, of course.'

'I mean – she seem all right?'

'Looks fine to me.'

'What's she doin' now then?'

'Opening the door. Gone in. Closed the door. Lights gone on,' Davey Shortt reported, keeping his mouth open a little when he'd finished just in case something new and unexpected cropped up that should be added to this commentary.

And then the church bell started to ring, slowly at first as Kitty warmed up, and then quicker as she got into the swing of it.

'Priest must be all right,' Connor Neill said.

'Of course he's all right,' Mrs Biddlecomb snapped, coming into the store from the kitchen and leaning against the counter as she pulled on her gloves. 'Ripping his heart out with his bare hands,' she scoffed. 'Just wait till he hears that one!' She took a peep at herself in the mirror behind the bar. 'I'm ready, Mr Biddlecomb,' she announced.

'Right,' Mr Biddlecomb said, jumping to it. 'Everyone out,' he ordered.

'Out!' Mrs Biddlecomb reiterated loudly as one or two of the men lingered.

'Mam?' I called from the foot of the stairs.

Ever since she'd told me what Dad had done Mam had changed. She'd gone very quiet, not sulky-quiet but gentle-quiet. When my Grandma was dying the doctor said he'd never seen anyone so serene, and that was what Mam was like now: serene. Somehow she'd stricken all that was cruel from her mind, and had taken herself back to when we were all happy together, back to the time when Dad was alive and I was still a child at school. She sang happily to herself as she did her housework, and took to making herself pretty again, combing and brushing her hair for hours the way she used to, and then tying it up with pretty ribbon, and primping in the mirror. 'Yes, Aiden?' she called back from her bedroom.

'I'm just going.'

'All right, dear. You run along. Say goodbye to your Daddy.'

''Bye, Dad,' I said.

'Daddy says goodbye, dear,' Mam told me, and as I left the house I could hear her talking away, and laughing cheerily as she busied herself caring for her ghost.

The church was packed, everyone wanting to see Father Cunningham for themselves and wanting to hear some explanation for the curious happening from his own lips, some of the women trying to catch Kitty Mercer's eyes, and quiz her, getting a jump on the others. But Kitty wasn't having any of that. She scuttled about the sanctuary getting everything ready, biting her lower lip and letting her hands flutter like two little sparrows caught in netting. From time to time she went to the sacristy door and peered in, each time retreating with a shaking of her head.

'Something's up,' Davey Shortt said. Connor Neill nodded. And so did Patrick Farrel, Billy Maken and Willie Little.

'See *he's* here,' Mr Biddlecomb pointed out.

'Who?'

'Johnsey. Up there. At the front. With Hannah.'

'So he is.'

And so he was. Bareheaded, his hair tumbling down to his shoulders, overflowing the collar of that heavy tweed coat of his, the one with the cape to it, his hands folded neatly on his lap, Johnsey sat as still as any of the statues that peered unblinkingly at the congregation from their cosy niches. Beside him, Hannah O'Mahony, with her straw hat at a jaunty angle, licking her fingers as she shuffled her way through the missal she carried, bending twice to retrieve retreat cards from her schooldays that slipped from between the pages and fluttered to the floor. And perhaps because of her constant fidgeting, Johnsey, unmoving, had an eerie air to him.

'Looks like he's just about ready to leap at someone,' was how Willie Little put it.

'He's not going to leap at anyone during the Mass,' Mr Biddlecomb said, as if such a notion was too fantastic to merit credence.

'Just saying he *looks* that way.'

'Looks more like he's having a doze to me,' Patrick Farrel observed.

'Bet that fella *never* sleeps,' Willie said to that. 'Or if he does it's with one of them beady eyes of his open.'

'Need to with the likes of you around,' Davey Shortt said.

'You can talk,' Willie told him. '*I* don't go round setting fire to humans,' he added, and then, wickedly, 'Mind you, don't let no bastard shove my head down no rabbit hole either.'

Patrick Farrel nudged Mr Biddlecomb and nodded towards the altar. Mr Biddlecomb craned his neck to look.

It seemed that something was about to happen. Kitty Mercer was moving across the sanctuary at the trot. She opened the sacristy door, bowed her head, folded her hands devoutly, and stepped back, allowing Father Cunningham, all decked out in his nice white alb and seasonal chasuble, to make his entrance.

He made it to the altar steps all right, preceded by Tommy Coyne who was altar-boy that Sunday. He handed Tommy his biretta, and Tommy took it with a bit of a smirk on his face, but then Tommy always had a bit of a smirk on his face like he knew something really funny about the world that no one else was privy to. Then Father Cunningham bent down and hitched up his alb a bit so he wouldn't trip on the steps: it had happened to him once before, years and years ago, and it wasn't going to happen again if he could help it. Yet, everyone who'd seen him trip on that one occasion remembered it as if it was yesterday, and now, each Sunday when Father Cunningham made it to the top step successfully, there was a hissing sort of sigh, hissing because most of the witnesses were pretty old and had long since lost the majority of their teeth. And there was that sibilant sigh now as Father Cunningham reached the altar and, holding his hands aloft, began to pray. 'Introibo ad altare Dei,' he intoned, and everyone settled back. But not for long.

Time for the sermon came, and Father Cunningham made his way to the little flower-bedecked platform that served nicely as a pulpit. Everything had gone smoothly up until then although, true, Father Cunningham had faltered here and there, seeming distracted, but who wouldn't be with his chest all clawed the way the priest's had been? He climbed onto the dais and folded his arms, shoving his hands up the sleeves of his alb. For quite some time he said nothing, staring over his spectacles at the congregation as if he was counting them or making sure everyone he wanted to be there was there. When his eyes rested on Johnsey he seemed to shudder a bit, but it could have been the draught from the sacristy that made him do that. He flicked his eyes to Hannah O'Mahony and then back to Johnsey's face again. He cleared his throat. He looked upwards, all his small actions giving the impression that what he was about to say would be very significant. But it wasn't really. Well, maybe it was to Father Cunningham but to the villagers it was the usual sort of sermon about loving one another, and seeing the mote in your own eye before accusing others of misdeeds; about not judging others, leaving that sort of thing to God since He knew more about that sort of thing and, anyway, everyone was answerable to Him in the end.

There was a bit of a stir when he finished his sermon. Usually he ended up by asking everyone to take a few minutes to pray for themselves, commune with Jesus he used to say, until he found out no one knew what that meant and changed it to saying, 'Just talk to God and tell him your troubles.' But now he asked all the congregation to pray for him, which made people sit up since the only time they were asked to pray for someone specific was when that person was as near as made no difference to dying. But everyone bowed their heads and prayed, only God knowing if they were doing what the priest asked and praying for him. And the few minutes allotted to this task dragged on quite a while too, and people kept taking peeps from under their eyelids to see what Father Cunningham was up to, whether he'd fallen asleep, maybe, or had a turn, or maybe he had died standing up there. Maybe he had dozed off but he certainly hadn't died, and eventually, when the men at the back started coughing, he lifted his head and gave everyone something like a friendly smile, and went back to the altar.

'Knew he wasn't right, I did,' Willie Little was to say later.

'Know everything, you do,' Davey Shortt told him. 'After it's happened.'

'Anyone with eyes in their head could see he wasn't right,' Willie Little retorted. 'Before it happened,' he added with a glare.

'We *all* knew *something* was wrong with him,' Connor Neill pointed out, shaking his head in disbelief.

'Didn't know he was going to –' Willie Little started to say.

'How could any of us know *that*?' Patrick Farrel demanded. 'Never seen anything to match that in all my life. Never *want* to see anything like it again in my life neither.'

'Christ, no,' Mr Biddlecomb agreed, standing up on his toes to see if anyone by chance was looking to order a drink and wishing someone would get a move on and do so.

'Can't believe it,' Billy Maken confessed. '*Still* can't believe it even if I did see it with my own eyes.'

'And what about what he *said* never mind what he *did*?' Patrick Farrel asked, but all he got by way of answer was shaking heads, and bewildered looks, and vague gestures that intimated disbelief.

And the women, gathered now in Mrs Biddlecomb's kitchen, were in a similar state of shock: the cups of tea Mrs Farrel took it upon herself to dish out – with Mrs Biddlecomb's approval, of course – rattled on the saucers as nervous fingers tried to raise them to mouths. Kitty Mercer wasn't there since she was beside herself with trepidation, and Mrs Finch had been forced to excuse herself – and none too pleased at having so to do – since she felt it her duty to see Kitty home and sit with her a while.

'Well, I don't know what the world is coming to,' was how Mrs Biddlecomb expressed her feelings.

'And him a *priest*,' Mrs Farrel said with a toss of her nicely combed head.

'A *priest*,' she emphasised again, and stopped handing round tea for a moment, standing there, arms akimbo, watching as the enormity of her observation sank in.

'If only he hadn't *told* us,' Mrs Shortt said vaguely.

'What do you mean by that?' Mrs Farrel asked.

But Mrs Shortt didn't know what she meant by that, so she ignored Mrs Farrel's question and took to staring straight in front of her just as she, and everyone else for that matter, had stared in consternation, numbed, as Father Cunningham began what years later were always referred to as his antics.

There was always to be argument as to the exact sequence of events, but everyone agreed that it became clear something was radically amiss with Father Cunningham just before he was about to distribute communion. Although it wasn't liturgically correct, Father Cunningham always said a few little prayers for the dead of the village before he collected the ciborium and made his way down the steps to the altar rail to face the gaping mouths and extended tongues of those eager to receive. He said it was his way of including the dead in the communion which was nice, and comforting for the very old since it meant they wouldn't be forgotten, be sort of brought back from the grave every Sunday.

Anyway, Father Cunningham named those he wanted everyone to pray for, and bowed his head to say his own prayers for them. It was very still and quiet, the way it is when everyone is praying. Suddenly, Hannah O'Mahony was on her feet, shouting at the priest, 'What about my little May? Aren't you going to pray for my little May?'

Well, you'd have thought God had turned everyone in the church to stone, and Hannah's words seemed to echo round the place, repeating the question over and over, and getting even more plaintive with the repetition.

Father Cunningham's shoulders started to shake, up and down as if he was sobbing.

'What about little May?' Hannah shouted again. 'Aren't you going to even *pray* for her?'

Mrs Farrel, sitting directly behind Hannah, leaned forward as if, somehow, to restrain her, but as she reached out Johnsey gave her a glare and she pulled her hand back like he'd snapped at it.

Father Cunningham was shaking all over now, and Tommy Coyne, the smirk like a petrified grimace across his face, was backing away from the altar, the communion plate still in his hands, backing away to the sacristy door, taking little looks over his shoulders as if making sure his escape was unhindered.

And then he let out a long, low moan like he was in terrible pain, and he gave a strange gurgle too which people later said was just like the rattle life made when it was slivering out of a body. He reached out and took the ciborium in both hands and stared at it for what seemed a very long time under the circumstances. Then he turned and faced the congregation, stared at them long and hard, a curious longing in his frightened eyes as if all he wanted, wanted more than anything else anyway, was to share in that indomitable faith he saw before him, an uncomplicated faith in a God quite different to his own, a God of compassion and understanding.

Suddenly, horribly, he was sitting on the altar steps, the ciborium viced between his knees, while with both hands he was thrusting the sacred hosts into his mouth, chewing and swallowing compulsively, slobbering and still shaking out of control.

It was as though everyone drew their breath in at once. A huge and appalled gasp filled the church, yet still no one moved. No one except Kitty Mercer, that is. She pushed Tommy Coyne into the sacristy out of the way and closed the door on him, and then, her arms reaching out as though to console and welcome a prodigal son, she started to move across the sanctuary towards Father Cunningham, although she did hesitate every few steps to size him up, adopting a comic pose like that of a matador, as if she half expected whatever madness had got into him to make him leap to his feet and charge her down.

She had almost reached him when Johnsey stood up, and said in a quiet voice, 'Leave him, Kitty.'

Kitty Mercer stopped dead in her tracks. She looked at Johnsey. She looked at Father Cunningham. She looked at Johnsey again. And as she was standing there looking, Father Cunningham began to babble. Hugging the now empty ciborium to his chest, cuddling it, rocking back and forth, he was apologising. 'I'm sorry,' he said. And then said it again and again. 'I'm sorry. I'm sorry. I'm sorry,' each time his voice rising until on the final utterance it was almost a scream. He looked about him with a wild sort of look, the look of someone in mortal terror, someone in mortal terror and lost. He was crying now, too, heaving his sorrow from his soul in great, choking sobs which made what he said difficult to understand, difficult to hear anyway. 'Why, why?' he asked. 'I didn't mean, you see. It just . . . she was so . . . I'm sorry . . . Oh, my God,' he wailed as if something terrible had just struck him. 'So cold . . . just wanted to warm her . . . in my arms . . . and then,' Father Cunningham looked about him again in a bewildered way now. It was as if, Mr Biddlecomb was to insist, as if he couldn't see any of them, as if he was alone, as if there was just himself and God in the place, himself and an angry God. Certainly Father Cunningham seemed to be trying to shield himself from something, bending his head and raising one arm as if to protect him from blows. Suddenly, in a crazed and terrible energy that came from somewhere, he screamed, 'Oh, May, May . . . forgive me . . . so cold . . . so cold. Forgive me,' and that for the moment seemed to remove the threat of attack. His body went limp and the ciborium rolled from his grasp and clattered away from him, bouncing down the steps. For a long time Father Cunningham stared at the sacred vessel: his look was quizzical, perhaps wondering if there was something significant about the empty ciborium rolling from his grasp. Then he seemed to shrink, become a shadow of himself. As everyone watched he curled himself up and toppled over, shaking again now, sobbing and moaning.

No one could ever remember how long they stayed and watched him, but it was certainly a very long time. Then Johnsey took Hannah O'Mahony by the arm and led her from the church. And soon after that everyone was leaving, trooping out in stunned silence. Even Kitty Mercer abandoned the priest, leaving the church last and closing the door behind her, and everyone getting the fright of their lives when it was jerked open again almost instantly, and then giving a couple of nervous titters as Tommy Coyne came out, white as a sheet and with his smirk twisted into something frightening. Then Kitty Mercer pulled the door closed again, and there was something very final about the way she did it, and the pain in her face made some people think she had shut away in the church all that was happy in her life.

Despite the cold the villagers hovered about the church, unwilling to leave in the way they often appeared unwilling to leave a grave after the burial of someone who had been a part of their lives for longer than they could remember. But the men started to talk to each other again in low and sombre tones, the women remaining silent, their faces drawn and ashen-grey, only moving from the church when the Gardai arrived as though they could not bear to witness the humiliation of the priest, walking slowly up the village street to gather in little groups, still unspeaking as if the tragedy they had witnessed was unspeakable, leaving the men to watch the outrage conclude. And most of them averted their eyes as the cars took Father Cunningham away, fearful that he might see their pain and himself suffer the more because of it, their anger at what he had done not yet conceived.

And before the sound of the growling engines had died away, the snow started to fall again, thick and dense, obliterating any chance that they might spy the cars as they climbed the hill beyond the graveyard, as if God had washed His hands of the priest and expected them to do the same.

Twenty-three

Maybe God decided He'd given the villagers tragedy enough to be going on with and that was why no one died in Ifreann that winter; no one except old Mrs Horgan, that is, but, as Mrs Biddlecomb pointed out, Mrs Horgan had been as good as dead for the past couple of years so her demise didn't really count.

And the whole business with Father Cunningham and the terrible sins he had committed were hushed up, of course. The bishops saw to that, explaining in their cunning episcopal way that it wouldn't be good for the faithful to know too much about such matters lest it weaken their faith in all the other representatives of Christ. For weeks nobody spoke of anything else. There was a rumour that Father Cunningham had gone totally mad and had been locked up in a special asylum for crazy priests: Willie Little started that one. But Patrick Farrel said Father Cunningham had been sent to a monastery where none of the monks spoke, which seemed more likely, although Mr Biddlecomb said he'd heard the priest was in Africa working with black children just like the one that bobbed its head when you put a penny in the box for the education of the pickaninnies, although Davey Shortt insisted it was South America and the Amazonians Father Cunningham was ministering to.

But then the bishops closed the church, calling it redundant, and laying on a bus to take the villagers to the town for the sacraments, and with the church gone the memory of

Father Cunningham receded with it, and soon he was rarely mentioned, and became part of the folklore, only to be called up on those occasions when something else happened to remind the villagers of him.

And Hannah O'Mahony took on a new lease of life, getting very cheery and sure of herself, walking with a bit of a swagger, and holding her head up like she'd never done. 'He was my son,' she told everyone who asked her who in the name of God that Johnsey fella was, but no one believed her until Kevin Keogh startled everyone in the store one evening by shouting 'That's it!' out of the blue.

'That's what?' Mr Biddlecomb demanded.

'That's who he reminded me of,' Kevin Keogh said.

'Who?'

'That Johnsey.'

'No, dammit,' Mr Biddlecomb, said testily. 'Who did he remind you of?'

'Liam Kelly.'

The men looked at each other in a puzzled way, some of them mouthing the name, Liam Kelly, as if so doing would make them understand what Kevin was on about.

'Don't youse remember?' Kevin asked. 'Way back. When Liam did the runner without telling a soul and Hannah –'

'Jesus, you're right!' Patrick Farrel exclaimed. 'Hannah had a child that was taken off of her. Forgot all about that, I did.'

Kevin Keogh nodded. 'Image of Liam, that Johnsey was.'

'So Johnsey *could* have been Hannah's son!'

'Could easily have been.'

'Christ!'

'And that'd explain it,' Kevin Keogh went on.

'Explain what?' Davey Shortt wanted to know.

'Why he was so mad keen to find out what happened to little May.'

'Oh.'

'She'd have been his sister, see?'

'Half,' Mrs Biddlecomb pointed out. 'Half sister.'

'Whatever.'

'That'd explain things all right.'

And so, accepting the explanation, the villagers regarded Hannah in a new light, being careful not to upset her if they could help it just in case she had the power to summon Johnsey back whenever she needed him. 'Wonder what did happen to him?' the men asked each other, but the only answer forthcoming was a shrug. None of them had a clue, and none of them wanted to hazard a guess either. Johnsey had simply disappeared as mysteriously as he had arrived, and although Hannah pretended from time to time to know where he was, you could tell by the furtive little look in her eyes that she was at as much of a loss as everyone else. 'But he'll be back,' she'd say with that small smile of hers, and enjoy the way most people cringed at the thought of that.

How are you, Johnsey? I ask. I go up to the woods most evenings and sit there just like we used to, and I can sometimes feel him sitting there with me. Not always. Sometimes. And when he's not with me I tell him what's happening in the village and what people are saying. I tell him about the badgers we'd seen, and about my dogs and about how the oldest one is blind in one eye now and how the younger one helps him by walking close to him and stopping him bumping into things.

And I tell him how Olly Carver's eldest daughter, Heather, took the bit between her teeth and ran off with a young lad from the city who'd been staying at the big house for the shooting, and how now all the daughters were getting itchy feet and driving Olly to distraction as he tried to keep them under control, and not having much success with it either.

And I tell him how Willie Little sneaked off to the new hospital in the town and got himself a false arm that sticks onto his stump, and how he says it's better than the real thing since he can screw it off and use it as a handy weapon if he wants to clout someone.

And I tell him how Davey Shortt is getting mileage out of the scar the rabbit snare made on his neck, giving a different explanation for it every time it's brought up, but shutting up quick enough when it's pointed out what a state he was in after it happened.

I don't tell Johnsey much about myself though. I think he always hoped I'd leave the village and make something special of myself, but I know too that I never will leave, and he wouldn't like to hear that.

It's nice to have Johnsey to talk to. Mam and I don't have much to say to each other now since she does most of her talking to my Dad. But she seems happy and peaceful in herself which is good to see.

And there's no one else I want to talk to. No one who'd understand me anyway.